Parent Imperfect is a book of beginnings and endings, the very pattern that makes life — it is our series of lines that make meaning in our world. This moving story takes us to the woods to live deliberately along with the family at the center of it, exploring the ways in which a place can hold hope for the past, the present, and the future, pointing to the consistency and foundations of the ever-shifting components of our lives, urging us to return always to what we know and those we love. Heart-wrenching and heart-warming, this is a novel about growing up and letting others see the parts of us we barely know ourselves, at whatever stage in life we need to do so. This book is a welcome reminder to seek solace and beauty in the quotidian and to pay attention to the small things.

Wesley Scott McMasters
author of *In Which My Lover Tells Me about the Nature of Wild Things*

Against a backdrop of enduring nature, a gay couple and their son struggle to overcome rejection and learn to welcome acceptance in this emotionally powerful portrait of modern manhood.

Brian Keaney
author of *The Alphabet of Heart's Desire*

A thoughtful exploration of love, understanding, kindness, and forgiveness, amid the ever shifting but always enduring landscape of family. A solid work for our times.

Tetman Callis
author of *High Street: Lawyers, Guns & Money in a Stoner's New Mexico*, and *Franny & Toby*

Parent Imperfect

a novel

by

Paul Lamb

Blue Cedar Press
Wichita, Kansas

Parent Imperfect, a novel
Copyright ©2024 Paul Lamb

This is a work of fiction, and all characters and scenes are the product of the author's imagination.

All rights reserved. No part of this book may be reproduced in any form or by any electronic or mechanical means, including information storage and retrieval systems, without permission in writing from the publisher except for brief quotations quoted in critical articles and reviews. Inquiries should be addressed to:

Blue Cedar Press PO Box 48715
Wichita, KS 67201
Visit the Blue Cedar Press website: www.bluecedarpress.com
10 9 8 7 6 5 4 3 2 1

First edition June 2024
ISBN: 978-1-958728-24-6 (paper)
ISBN: 978-1-958728-25-3 (ebook)
Library of Congress Control Number: 2024936212

Cover photo: Rachel Johnson
Cover and interior design: Gina Laiso, Integrita Productions
Editors: Laura Tillem and Gretchen Eick

Printed in the United States of America at IngramSpark

Several chapters first appeared in slightly different form
in these journals:

Hush Arbor — *fron//tera* — July 2021
Three Small Words — *Adelaide Literary Magazine* — August 2019
Forest Succession — *Heartwood Literary Magazine* — April 2019

For David Panian, forever my friend and fellow adventurer.

I went to the woods because I wished to live deliberately,
to front only the essential facts of life, and see if
I could not learn what it had to teach, and not,
when I came to die, discover that I had not lived.

Henry David Thoreau
Walden

'Father, father, where are you going?
O do not walk so fast.
Speak father, speak to your little boy,
Or else I shall be lost.'

The night was dark, no father was there,
The child was wet with dew;
The mire was deep, & the child did weep,
And away the vapour flew.

William Blake
"The Little Boy Lost"
Songs of Innocence

Table of Contents

Prologue 3
One - Trial by Fire 5
Two - Looking Forward, Looking Backward 25
Three - Expedition into a Dark Forest...................... 33
Four - Nature Always Wins....................................... 47
Five - Home Run 55
Six - Name Calling.. 63
Seven - You Pushed Mountains Out of Your Way 75
Eight - A Tree Grows in the Forest............................ 87
Nine - STOP! STOP! STOP! 97
Ten - A Multitude of Sins 109
Eleven - Battles and Skirmishes............................. 119
Twelve - How to Really Make a Mess of Things with Your Son ... 133
Thirteen - Hush Arbor... 147
Fourteen - Motherlove 155
Fifteen - The Journey is the Destination 161
Sixteen - Catch and Release 169
Seventeen - Three Small Words 179
Eighteen - Forest Succession 189
Nineteen - to love that well which thou must leave ere long 195
Twenty - Flint and Steel 205
Twenty-one - Invisible Wounds 217
Twenty-two - yellow leaves, or none, or few.......... 225
Twenty-three - Barbarian at the Gate 231
Twenty-four - The Woman at the Fair 239
Twenty-five - The Old Man of the Forest................ 249
Twenty-six - Running Naked 259
Twenty-seven - The Liminal Animal 269
Coda - Two-Match Fire 279

Prologue

Where to begin? To realize you're never going to understand and the best you can do with your life is laugh at it?

Curt was already swept into the flow of the interstate, his rotten muffler joining the roar of the traffic, before he considered how poorly dressed he was for what he was about to do. Kelly would say that "about" wasn't the correct word. He had a three-hour drive before he could "do" anything. But he'd snuck out and left Kelly behind.

You can wear skimpy clothes in early March if you're running, but not at a cabin deep in the Ozarks. If he'd had time, if he'd thought it through, he would have changed into warmer clothes. He didn't have time, though, and he hadn't thought it through. He'd acted impulsively, which surprised him. That wasn't his nature. It was as though a different Curt had taken charge. A Curt of feeling, not analysis.

That was why he hadn't taken the first exit and returned home to pull on some sweats at least. Instead, he remained in the flow, and he thought, no, he *felt*, that he shouldn't stop, shouldn't reconsider, shouldn't postpone what had to be done.

And what had to be done? He'd work that out once he was away from the city, when the pack thinned and he could refocus his attention, and when, he knew, he'd have gone far enough that he'd keep going.

He knew he shouldn't meet outrage with outrage. Anger with anger. What the boy had done was clearly a provocation. Intended to draw him into a fight, which would only make a bad thing worse. A fight would be a child's solution, and Curt needed to present an adult's solution. Reasoned. Measured. Appropriate.

With three hours to think, he could come up with a half dozen sensible scenarios to present. What exactly is the problem? Well, I see it as this, or this, or this. How do we fix the problem? By doing this, or this, or this. How will our lives be going forward? I imagine this, or this, or this.

He'd work it out rationally and give the boy options to right the wrong, accept the discipline, choose a better path. It couldn't continue the way it had. He'd make the boy see that. He'd explain the sensible options he would set before him. And the boy could make his choice.

Which was what Curt did for three hours. He thought he did well too. In that time, he'd come up with several rational scenarios for moving forward.

What he couldn't resolve during those three hours, however, were other questions. How had it gotten this bad? Who was really to blame? Was the boy's behavior reasonable considering how he had been treated? How had he been treated? What kind of adult had Curt let himself become? Was it really Curt who was at fault?

Those were difficult questions, and he didn't have answers for them, or didn't *want* answers for them. So he took refuge in the reasonable scenarios he'd prepared for the boy, in his certainty that each made perfect sense, that the burden was on him. He would assert his authority, gently if he could but firmly if he must. He would change the boy, but he would remain the adult.

When he finally reached the cabin, though, and saw what the boy had done, Curt realized that he didn't even begin to understand the problem. That he could never have been prepared.

Chapter One

Trial by Fire

Despite his fears, Kelly had made it home alive. He'd survived a long day trip to a remote cabin with the man who would soon be his father-in-law.

He'd shed his bug-laden, soot-smudged clothes onto the tiles just inside the door of their apartment as Curt had instructed. Smelling of woodsmoke and sweat and forest, he would jump directly in the shower where he would scrub hard, also as Curt had instructed. Curt would check him for ticks before they fell into bed together. Only then could Kelly tell him every detail of his day for as long as they could keep their eyes open.

The day would be a harmless, get-to-know-you trip, Curt assured him when Kelly had voiced his wariness. A chance for him to see David in his natural state. Kelly wasn't sure if that was a good thing or not.

"Relax," Curt had said. "Dad is his finest at the cabin. He loves that place. He's taking you there because he wants you to love it as well."

And to his surprise, that's what Kelly had seemed to find. He'd met Curt's parents several times already. A backyard lunch at their little house in Richmond Heights, full of jollity and polite questions that broke the ice. There was no mistaking the strength in David's grip as he shook Kelly's hand or the warmth of Kathy's embrace. An evening at an Italian restaurant that was never crowded, so they could linger at their table for hours and tell funny stories about each other. Even a well-mannered trip to the art museum — Kelly's suggestion that they had dutifully gone along with, though Kelly could see only Curt's mother was interested. Curt had cautioned his parents not to ask about Kelly's family, who still weren't talking to him after he'd come out the year before. "Let him bring it up if he wants to." And they were careful. But David finally pushed past the harmless chitchat and suggested that he and Kelly make a trip to the cabin. "Just the two of us," he boomed, clapping his two big hands together. "To see where Curt *really* grew up!"

Kelly was uncertain. He'd already snuck out to the cabin once with Curt, before his parents knew they were a couple, and while he thought the place had a rugged charm, it was undeniably remote, "out there in Bugbite County." Off the grid. Wild and fecund and hot. No running water. No flushing toilet. No electricity. No cell service. No way to call for help. No witnesses. A place full of snakes and chainsaws and all manner of grisly accidents. Kelly still carried the emotional scars of his own father's violent rejection, and now here was another father, a man he barely knew, proposing to take him deep into the wilderness. Alone.

Not so, countered Curt. There was no safer place for the human heart than the Clark family cabin, he insisted. "Dad wants to take you there because this is his way of welcoming you to the family. That cabin is my father's holy place, and he wants to share it with you, Kelly. You can't deny him this."

But Kelly wasn't convinced. Weren't holy places where blood sacrifices were made? So Curt ran him through some scenarios the night before, laughingly at first until he saw Kelly wasn't laughing. What the two of them might do while at the cabin. Maybe hike in the hills. Maybe liberate some cedars from their earthly toil. Or cut down a tree together. "That's actually a bigger emotional experience than you might imagine!" Split some logs. Fish in the lake. *Swim* in the lake.

"Ask him to teach you how to build a one-match fire. You'll live in Dad's heart forever."

"But what if I can't light it with one match?"

"He won't let you fail, Kelly."

And Kelly slowly, warily began to think that there really might be something warm and loving in this new family he was joining. Something better than the family he had known. Something, he was learning, he deeply wanted.

Kelly had paced at the front window that morning, watching for David's truck. He had girded himself for the day; he'd already tucked his jeans into his socks, having learned the value of this after a week of itching torment when he'd dismissed Curt's suggestion on their earlier trip. He wore new boots with thick soles. He'd pulled on one of Curt's flannel shirts, though the day promised to be warm enough that he wouldn't need it. And he deliberately did not shave the past two mornings to look as virile as he could. He intended to show David that he could be just as manly as any man in the woods. Plus, he'd made a mental list of the things he would and would not talk about. How he could hide his reaction if stung by the wrong questions. Put on a mask of nonchalance if necessary. Change the subject somehow.

"You won't need anything," Curt said after Kelly had collected a backpack of supplies. He slid the pack from Kelly's shoulders and dropped it on the kitchen counter then stood in front of it. "Dad will have everything for the day."

When David's truck pulled up before their apartment, Kelly saw two coolers in the back. They were supposed to be having burgers and chips for lunch. Not even beer since they were driving home that evening. What could they possibly need for their day trip that would require *two* coolers? Just how big were those burgers going to be?

In his robe, Curt followed Kelly onto their front step. He waved and then shouted to his father, "Remember, he's new at this!" They'd agreed not to tell David that Kelly had already been to the cabin once. It would dampen his dad's enthusiasm, Curt had said, his pride at showing off his special place.

Kelly took a deep breath then stepped into the pre-dawn light. As he was walking to the truck he heard Curt call to him, "Don't be intimidated by my dad's enthusiasm," which instantly put Kelly on edge, all his fears flooding back.

Kelly had decided that on the long drive, if the vibe was right, he would try revealing bits of his background. Not the deep stuff. Nobody got that. But maybe some of the things they had all politely avoided discussing but that he knew they were curious about, so he didn't have to remain a complete stranger to them. When Curt had described how effortlessly his father had embraced him after he came out, Kelly hoped the man would be equally open if his future son-in-law shared some bits of his own messy life. He'd read the signs. He'd watch how David reacted, puzzle out the hidden meaning behind whatever questions he asked, see if David tried to change the subject because he was uncomfortable. Uncomfortable not because the man sitting beside him was gay but because the family rejection Kelly might reveal was brutal and unabating, and how could anyone be comfortable hearing about something like that, still so fresh and raw?

But about this, he saw that his fears were unfounded. David had listened politely as Kelly sketched some broad strokes about his life, and he had asked a few safe questions. "So you're an English major?" and "Did you grow up in St. Louis?" and "Three older sisters?" and the one he knew he was required to ask: "Where did you go to high school?"

Sure, David's questions were intended to get a better picture of Kelly's life. But he could hear reluctance in Kelly's voice sometimes. David knew how burdened Curt had been with his own secret, keeping it for *years* because he feared his father's reaction, and how relieved Curt was when he finally felt safe to speak his truth. So David saw he had a chance to let another troubled soul gain some relief simply by listening. And it wasn't as though a three-hour drive was a long time to lend a patient ear to Kelly's words. Rather, David could tell, it wouldn't be nearly long enough.

When they turned off the paved county road, David stopped the truck.

"Are we there?" Kelly said.

"Not quite. We still have about two miles to the cabin. But here is where I normally turn off the air conditioning and roll down the windows. Take off my sunglasses, breathe the country air, and start to experience the forest on its terms. Okay with you?"

Curt hadn't done that when they'd come before. Had he been trying to shield the city boy from the wild just a little longer? Was that what the Clark men did? Think about others all the time? Did people really do that?

"Sure," said Kelly, tossing his sunglasses onto the dash as he had seen David do. He thought about rolling up the sleeves of his flannel shirt but didn't.

"You might want to stay buckled," David said as they began driving across the rutted gravel. "It's rough going from here. And be careful that the forest doesn't slap you in the face. There's some low branches ahead I can't really steer around."

They rattled across washboard for the next two miles. At one point, David stopped the truck and pointed ahead. "We cross that stream, and if we do it right, we splash a lot of water in the air.

When Curt was a boy, he'd hold his arm out the window to catch the drops."

Kelly laughed.

"What?" said David.

"Oh, I was just trying to picture Curt being playful like that."

David thought for a moment, the hint of a smile on his lips. "He was a sweet boy. I still see some of that in him when he's around you, Kelly." He lifted his big hand from the steering wheel as though he were going to pat Kelly on the knee, but he hesitated and then gripped the wheel again. "I'm grateful for that, Kelly."

David stepped on the gas and roared ahead, splashing through the stream as Kelly held his arm out the window. He did catch some drops and got his sleeve nicely wet. They crossed the valley and then mounted a ridge, spraying gravel behind them as they climbed. At the top the road split. "Jimmy lives down that way," David said, pointing to the fork they did not take. "He's our unofficial caretaker. Been around forever. I hope I'm as spry when I'm a thousand years old."

They bumped along before turning into a meadow with a barely discernible track that may have been a road once. Kelly heard the tall grass thrumming against the truck as it passed over. Grasshoppers landed on their windshield and then jumped off. One jumped into the cab, and Kelly tried not to flinch.

"The hundred acres begins at that line of trees ahead. Our land is more or less a rectangle. We're at the southwest corner right here. It's mostly second growth forest. And the lake. And the bit we keep clear around the cabin. I can't wait for you to see it!"

Kelly decided to accept David's barely contained excitement as genuine, and on they drove. His eyes adjusted quickly to the broken sunlight; he could see deep into the forest around him, into the light and dark, but what he saw was mostly scrub amidst an unending rank of vertical tree trunks. A hundred acres of this, he thought. Easy to get lost.

"Along here," David said, creeping the truck down the road that had been carved through the forest decades ago, "we sometimes see deer dashing past. Not sure why they favor this part of the woods. Farthest from the cabin maybe."

Kelly watched for deer. That would be something he could report to Curt when he got home. *If* he got home, he reminded himself with a half chuckle.

"Right here," David said as he stopped the truck, "an old hackberry fell across the road." He surveyed the forest around them, seeing things Kelly guessed were invisible to him. "Last spring. Curt and I cut it up. That was a good trip."

Did David pause longer there than necessary? He wasn't even looking into his forest anymore, it seemed to Kelly, but into himself. Yet there was a smile on his face. Kelly took that as another hopeful sign.

The road ahead turned and ran beside a cultivated field to their north. "I think that's soybeans," David said. "Every year my neighbor plants something new. Watch for turkeys. They pick whatever they can in the field, but then my noisy truck comes bouncing along and they run for the safety of the forest, right past the front of the truck. Curt says their little turkey brains don't appreciate the irony in that."

A turkey in the wild would be another thing he could report to Curt, but in this he was also disappointed.

"Long ago this used to be a muddy spot," David said, stopping at another point. "Water doesn't drain too well since this part of the ridgetop is so flat. My dad hired a man to lay a pipe under the road — see there? — and spread some gravel over it. It's been twenty, thirty years. We've never had a problem since. Money well spent."

They'd never get to the cabin at this rate, but Kelly could see

Trial by Fire

David's delight in sharing his lore, and he thought these were the kinds of homespun details Curt probably wouldn't share with him, things that Curt might not even know. But Curt was right. This really was a holy place to David.

They rattled down the gravel road as it descended the ridge, and David's hand flew from the wheel to point into the forest. "There's the lake, Kelly! Can you see it through the trees?"

Soon Kelly could see the cabin taking shape among the trees too. He tried to look at it with fresh eyes, to maintain the fiction that this was his first visit. Did David know that he and Curt had snuck out here for a romantic weekend? And if he did, would maintaining that fiction be wrong? Or at least embarrassing? Or was it perhaps not important? That maybe he could simply be here on David's terms for the day, soak in what was offered, and start finding his place in the family?

David parked the truck on the weedy gravel and they both hopped out. Unconsciously, Kelly pulled together the open front of his flannel shirt.

"Have a look around, Kelly. I'll unload the truck and unlock the cabin."

Kelly had intended to help David unload their gear and show he was vigorous, but before he could, David had grabbed both coolers and was carrying them, one atop the other, toward the cabin. Kelly didn't want to do the wrong thing, so he didn't do anything.

The forest chirred. Birds were calling in the trees. Little gray birds, he guessed. Frogs and insects were buzzing all around him and from down at the lake he heard a squawk and sudden flapping as some startled waterbird flew away, alarmed by their arrival. He wished he'd seen whatever it had been so he could report that to Curt. Instead, he'd have to report a day of *not quite* seeing what must be all around him.

Kelly wandered around the area, looking again at what he'd seen before but trying to look anew. There was the fire ring, where Curt had told him he'd eaten countless meals with his father and grandfather. The black ash really was a foot deep. How many fires had they kindled to produce so much? The gray gravel spread around the cabin — as a firebreak and to make walking in the area easier, less buggy — was littered with early fallen leaves. There was the lake below, glinting in the sun, and when he stepped onto the porch, the nice view. The new dock, half-finished. He could offer to help with that though he was miserable with tools. The ever-moving ripples on the water. The sunlight dancing off them a thousand different ways. Dragonflies patrolling the surface. And the forest on the other side of the lake, beyond the brown water, its branches swaying in the breeze, rising to the south ridge where turkey vultures were said to soar.

"There's a turtle, coming up for some air," David said, pointing to a glint on the water that to Kelly's eye was just a floating leaf. David rested his other hand softly on his shoulder. Curt had cautioned him that Kelly was a city boy, but from what David could tell, Kelly was more a person open to new experiences. Even eager for them. He supposed if Curt were showing Kelly around the place, his explanations would be more specific, maybe even scientific, but David thought that Kelly wasn't after schooling this day. Maybe more like finding a feeling of welcome? Well, that had been David's plan anyway.

"The turtles come up and float for a while, taking deep breaths and soaking up the warmth of the sun before disappearing again. Keep watching. You'll probably see more."

Kelly thought about swimming in that murky water filled with turtles. Were they really going to do that? He'd done it before, so he supposed he could again. And it was then that he realized his swimsuit was in the backpack that Curt had convinced him to leave at home.

"So our day's wide open. It's a little early to fix lunch but —"

"Can you teach me how to light a fire with just one match?" He'd almost added "David?" which probably would have been better than "Dad?" but Kelly wasn't sure how to address him. This was a subject he and Curt hadn't talked about yet. Would he feel off balance hearing Kelly refer to his father as "David." Would he feel jealous if Kelly called him "Dad?" And how would David feel? How would *he* feel?

"A one-match fire? Easy." He slipped a hand on Kelly's shoulder again. Gave it a squeeze. "It's all in the preparation. Do that right and you'll succeed every time. But I'm going to walk down to the lake first, just to look around."

"I'll come with you."

"I was hoping you'd say that." And David had almost added "Son," a word he guessed Kelly yearned to hear, but maybe it was too soon, maybe it would be better spoken after lunch when they would be sitting around the fire, stupefied by digesting their burgers. Relaxed, with a little more shared experience between them. He'd watch for a chance.

They walked down the old sandstone steps.

"So these are the stone steps Curt told me about. He said you and your father laid them. That must have been a big job."

David stopped abruptly and gazed across the water. Kelly feared he'd said something wrong, that David was preparing to throw him in the lake.

"I miss Dad," David said. "I miss him every day." Then he turned to Kelly. His face was solemn, not angry. "But I'm closest to him when I'm here. I hope you come to love this place in your own way, Kelly. Leave your mark. Sink roots. I really do. You're always welcome here." With a smile he continued. "We didn't do it all at once. Dad and me. One or two steps at a time. Put a quarter under each one to show the year we laid it down. If you're ever out here and need a few dollars real quick, this is where you can find them!" He stomped on the step.

To Kelly those quarters were suddenly as sacred as any holy relic he could imagine. Curt hadn't mentioned the quarters when they'd descended and climbed the sandstone steps for their skinny-dipping adventure that day. Did he even know about them?

"I should probably just hire somebody from town to finish rebuilding this," David said when they walked onto the completed part of the new dock. The brown water began where the planks ended. "I pick at it a little when I visit. When I feel motivated. It's a losing battle. Dad said nature always wins, and I guess when you put wood near water, it's not even a contest."

Kelly soon saw that for David it wasn't just the two of them in the woods that day. His own father was with them. He always would be when David was at the cabin. And that felt good to Kelly. Yes, it felt holy. He wanted to be a part of something like that. He wanted to find his own path in.

David stared down that the unfinished dock, shaking his head. "So let's get started on that one-match fire of yours, Kelly. Grab any sticks you see on the way."

They mounted the stone steps, Kelly in the lead and pausing to pick up the few sticks that he thought might be good for a fire. But when they got to the ring, he saw that David had collected twice as many.

"Those steps are getting steeper every year," David said with a chuckle. He looked at the pile of kindling. "We'll need lots of this, so see what you can find around the cabin. Twigs. Branches. They're always falling out of the trees."

Kelly started off, but David said, "Wait!" He trotted over to the truck and reached inside then tossed a pair of leather gloves to Kelly. They were curled into the shape of the hands that had worn them many times. "Make it a little easier. Or cleaner anyway." Kelly slipped them on gratefully even though they were too big for him.

Kelly and David went different directions to forage, and when Kelly had collected enough small branches — clutching them to his chest and glad he'd worn the flannel shirt — he brought them to the fire ring, dumping them on top of the stack David had already delivered.

"About that much more and we should be set."

So off Kelly went again, going a little farther to find more and returning when he had all he could carry. The pile of kindling looked big enough to roast one of those wild turkeys he hadn't seen, but he guessed David knew more about the job than he did.

While Kelly was foraging, David had gone into the cabin and came back with an old paper notebook and a cardboard egg carton.

"Curt says this is cheating," David said, waving the egg carton, "but it really makes a difference." He knelt in the gravel beside the fire ring and waved Kelly over. "So the tinder is the paper stuff that lights easily, but it burns fast so you have to cover it with kindling to take the flames and burn a little longer. After that you can begin adding the bigger pieces of wood for flames and coals you'll cook with. And sit around. A successful fire is one you can sit around and jabber or just sit around and think." He tore pages from the notebook. "My college career continues to serve me."

Kneeling in gravel was not something Kelly was used to, but his jeans protected his knees from the worst of it. He took that as a lesson of the day. He needed to clothe himself from harsher realities of the forest. The sharp edges. The stinging insects. Those gloves David had given him were a good idea; they protected his hands as he rooted in the leaves for sticks. A hat would have been good, to swat at the flies that buzzed him occasionally. And how had he forgotten sunscreen? It wouldn't take much thought, really, to come up with an outfit he could wear to the cabin to protect his body.

Before him in the black ash, Kelly could see what looked like dozens of bent and rusty nails. The more he looked, the more of these he saw, and he remembered Curt telling him that David had burned an old fence in this ring. It seemed to him that these nails were another kind of family lore. Stories that the ash had to tell if he could learn how to listen. But David had continued talking, and he needed to listen to him.

"So you crumple the paper loosely — like this — and lay it on the ash. Here. Give it a try."

Kelly followed David's example, though he took off the gloves for better dexterity. David had not made a ball of the paper but had crumpled it lengthwise. Kelly did the same and laid his beside the one David had done.

"Just like that. Maybe a half dozen of these for a good base, and then we lay the open egg carton on top. After that comes the kindling. Takes a while, but it's all in the preparation."

They knelt together, David giving patient instruction and Kelly listening and learning. He crumpled more of the torn paper and set the pieces beside the others on the cold ash. He was building a fire that would add its own ash to the ring. For the rest of his life, Kelly thought, even if he never built another fire, a part of him would be a part of this thing that meant so much to his new family. His effort would join theirs, be mixed in the ash of their generations of fires.

"Um, I have to pee," Kelly said.

"Anywhere across the road," David said, gesturing beyond the truck. "It's not in the lake's watershed over there. I'll get the matches and wait for you before we light it. I mean, before *you* light it."

Kelly pushed up from the gravel and walked quickly over to the road. He chose a spot that hid him behind David's truck not from modesty but because he didn't need to go. He would stand there as though he were, and he'd wait sufficient time, but what he would really be doing was wiping tears out of his eyes and coughing a few times to clear his throat.

Had his own father ever sat with him and explained anything in a calm manner? Had he ever been eager to share knowledge and experience with his son? He must have, Kelly thought. There must have been times like that, but all he could remember was frustration that most often led to harsh words, insults, failure.

When Kelly returned to the fire ring, he found that David had set a box of matches on the gravel. An entire box, in case his first effort at a one-match fire was a failure, Kelly supposed. But beside it was also a bottle of water. "For rinsing your hands if you want," David said casually. And Kelly went through the motions, as much to respect the man's thoughtfulness as to continue his own charade. But he wondered if maybe he was supposed to make a ritual cleansing before he performed this sacred rite.

When Kelly had finished arranging the kindling over the tinder, taking David's occasional suggestion and putting, he felt sure, far more sticks in place than were needed, he took a deep breath.

"This is it," he said, kneeling next to David.

"Nothing to it, Kelly. You've done real well."

He handed the box of matches to Kelly and then leaned toward what he'd built in the fire ring. "Touch the match here. And here. Wherever you can to get the paper going, and then when you can't hold the match any longer, just toss it into the kindling. Make sense?"

"In the abstract." He slid the box open and removed a single match. The striking patch on the side of the box was scarred from use, and Kelly wondered if he could even light one *match*, let alone a one-match fire.

He stroked the match against the box, but nothing happened. So he tried again, and the match snapped just below the tip.

"That doesn't count," David said. "Happens to me all the time. Next time I need matches, I'm going to get the kind you can strike against a rock. I just don't go through a box fast enough."

Kelly tossed the broken match, the one that didn't count, into the kindling and took out another one.

"Sometimes helps if you hold the match close to the tip. You just gotta move your fingers pretty quick when it flares."

Kelly, being closely observed in his trial by fire, tried again. He struck the match, and on the second try, it flared. He dropped the box onto the gravel and then bent low to touch the match to the paper. Without burning himself at all, he managed to do this, and soon the orange flames were climbing into the kindling, finding purchase there.

"First try!" David cheered, giving him a clap on the shoulder. "Well done!"

Kelly felt a smile forming on his face. A silly thing to be proud of, but he couldn't deny what he felt. He'd done this thing. What Curt had spoken of so many times. What David had guided him through. What *he* had done. He looked at the orange flames climbing through the sticks, reaching into the air, sending white smoke ahead of them.

"My first one-match fire!" he heard himself saying, a mix of awe and delight in his words.

"First of many! In a minute we can add the larger pieces of wood," David said, handing a thick piece to Kelly. "The kindling will collapse under the weight, but you have a good foundation already."

Kelly didn't want to stop tending this fire he'd created. He placed more wood on it and lined up further pieces for later. Somewhere along the way he had taken off his flannel shirt and laid it across the back of a chair. He watched the orange flames dance. Heard the wood snap. Sure, they'd cook their burgers over it, and later they'd sit around it and muse for a while. But for now, it was perfect itself. Something he had done, something that was showing him a meaning and purpose he was only beginning to understand. Had he passed the test? Proved himself worthy of David's welcome to the family? Was it a fire that could forge a lasting bond? He stared into the flames.

David had kept quiet as Kelly followed his thoughts. He'd been watching the boy. Noticed how he asked questions, if he was doing it correctly, if he had enough tinder, enough kindling. Was it stacked the correct way? Did he need more here? Less there? He seemed to want to do it exactly right, and David worried he thought he was being judged. Did Kelly really care what he thought of him?

They burned the burgers enough to be called cooked, and then they sat around the fire eating them and chatting about nothing specific. How old the cabin was. "Almost as old as me," David had said. What it was like in the winter. "Nice with a fire in the stove." What wildlife they had. "I saw a fox once. Across the lake." How bad the ticks were. "Just a nuisance as long as you find them right away.

"Long ago," David said from behind closed eyes, "Dad said he wished he had planted short-leaf pine trees all around the cabin. How nice it would be to have a little cabin in a pine forest. I'd always meant to do that. They'd be big by now, though I'm not sure pines would do well in this soil."

Kelly watched his fire burn, watched his logs slowly turn to ash and join the decades of ash beneath. He wanted to add more wood, and so create more ash, but David cautioned that if they had any other plans for the day, especially plans that would take them from the cabin, they wouldn't want to leave the fire burning or even smoldering. Best to let it burn out.

"I guess I'll light another one-match fire someday."

"Someday soon, I hope. And *many* more, Kelly."

He might have been dimly aware of David's plan to help him feel relaxed around the campfire. He certainly *was* relaxed, and whether it was medical or magical, Kelly was content right where he sat. Sunlight dappled where it touched him through the trees. A horsefly buzzed past a few times. Bullfrogs harrumphed down at the lake. From far away someone's chainsaw whined. Kelly thought that if he closed his eyes, he could easily fall asleep in that comfy chair before his dying fire. And wouldn't that be just one more way to experience the cabin? Wasn't sleeping your most relaxed, your most vulnerable state? Stripped of defenses? Would it show David that he felt safe there? Safe with him? There was nothing, absolutely nothing intimidating about this man! This gentle, kind man who could be his new father. He knew then that he wanted to come to this holy cabin many more times. To come again with David. And with Curt. With their whole family. Present and past. To taste this life more fully, not as a comical city boy stumbling around in the forest but as a son, newly born into a loving family. Embraced in their nurturing place.

There had been not one second of hesitation when Curt had introduced Kelly as his fiancé at that backyard picnic. Not his roommate. Not his boyfriend. Not even his lover. But his fiancé. The person he wanted to share the rest of his life with and that he wanted his parents to welcome into their hearts. And to Kelly's surprise, they instantly had. And they would continue to welcome him for as long as their hearts beat in their chests. Maybe longer. No, there was no need to shelter his heart from this father.

"How about a swim?" Kelly said, his thoughts reaching their inevitable conclusion.

"About that . . ." David said with hesitation. He leaned forward but didn't look up.

"I know. Skinny-dipping. Curt says it's the most natural thing in the world." Kelly hoped he was sounding dismissive and carefree. Comfortable. Relaxed. At ease. All the adjectives he wasn't quite feeling in that moment.

"You're okay with it? You and me?"

"Yeah. I mean . . . yeah." He found himself smiling. Not leering. Not smirking. But smiling.

"Well, I need to put out these coals first," David said, rising from his chair and poking the embers with a stick. "There's a bucket in the cabin. I'll get some water from the lake. Should have done that earlier, really."

"I'll do it," Kelly said, jumping from his chair and dashing to the cabin. His suggestion of a swim was heartfelt, but he feared that as the seconds passed his spontaneous courage might falter. He needed to stay in the moment, not second guess or change his mind. He flew down the stone steps with the bucket and returned to the fire ring, breathing hard as he handed the water to David. "Show me how it's done," he said.

David sloshed half of the water on the coals and stirred them. They hissed and sent steam into the air. Then he sprinkled the rest of the water. David was confident they were sufficiently quenched to leave them alone for a while. He'd return with another bucketful after their swim, he said.

They undressed separately in the cabin — David's concession to decorum — and each emerged on the porch with a towel around his waist. So far, so good, Kelly thought, though a little reluctance still bubbled in his chest. But then he smiled with the thought that if he were David's future *daughter*-in-law, this wouldn't be happening. Probably.

"The turtles are going to leave me alone, right? And by that, I mean *all* of me." He suddenly realized a broader meaning to letting himself be vulnerable.

David laughed. "Yes. The turtles will swim away, and as long as you keep moving, the fish will too."

"The fish." What else? Kelly wondered.

"They always go after Curt's freckles."

David led the way down the steps and walked onto the dock. Kelly held back a moment, and David noticed. He could turn away as Kelly slipped out of his towel. Or he could already be in the murky water when it was Kelly's turn.

Or he could do what he did.

He threw off his towel and shouted, "C'mon, Son!"

In that moment Kelly found himself leaping off the dock after David, shouting "Wait for me, Dad!" His towel and his hesitations left behind.

Chapter Two

Looking Forward, Looking Backward

David was surprised when he stepped onto the back patio, darkness nearly fallen and a chill in the March air after a day of glorious sunshine. He'd taken a beer with him and stood in the quiet, the first moment of solitude he'd experienced the entire day. That was how it felt anyway. A day of giddy excitement and handshakes and hugs all around. Of goodwill and good wishes. Hope and promise. A few tears, even a few of his own. Dashing here and there. Photos. A big meal at a restaurant he couldn't afford. A little speechifying, which was the most uncomfortable he'd felt in years, but it fell to him as father of the groom. "Bridegroom," Kelly had corrected. "A groom is a person who takes care of horses." Then Kathy had jumped in, "Well that must be me then!" And they all laughed, though none of them brayed.

A few quiet moments with Kathy at the end of it all, a chance to acknowledge their own wedding anniversary on the day their son had chosen to be married. Curt had insisted on the same March date that his parents had had their wedding, a long-ago courthouse ceremony that his sainted grandmother had not considered legitimate — she'd insisted on a church wedding later — but it was the anniversary they'd all held as the real one through the years. And she had come all the way from Kansas City to be a part of Curt's courthouse wedding. Remarkable, really. The devout Catholic woman, who had taken few pains over the years to hide her disapproval of her son-in-law and wasn't about to make an exception now, coming nonetheless to the wedding of her grandson *to a man*. A gay wedding. A same-sex marriage. Unspeakable among her friends. Utterly outside their experience. Scandalous. Even sinful. They certainly couldn't have had this kind of ceremony in a church! She understood that part, why it had to be a civil ceremony. And yet, her daughter had suspected, it was something that would grant her a touch of the exotic among her friends, that would show she had a breadth of mind to accept, or at least to acknowledge, the way the world was changing. Kathy doubted, though, that her mother caught the significance of the date Curt had chosen.

She had been coolly civil with David, excessively motherly with Kathy, kindly gracious with Kelly, and unstintingly adoring with Curt. Kathy and her mother were in the house then, catching up over glasses of wine, having their own moments of quiet before Kathy drove her back to the hotel she'd chosen to stay in for her week-long visit. And just as well, too, because Curtis David Clark, M.D., their grown son, the bridegroom, had asked to stay in his childhood bedroom on the night before his wedding. He'd said it with a laugh — he'd been living with Kelly at his tiny apartment since the summer before — but David could tell from the wistfulness in his words that his request held a deeper meaning than he'd ever let himself admit openly. One last night in his own bed perhaps? Not show himself to his husband before the ceremony as though he were a blushing bride? A little madcap mayhem with his family in the morning as he'd pretend he was nervous? Or maybe he wanted a few final moments with his mother and father, his first family, before he embarked with his new family. In any case, it gave them a plausible excuse not to host Kathy's mother in their tiny house.

So while the two women picked apart the day over their glasses of wine, David had excused himself, fetched a beer from the refrigerator, and stepped out the back door and onto the patio. Someone nearby had a fire in their fireplace. A dog was barking down the block. He heard the drifting murmur of voices, a conversation on a back porch nearby, too low to understand but part of the commonplace of his neighborhood.

And it was in that moment, the bottle of beer paused halfway to his lips, that David was surprised by an unexpected thought. It was time for him to go to work. To head off to the warehouse and start loading the trucks. On evenings like this, at this twilight hour, in this kind of quiet, he'd left home and family thousands of times and gone to work on the night shift, back in his Kansas City life. Except that he hadn't done that for ten years. He was management now. Had been for a long time. He no longer worked nights. And yet some memory, some reflex, had fired, and he felt again the exhaustion he'd felt then. The anticipation of a night of lifting and carrying. Of loading and unloading as quickly as he could. Of being on his feet for long hours, constantly moving, in the glare of the warehouse lights, to the sound of the trucks and the stink of their diesel exhaust at the hour when everyone else in the world was asleep. It was just supposed to be a starter job to get the two of them going in their life together, but somehow it had hung on. The laughter. The jokes among the crew. Most of it coarse. Often obscene. He'd been an innocent kid with no life experience, no knowledge of the world, yet suddenly with a wife and son and the desperate need to provide for them because that was the choice he had made. He'd always felt he didn't fit in with that warehouse crowd, that he was just biding his time, deflecting their influence as much as he could, waiting to get out, to find something better. That took him longer than he'd expected, but he'd done it. Though now, it seemed, he'd not fully gotten out.

He could go in the house after he finished his beer, after Kathy took her mother away for the night, and fall into his bed. Sleep when most people sleep. Rise in the morning, brush his teeth, dress in presentable clothes, and go to his job in the daylight. Sure, he still spent so much time on the warehouse floor that it might as well be his office, and the clipboard he had carried — now a tablet — served as his real desk. But he wasn't a grunt anymore. He'd paid his dues. Worked his way up. Crafted a little self-esteem. He'd paid his bills through all those years too, and now it was a little easier to do that. A little less of the dread of going from paycheck to paycheck. But you never quite forget that kind of thing.

That morning when they arrived at the courthouse, past the security wands and down the anonymous, nondescript hallways, they had to wait as the other happy couples ahead of them stepped before the judge and exchanged their vows. They sat in the same courtroom where four other days of the week justice was dispensed. But on this day, the judge had a happier duty. And dozens of couples were there to partake.

Among them, David noticed, and he thought Kathy must have as well, a boy and girl who had to be all of one hour older than eighteen. Big smiles on their faces, their hands held tightly as they fidgeted in their chairs, waiting to be called. This courtroom probably saw plenty of kids like them each week, but it brought David back to his own wedding day in a similar courtroom and the urgent, growing need to make their bond legal.

Kelly had met them in the hallway outside of the courtroom. He was alone. Curt introduced him to Kathy's mother, who shook his hand rather than accept his hug, but Curt had warned him about this. They were the only same-sex couple there as far as they could tell, but no one seemed to give them any special regard. Not like the woman in full wedding regalia: a big white dress with a long train and a veil. A huge bouquet of flowers. All dressed up for a ceremony that would last five minutes tops. She had caught everyone's eye. Yet in the courtroom there was no aisle for her father to walk her down. And for this David was grateful. Would he have had to walk Curt down the aisle if they'd had a church wedding? How would that have worked?

He'd found a chance to take Kelly aside as they had waited outside the courtroom. He saw that Kelly had a rose on his lapel, as close, he supposed, to a bouquet the two of them would allow themselves.

"Here, this is for you." David handed him a brass key with a red ribbon tied to it. "It's not much, but it's the best gift I can give you, Son."

"The key to my future?"

David smiled. "In a way, I guess. It's a key to the cabin, Kelly. Your own key. You're a part of the family now."

They'd begged off gifts, hadn't registered anywhere. They needed to find a bigger place, they'd told everyone, before they could fill it with kitchen gadgets and place settings and monogrammed towels. They hadn't even had a bachelor party since there were two bachelors and that would have been awkward.

In the months he had known him, Kelly learned that David was not an emotional man. Or rather, like his son, he didn't let his emotions show very easily. Curt had hinted how deeply his father cared, and Kathy had warned Kelly how David would soon unleash this deep well of care on him. But he'd have to watch for the signs, the subtle ways David expressed love. David had welcomed Kelly from the start — they'd even gone skinny-dipping together at the cabin, which had been a revelation and a relief — but this simple gesture, giving him his own key to a cabin that meant so much to the family, seemed to Kelly to be a bond as deep and meaningful as the wedding vows he was about to make. This was David speaking his love to Kelly.

"It's not really fair," Kelly whispered. "Giving me this right now. You're going to make me ugly cry before the ceremony. *That's* when

I'm supposed to cry." And it was true because he was struggling to hold in a surge of something he couldn't quite define. "This isn't even a real handkerchief in my pocket. It's just for show. I can't use it to dry my tears."

"I wanted to find a quiet moment to give it to you. Not draw a lot of attention to it. Everyone would think it was silly, Kelly. Me giving you a key as a wedding present."

"No one in this family would think this key is silly! Least of all me. Thank you, Dad!"

He gave David a hug that lasted longer than it needed to, but it was a day for big emotions, and nobody noticed.

"Take good care of my boy, Kelly."

"Now I'm really going to cry!"

After they had found seats in the courtroom, they waited their turn. The boy and girl ahead of them giggled through their vows, kissed quickly before the judge as he'd pronounced them husband and wife, and then darted toward the door. David wondered if they were late for class.

When Curt and Kelly were finally called up, David saw no hesitation in his son's eyes. He rose from the seat between his parents, kissed his mother and grandmother, shook his father's hand, then joined Kelly as they walked toward the judge.

Until the last moment, their ceremony was no different from the dozen that came before them. The judge did a good job, not racing through vows he had already recited many times that morning, not calling attention to the fact that here were two men getting married. Giving them the same official care that he'd shown for the others, even if it lasted only a few minutes.

At the end he said, "I present to you Kelly and Curtis Shepherd."

David and Kathy looked at each other with surprise in their wet eyes. Their boy had taken his husband's last name. It took only a second to sink in before they both beamed at their two sons.

The rest of the day was the frenzied whirlwind they all expected. They dashed from the courthouse to the art museum where they discreetly took some photos — none of them knew if such a thing was allowed and were afraid to ask in case it wasn't — and then the young couple returned to their apartment to change out of the wedding suits and finish packing for their trip to Italy the next morning. They all met at the restaurant for a celebratory dinner on David's dime and maybe had too much to drink. Then evening came, and they parted with tearful hugs.

When they finally got home, David shrugged out of his coat and jacket and loosened his tie then paused to realize how tired he was. He would sleep well beside his wife that night.

Inside the house, Kathy continued to talk with her mother, and he wondered how long that would last. He'd mostly dodged his mother-in-law's scornful eye during all his years with Kathy, and he would stay out in the chill that was penetrating his thin dress shirt until she left. Kathy had taken the week off work to spend with her mother, but he would go to the warehouse in the morning as he regularly did, to give them space. Maybe he'd go to the cabin that weekend. Maybe for an overnight.

Curt had taken Kelly's name. That surprised him, and, as he nursed his beer, he wondered why Curt hadn't told him before it was announced. Was it a gift he was reserving for Kelly? Or did he not want to hurt his father until he had to?

"If we'd had a daughter," Kathy had said in a moment they'd found together in the long afternoon, "and she had taken her husband's name, we wouldn't have thought twice about it." She worried that David would brood on that small detail of the big day.

For long years Curt had let him know in subtle and not-so-subtle ways that, well, he didn't measure up as a father. That maybe he had been okay once, but he was no longer needed. That having a father who had loaded trucks was an embarrassment to the brilliant, high-achieving boy Curt had been. That maybe his father didn't have the emotional intelligence to understand his son.

That had resolved itself finally, except that it hadn't. Neither man would ever be fully free of his doubts about the other's feelings. Curt had kept an emotional distance from David for too long, and David had lived years certain of his own inadequacy in all things despite Kathy's insistence that he was the finest man and husband and father on the planet.

Yet this simple thing, Curt taking a new name, was all that was needed to tip David into the depths of well-practiced self-doubt and trigger a muscle memory that it was time to go load trucks again. He spiraled back to the time when self-doubt and his son's distance defined him. He knew he was wrong, of course, but David was certain Curt taking on a new name, forsaking the Clark name, could be one more sign that he thought his father was inadequate, whether he meant it consciously or unconsciously. And David would brood on it, never fully shaking himself free of the belief.

Chapter Three

Expedition into a Dark Forest

They believed themselves properly equipped for their expedition into the far reaches of the forest. They each had a backpack, weighed down with pocket knives, water bottles, granola bars, handsaws, hand shovels, old-school compasses (in case they got lost, which Curt knew was impossible for him and unlikely for Kelly, despite his silly fears), topographic maps of the hundred acres, two rolls of red survey tape each, one roll of toilet paper each, leather gloves, sunblock, insect repellent, more-than-basic first aid kits, nail clippers, snips, flashlights, lengths of twine, extra dry socks, zip ties, and good intentions. They wore stout boots on their feet, comfy flannel shirts on their bodies, and orange caps on their heads. They tucked their jeans into the tall socks they'd pulled on that morning. Each grabbed a lopper as they stepped out of the cabin and stood on the porch, ready for anything.

Their chore for the day was to hike along the unfenced quarter mile of their southern property line and tie fresh red tape to the posts that David and Curt had sunk along there years before. It had been David's good faith attempt to define the line. He had never met the man who owned the land south of them, and, for all any of them knew, that property could have changed hands several times in the decades the Clarks had been stomping around their hundred acres. Thus the good faith line of approximation, sporadically renewed with red tape. They wouldn't dispute a legal survey, if one ever happened, but no one seemed interested in spending money to formally draw that imaginary line, so the posts had sufficed for years.

"Remember," said Curt as he stepped off the porch, pulling his pack onto his shoulders. "If you get lost — and you won't — just go downhill. That will take you to the creek. Follow that and you'll reach the lake, and then you'll know where you are."

That *sounded* sensible to Kelly, but he'd been raised in the city, where a person tread on smooth sidewalks, beside paved and orderly streets that met mostly at right angles, all with names that hung on tall signposts. Traffic lights, crosswalks. Not old posts with fading red tape, marching through a trackless forest where there was no order any sensible person could see. Walking downhill to safety might make perfect sense in the calm of the cabin porch, but if he got lost, random panic, Kelly felt certain, would guide his stumbling feet. He stepped off the porch and joined Curt.

"How about I just stick to you like a tick on a dog?"

"That's a metaphor, isn't it?"

"Yes. Well, it's a simile. And it's my desperate plea that you never leave me."

"Now why would I do that, Kelly?"

His question was meant to be rhetorical, Kelly understood, but Curt was about to take him deep into the trackless wilderness and, well . . .

"Kiss for luck?"

They shared a quick kiss.

"I just hope luck doesn't factor in during our little expedition." He was trying to motivate his feet to move.

Curt smiled. "C'mon, Kelly. Let's go across the dam and along the north-facing slope."

It wasn't going to be an easy hike. The distance from the cabin to the unfenced property line wasn't far, but they would follow an indirect path a half mile through an Ozark forest, filled with hidden rocks they could stumble on, briars that would reach for their flesh, deadfalls they'd have to steer around.

"When Dad and I put these posts in — I must have been eleven or twelve at the time — he would toss a half dozen of them on his shoulder like it was nothing, and I carried the post driver, doing my best to keep up. I was a scrawny kid, and that thing was *heavy*! It's packed with lead so it can slam a post into this rocky ground." He spoke to the trees around him, revisiting a memory that had grown misty and fond over the years. "Took us about four trips to get the full line of posts in place, and I think Dad would have put in more if he'd had a better helper. My dad carrying all that steel on his shoulder, never showing any sign of fatigue. Never annoyed with me dragging the driver through the leaves behind him, complaining the whole time. I remember he'd take breaks to sip water he probably didn't need just so I could lean on him and gasp for a while. He'd put his hand on my shoulder, like he was the one who needed to rest. And when we were done for the day, he'd take the post driver from me and carry it back. I remember one time when we got to the cabin, I fell into a chair by the fire ring, and the next thing I knew, he was waking me up with a burger on a plate for my lunch."

But Curt was talking to himself. When he turned, Kelly was thirty feet behind him, carefully extracting the sleeve of his flannel shirt from the thorny grip of a smilax vine.

"Sorry," Curt hollered. "I should have warned you about that."

"Don't worry. I *should* be able to get the blood out of my shirt," Kelly hollered back. "And despite that, I do love this forest of yours, Curt."

"Technically, it's Dad's. Or Mom's and Dad's. I've never seen the deed. But nobody thinks like that. It's ours. Mom's and Dad's and mine. And yours, too." He touched Kelly's cheek. "Yours, too. *Ours*."

Expedition into a Dark Forest 35

"I feel like I should do something to earn my way in."

"You're going to make me get mushy, aren't you?"

"Maybe. You should probably just consider that my permanent *modus operandi*."

Curt adjusted his cap, stuck his thumbs under the straps of his pack, and puffed out his chest. He stared up at patches of blue peeking through the treetops for a moment. "Okay, Smarty-pants. You've already earned your way into my heart. That's all you ever had to do. Is that what you wanted to hear?"

Kelly smiled. "Pretty much. So how much farther?"

"It's not marathon distance." He pointed to the west. "Thataway, more or less. Follow me."

They could have continued talking over the crunch of the leaves beneath their boots, hearing the call of the birds, the wind in the trees, but Kelly wanted to conserve his breath for, well, breathing. Curt would occasionally say something like "watch out for that root," or "careful here," or "low branch," and especially "thorns," but mostly they trudged in silence. One time he stopped abruptly and held up his hand, signaling Kelly to be silent and not move for nearly a minute, peering into the trees. Then he dropped his hand in disappointment. "I thought I heard something big down by the lake." Kelly wasn't sure whether to feel excited or frightened by this.

Kelly mostly believed that they really would reach a line of fence posts somewhere ahead, marking part of the southern border, because he couldn't come up with any other reason why Curt would drag him deep into their forest, except for nefarious stuff that he dismissed. Mostly.

They stumbled on, past an uncounted host of trees that all looked the same to Kelly, skirting deadfalls, and he lost his sense of direction.

"And here we are." Curt stopped them beside a green steel post rising incongruously from the ground in the middle of the forest. A scrap of tape, faded to pink, still clung to the top of the post. "There's the next one over there. See?" He pointed into the trees, but Kelly couldn't see any post. It would be vertical like the trees, and green like the scrub. Were there really more of them out there? He doubted he could get back to the cabin on his own.

Curt turned his back to Kelly. "If you would kindly extract a roll of red tape from my pack, Mr. Shepherd, we can begin our work for the day."

Kelly dug around in Curt's pack until his fingers felt the tape, and he brought it out. Curt pulled a couple feet from the roll, ripped it free, then gripped the roll between his teeth while he tied the tape around the pole, leaving long strands, which fluttered in the breeze.

"Easier to see this way," he said, taking the tape roll from his mouth. "Though I don't know who will ever see it but us. Still, it's important to show we're paying attention. Keep things neat and orderly."

Kelly looked at Curt's handiwork dancing in the breeze. "I'll bet even I could do that." He took the roll of tape from Curt. "Assuming I could find another post in this wild wood."

"Well, you could use your compass to take a west bearing, accounting for the angle of declination, of course, and then march through the scrub until you reach the next post. Or I could show it to you."

"Easier if you showed it to me."

"Then stick to this dog."

Curt began crunching through the leaves again perhaps a hundred feet to the next post. Any tape it once held was gone.

So there *is* more than one of these posts, Kelly thought. Maybe there were more. Maybe a long line of them. If so, he could try to dismiss his mostly light-hearted worry about whatever it was he worried about being deep in a forest.

Since Kelly still held the red tape, he rolled off a length and tore it free, then he put the roll in Curt's mouth. "Here. Hold this." They both chuckled at this, though Curt sounded like he was gurgling.

"How many of these posts are there, did you say?" Kelly began tying the tape to the top of the post, though his fluttering ends came out uneven, and he worried Curt would think his work looked sloppy.

Curt removed the roll from his mouth and wiped it on Kelly's shirt.

"When I was helping Dad put them in, it seemed like hundreds. But I think there's probably more like twenty. Twenty-five. I never counted. Somewhere along the way we'll come near The Old Man of the Forest."

"The Old Man of the Forest?"

"An ancient cedar tree. Much older than the other cedars around here. Kind of a council tree for me and Dad. Good place to have a heart-to-heart. It's where he told me about the birds and the bees. Heterosexual, of course, but neither of us was clear about me then."

Kelly looked back at the first post. He could see the fluttering red tape now, and he understood better why they had taken up this chore. He lined up that post with the one he had tied and looked farther into the trees, to spot the next in the line.

Once he knew what he was looking for and how to find it, he could see the next post, so he hurried to it. When he stopped beside it, he realized he didn't have the tape, but then he turned and saw Curt was gripping it in his teeth again. Curt could be emotionally aloof. When they'd eat out or shop for groceries, he'd be polite to any stranger he had to talk to, but he was never warm and certainly not playful. Yet here at the cabin, deep in the woods and far from the rest of the world, Curt let himself be a different person. Or rather,

Kelly judged, let himself be more himself. Kelly liked seeing this Curt. It was going to be a great life!

He grabbed Curt in a bear hug. "I love you, Curtis Shepherd! I really, really love you!"

With his arms pinned to his sides, Curt couldn't remove the roll of tape from his mouth, so he turned his head and spat it out, careful to see where it rolled in the leaves so they could retrieve it later.

"I love you too, Kelly Shepherd."

They stood like that for what may have been only moments. Or the seasons could have changed, but the time was sufficient for both of them. Finally, Kelly released his hold and stepped back.

"It's just that you bring me to this perfect place. To your perfect family. You let me in. You let me *belong*." Kelly looked away, into the trees. "You don't know what that means to me, Curt. I get overwhelmed sometimes. I run out of clever words and metaphors."

"We're both better with each other." A breeze sighed through the trees above them. This is right, the breeze was telling them. Do this. Do lots of this.

When they got back to work, Curt was able to find the roll of tape and Kelly was able to find the next post.

"Next in line."

As Kelly was tying the tape onto it, Curt noticed that Kelly's sleeve was torn.

"Did you really cut yourself on that smilax?"

Kelly smirked. "I'll guess we'll find out when we do our tick check later."

"In other words, you *didn't* draw blood because if you had, you know I'd be applying antiseptic ointment and a bandage before we took another step. Do I need to rip your shirt off your body?"

Curt the carer. Curt the nurturer. Early in their relationship, when Curt slowly began creeping out of his shell and started revealing the kind of man he was, this had surprised Kelly. But Kelly kept seeing it, the goodness and kindness that he judged was genuine and not a performance intended to get him in bed. And soon he saw it was a fundamental part of Curt's nature. And so, there, deep in the woods with no one around to hear, Kelly decided to bring up a thought he'd been mulling.

"Who's our next in line?"

"What do you mean?"

"After us. Who's next in line to be lord or lady of the manor?" He gestured toward the forest around them.

"That's not exactly a metaphor, is it?"

"It's more like rhetorical phrasing. With a playful flourish."

"I've never considered that. The cabin. The woods. The lake. They seem eternal to me. Like they were always here for us and always will be. It never entered my mind, until you put it there, Kelly Shepherd, who or what would come after us."

Kelly liked that he used the word "us." Curt *did* see him as an equal member of the family. It was the kind of casually dropped word, the unhesitant gesture that he'd seen from Curt, and from Curt's parents, that made him feel like he really was welcomed among them, that he truly belonged. That he was part of a family again. Only a good one this time. It hardly seemed possible sometimes. Curt would probably laugh at the notion, if Kelly dared mention it, but then he'd reflect on it and understand the importance little gestures can have in a relationship. Especially for someone like Kelly.

"Because I was thinking about something, Curt."

"That's never good. Do I need to sit down?"

"About us maybe having a child."

Curt's face went blank. He was silent for a moment then said crisply, "The apartment's too small for another person!" He turned and started walking to the next post.

Kelly trotted after him, persisting.

"I mean it, Curt. You and me. Fathers to a little boy or a little girl. A family of our own. We'd be good at it. I know we would."

Curt didn't slow his step, so Kelly stopped.

"You know this is a conversation we were going to have eventually!" he called to Curt's back.

Kelly understood the cabin was their place of peace, and he was introducing conflict. But if it escalated to a fight, better here than in their thin-walled apartment. Anyway, it wouldn't escalate. Kelly felt certain of that. Curt wasn't the kind to raise his voice. Here at the cabin, their safe place, they could have a quiet, thoughtful conversation about something that was important to him.

Curt had reached the next post and shucked his pack so he could retrieve the second roll of tape.

"Curt!"

"C'mon, Kelly," he barked. "We don't have all day."

But they did have all day, and they both knew it.

Kelly sat on the ground. His backpack clanked and rattled as he pulled it off. "I'm going to get full of ticks now!" He grumbled as he began shredding an oak leaf.

"Suit yourself."

Curt finished with the tape and marched to the next post. Kelly watched his orange cap bobbing among the trees, getting farther from him. He began to wonder if he really could get himself back to the cabin. And if he did, would their car still be there? Or would Curt have left without him? He guessed he could survive a few days on his own, but sooner or later some wild beast would carry him off and that would be that.

He turned again to look for Curt, but he was gone. All Kelly saw were trees and more trees. He closed his eyes and tried to calm his thoughts. What kind of father would he be if he panicked at the first sign of trouble? And what kind of husband would he be if he grew angry at Curt's sudden coldness. Curt was that way sometimes. Kelly knew Curt needed to withdraw, and he knew he needed to wait him out and not make it worse by getting angry about something that was part of his nature. But knowing that didn't make him feel any better. Not in that moment. They'd welcomed him to this place, to their family, to their hearts. He wasn't going to repay them by being stupid.

He tried to relive his first time Curt had brought him to the cabin. He'd been ridiculously worried, fearful that he was going to be fed to bears or something. Why would anyone be kind to him? No one ever had. Yet Curt *had* been kind. And patient. He showed him things and taught him things. He'd cooked a meal for him. Shared a fire with him. Shared a bed with him. Showed Kelly that someone thought he was worthy of love. Slowly his worries had melted in Curt's embrace. All of that had convinced him that Curt could be a good father.

He didn't know how long he had been sitting there. Did he fall asleep? He wasn't sure, but when he heard crunching in the leaf litter, he knew Curt was coming back. At least he hoped it was Curt, but maybe it was a bear.

"Was that a metaphor?"

Kelly looked at a pair of boots planted before him. "What?"

"What I said. 'Suit yourself.' Was that a metaphor?"

"Not sure. Maybe."

"I'm sorry I said that, Kelly. I'm sorry I walked away from you like that." Curt was doubly sorry because it had been how he'd treated his father sometimes when he had been a stupid teenager. He thought he'd outgrown that kind of pettiness. He would have to work harder.

"Are there bears in these woods, Curt?"

"I've read something about them coming up from Arkansas, but I don't think they've gotten this far north yet."

"I thought I was going to die."

Curt laughed softly until he wondered if Kelly meant he would die emotionally. Did he have that kind of power over another person? How badly had he hurt his father all those years ago? It frightened him. Emotions frightened him. Kelly still hadn't looked up, so Curt seated himself cross legged on the ground before him and took both of his hands.

"Now we're both going to be full of ticks," Kelly said.

"We do things together. We'll do our tick check later!"

That brought a smile to Kelly's face.

"Look at me, Kelly." With a finger under Kelly's chin, he lifted his face. "Let's talk about this because I know it means a lot to you. And you mean a lot to me. We can talk about it here, sitting on this rocky ground like two crazy people. Or we can go back to the cabin and sit in chairs before a fire like adults. Or we can climb in bed and talk about it in each other's arms like two people who love each other. But we'll talk about it."

"What about the tape on the posts?"

"We'll leave defining boundaries for another day. I left my loppers over there somewhere, so we'll need to come back anyway."

"Do you want to start? Because I think you know where I stand."

"Okay. Bottom line: I just don't think I'd be a good father for any child."

"You're wrong, Curt."

"And the second big problem: how would we do it? The most likely avenue is adoption. And maybe it's selfish, but I don't know that I can fully love a child that doesn't share some of my genes."

"But you love me, and I don't share any of your genes?"

"That's different, and you know it. We're raised from infancy with the idea that we'll find someone to love. Be our partner. We share our souls, not our genes."

"I thought you didn't believe in souls."

"You know what I mean."

"Why can't that be the same with a child though? Love is love. Why is love for a child reserved for only a child who shares our genes? There are other things we can share with a child. Deeply. Intimately."

"I hate it when you outsmart me, Kelly. Or half outsmart me. I'm not saying it's that way for everyone. Just that it seems to be the case for me. I know I'm not going to pick up an infant for the first time and suddenly feel an immense love. I certainly don't in the hospital. And you'd be surprised the number of new mothers who find they feel the same way. Who don't bond with their baby even with shared genes. A person can't just turn their love on and off like a light switch."

"But if it was *your* baby? Your child?"

"I don't know. I don't feel like I could, Kelly. And what if I *didn't* love the child? What if we did this thing, adopted or had a surrogate or whatever, and I didn't love the outcome? What if I became a father by assignment rather than desire? Wouldn't that be worse? The poor kid."

Kelly thought for a moment, a moment that Curt was certain was allowing more ticks to crawl up their clothes.

"Actually, you know what? I've pretty much decided that my parents didn't love me. Not really. Not in a deep, soulful way.

What they felt for me might have sometimes been affection, maybe early on, but it was mostly obligation and routine and habit. Their assignment, like you said. What they'd been raised to believe was socially acceptable and inevitable. You get married. You have kids. You raise them. Do what you can for them. That kind of thing. Or maybe they started out loving me but got lost on the way. So when I stepped out of line, well, the kind of feelings they had for me really were something they could turn off. Just like a light switch." He looked down at the ground. "And then in the dark, they could do awful things."

Kelly never talked about the awful things had happened to him. Maybe he never would, and Curt thought he would be saddened to know most of it. But he knew it affected Kelly, and so it affected him, and he knew the two of them would find ways to work through it in their lives ahead. Most of all, though, he didn't want Kelly to fall into one of his spirals. Not ever. And certainly not at the cabin.

"That light switch was a pretty apt simile you came up with, Curt."

"The one time in my life I'm creative, and I wish I hadn't been."

"No. It's good. It's really good. It helps me clarify my thoughts." He rose from the ground with a little struggle. "Mostly the kinds of thoughts that don't belong in this forest." His family, his former family, had no place here. He reached for his backpack, swatted it a few times to knock off the ticks, and shrugged into it. Then he grabbed his loppers.

Curt studied him for a moment. Kelly was putting on his brave face, but was he giving up this easily on his hope for a child? Did he yield because he knew what bad parenting meant? Maybe around the campfire that evening, after a few beers and in the comfort of the chairs and darkness they could try again. Easier to talk in the dark. Maybe a whippoorwill would call. And they would not talk about ugly things, only healthy things. Yes. Happy things. Restorative things. Maybe a child, trying to raise a child right, was part of the medicine Kelly needed to heal. He'd have to think about that.

Curt rose from the ground. He brushed the seat of his jeans.

"I don't think I could have gotten myself back to the cabin, Curt."

"Sure you could. Just go downhill, remember?"

"Curt, going back alone, doing anything without you, well, that really would be going downhill for me." And then, "That's a metaphor, but you know what I mean."

"You should have been an English teacher."

"I should have been a lot of things, Curt. But I like who I'm becoming." He looked into the tree canopy. "I like where I am now." He looked at Curt. "I like who I'm with. I like it all so much that I want to share it, bring another heart and soul into it."

"I know, Kelly. Let's go back to the cabin. I can see things more clearly before a smokey fire. We can talk more there. It's not far."

Chapter Four

Nature Always Wins

"When you think about it," Curt said. "Having a fireplace is literally inviting your home's worst enemy through the door. Literally is the right word, isn't it?"

"Probably, but how so?"

"Fire. It can burn the place to the ground, and yet people pay extra to have a fireplace inside these houses made of toothpicks and glue."

They were seated before the condo's fireplace, in opposing wing chairs. Gas flames danced behind the glass screen though the day outside had grown warm. It was an open house, and they'd come to look the place over, after two duds they'd already seen that afternoon. There were a few more on their list but it looked increasingly like they weren't going to see them that afternoon. Reluctance or inertia or fatigue kept them seated in the wing chairs, which didn't seem to bother anyone.

"You boys class up the joint," the realtor said when they asked her if they could sit there and talk. "Deep in earnest discussion. You look like serious buyers. That nudges the other lookers to act. Stay right where you are as long as you like and chat away." She hurried off to find the prospects wandering upstairs.

Curt gestured toward the fire with the condo's information sheet. "I'm just saying we shouldn't pay a premium for a fireplace we don't want and won't use."

"We don't? We won't?"

"And think of the ash you'd have to clean out all the time."

"*I* would?"

"We can have all the fires we want at the cabin. Honestly, I don't think I could relax before a fire, stare into the flames and ponder the mysteries of the universe, unless it was at the cabin. And we don't have to clean up the ash there. It's the same reason I don't want a lawn to mow or even a flowerpot on the patio if I can help it. A hundred acres of Ozark forest is enough yard for us to maintain."

"Us?"

A youngish, very pregnant couple came in the front door and looked around.

"Is this the open house?" the man said, looking at the two men sitting comfortably before the fireplace as though it was their own home and the couple had gotten the wrong address.

"Yes. The agent is upstairs," Kelly said with a genial smile. "There's a bowl of chocolates in the kitchen, so be warned." He had been twisting the wrapper of one he'd already eaten, trying to stop himself from getting another.

"You're not the agent?"

"No. We seem to have become part of the décor. We're a couple of potential buyers having a little squabble."

The couple offered weak smiles and then hurried past them into the kitchen.

Curt leaned toward Kelly and whispered, "We aren't having a squabble,"

"Sure, we are. And it's not about fireplaces or lawns to mow or flowerpots."

"What's it about then?"

Kelly plucked at the crease in his slacks and crossed and uncrossed his legs. Curt was going to find fault with every place they looked at. How could he think that Kelly didn't see through it?

"It's about whether we want two bedrooms or three."

Curt rolled his eyes. They'd settled that. The cost of a three-bedroom condo in the city was too much, and finding one that wasn't part of some soulless, corporate development was close to impossible anyway.

"And what we're really squabbling about is who might sleep in the extra bedrooms."

"Let's not go into that here!" Curt snapped. The very pregnant couple had ascended the stairs and were out of earshot. But then his voice betrayed weariness. "I thought we were done talking about that, Kelly. I really did."

"I'll never finishing talking about it, Curt. And I don't think you're through with the matter either. I think you're secretly on the fence, despite your occasional, sharp words and postures of certainty."

Curt's eyes fell to his hands. He hadn't wanted to revisit the subject. Not that morning, and not ever. They could dress like adults. Have a nice brunch. Tour several open condos, only half seriously. Snipe about the décor. Have a fun day. Then regroup at their tiny apartment to digest what they'd found and see if they needed to reassess their requirements, settle on absolutes, consider compromises, maybe cast the net wider. But Kelly had to play his wild card. Again. Now. Here. And Curt feared he held a losing hand, despite his poker face. He could only bluff so long. Was he bluffing himself?

"You're going to make me go through it again, aren't you?"

"Only until you no longer think you believe it."

"Sometimes you're a stubborn ass, Kelly."

"Another metaphor! But isn't my stubbornness what you like about me? That I won't let you hide behind your wavering certainties or run away from your pestering uncertainties! That deep down inside you, there's a core, a soft, fuzzy place, a baseline Curt that you put a lot of effort into ignoring? Or hiding. You know you find it easy to talk to me. Eventually, anyway. So, talk."

Curt sighed. It was true. Kelly was easy to talk to, to confide in. He was safe. He listened closely. He cared. That was a quality that had strongly attracted him. That Kelly, who carried so many wounds himself, could still take on another's burdens. Kelly wrapped Curt's confidences in a blanket of quiet assurance, held them close, and respected them. He knew Curt had never felt safe doing that with anyone else.

"I don't feel this is an uncertainty. I feel that I know my mind about this."

"It's not a competition, Curt," Kelly said, getting right to the point. "You don't have to be better than your father."

Curt sighed. This was another beguilement about Kelly, that he could always lead Curt where he needed to go, whether Curt wanted to go there or not.

"There was a time in my life, Kelly, a time when I was a stupid kid, that I would have laughed at your comment because I would have thought you got it so backward. But now I shrink before it. No, it's not a competition. It's not even a contest! Not only could I never be better than my father; I'd be lucky if I could be half as good as my father. One quarter." He looked again at the flyer he was holding, trying to hide his rising emotion behind it, but Kelly's silent patience wore him down.

"If we had a child, I fear I'd withdraw and be neglectful and put too much of the burden on you. All the time knowing I wasn't measuring up to Dad's example. Or I'd micromanage the poor thing and second guess you all the time and try to force logic and order into parenting a child and botch it up atrociously and ruin some kid's life. There is no middle road for me, Kelly. I've seen how it should be done. I've seen how it *shouldn't* be done. I see it all the time at the hospital. It's not in my nature to be a parent."

Kelly allowed a moment to let Curt's carefully raised passion recede. They needed to remain calm if they were going to continue classing up the joint.

"You won't ruin a child's life, Curt. You haven't ruined mine."

"Give me more time. Plus, you were already an adult when I met you. Mostly." He permitted himself a smile.

"As are you."

"Thanks." And then, "I feel judged." But he tossed out another smile.

In his life with Curt, Kelly could feel himself being drawn into his father-in-law's orbit. There was no mistake; it was real. Maybe having such a crappy father made him more susceptible to David's guileless heart. He *wanted* a father like David. Wanted to fill the void in his life, the chasm that opened after his father had thrown a coffee mug at him and shouted at him to get out. David Clark had filled the emotional void that had always been there.

Kelly knew that what Curt was reacting to was not David's effortless love for his new son, but David's effortless love for his *first* son. Curt was in an orbit around a bright sun he would never escape, an orbit that was an embrace, and like the sun, it brought gifts of warmth and light. He was blinded by his father's love for him. And Curt thought he could never love a child as well as his father loved him, so he shouldn't even try. Other people tried and failed. Curt saw it every day at the hospital. They'd make a hash of it. He saw enough messed up kids to understand that he was part of a very tiny group of children from truly good parents. Two people who had done everything right. And if he couldn't do everything right, he didn't want to try at all. The risk was too great. And the consequences of doing it wrong were too great. Maybe if they could just get his dad to raise their child . . .

"My point is, you were already fully formed by the time I met you, Kelly. I didn't have the terrifying responsibility of molding your personality, your personhood. You already were who you are." He smiled. "For better or worse."

"Now who's being judged? In the spirit of fair and honest conversation, Curt, I'll take that as a compliment. But sometimes I think we're all fully formed when we're born, and the rude realities of our lives just assist or interfere with how that manifests itself. Your dad once told me that you can't really raise a child. That the best you can do is nudge them in the direction you think they ought to go."

"My dad said that?"

"Sure did. When I was over there doing laundry one day."

Curt threw his hands in the air. "What further evidence do you need that I'd be a poor father for some luckless child? I could never have such an insight! My dad thinks with his heart. I can't do that!"

"I think you've misdiagnosed your patient, Dr. Shepherd."

"I don't know about being fully formed at birth. I mean, look at a person. They're the product of all the influences in their life. Raise a child in a quiet household, and you're bound to have a quiet child."

"Not always, Curt. Not if the child is born with a boisterous personality. It will come out. Or the other way around. The shy child in a family full of high achievers. Or the big one: a gay child in a family of heterosexuals. I happen to know one of those who turned out pretty well."

"So do I. Okay, I'll give you that one. But it's still a big responsibility, raising a kid, and you must do it right."

"We *can* do it right. We *can*! You know we can, Curt. Or as right as our part needs to be, and the child fills in the rest."

"I just worry that if we adopt, we're going to abduct the child's personality. That they won't be whoever they were born to be because we got in the way. Nudged them the wrong way. Would I be a doctor today if some other family had brought me up?"

"Curt, you would have been something beyond commonplace if any other family brought you up. You would have reached high. It's in your nature. I mean, look back right now and tell me what specific influences you had from your parents that steered you into medicine. Did your mom and dad sit around the dinner table and talk about first aid every night? Did they watch doctor shows on television? Or volunteer at a hospital? Did your mother pine that her family always wanted a doctor?"

Curt was stymied. Kelly seemed to be right. Neither of his parents had ever suggested becoming a doctor as a career. Even the counselors in high school didn't. It had started with him. Something about it was in his nature.

Except Kelly was also wrong. There *was* one specific influence. When he discovered that his dad had been very sick as an infant. That he maybe could have died from whatever it was, though he had no proof of that. Curt still had the photo of that recovered boy, just a few months old and visibly weak, but with a smile. "Healthy again" it said on the back. Curt was sure that specific photo had steered him into becoming a doctor.

But then he thought maybe Kelly was right. Only a compassionate person would have been so affected by a photo like that, would have read and understood the message in it. His dad had never spoken of the sickness. He wasn't sure his dad even knew he'd been sick as a baby. Curt was affected by it because it was his nature to be compassionate, and it merely manifested as Curtis Shepherd, M.D. because his parents had nudged him to be a good person, however that presented itself.

He sat up straight and looked squarely at Kelly. "My folks gave me a stable, healthy childhood. They are excellent examples of excellent parents. They gave me permission to be curious and follow my interests. They let me follow my nature."

Kelly smiled. Curt had seen his point.

"And it was my nature that led me into medicine. The nature I was born with." He sat back, thinking he had just won the argument. Then his face fell. "I walked right into it, didn't I?"

"That same nature will make you an excellent, loving, and caring father. One who won't thwart a child's nature but nurture it."

"I can't believe I'm weakening, Kelly." He raised his finger. "If we do this thing, Kelly, if we do it, *I'm* the one who will be called Dad! Understand?"

It was then that the very pregnant couple came down the stairs, followed by the agent.

"I'm sorry I've run out of flyers," she was saying to them. "But I can email the information."

"Here, take this one," Curt said, rising from his chair by the fire. "We're not going to need it."

The husband accepted the flyer and began to study it. The agent smiled, but there was a query in her eyes. Maybe letting them class up the joint had caused them to talk themselves out of buying it.

"We have a few more places we want to see today," Curt said, and he began walking to the door. Kelly rose and followed him.

Curt stopped and turned to the agent. "Thank you," he said. And then to the very pregnant couple he said, "I hope you two find a place you like. And good luck with the big job ahead of you."

As they walked across the street to where they had parked their car, Kelly asked why he'd made the sudden exit.

"We clearly don't want that place," Curt said, fishing for his keys. "There aren't enough bedrooms, and it's too far from the elementary school."

Chapter Five

Home Run

They were waiting just past the Wall of Sound when Kelly got the call. He'd been tracking Curt's phone but lost him when he got on the lower deck of Queensboro Bridge, and all Kelly could do was wait for him to emerge on the Manhattan side to catch a satellite and show up on his phone again. Kathy and David were with Kelly, scanning the living mass of runners moving up First Avenue, to spot Curt's bright green shirt, the one he always raced in. Thousands of people lined both sides of the street as far north as they could see. The three would cheer and wave when they saw Curt, but he might not wave back, might not even see them among the crowd, and he certainly wouldn't stop to chat.

They'd agreed that trying to navigate the New York subways was too fraught for their Midwestern sensibilities. They had wanted to see Curt earlier on the marathon route, somewhere in Brooklyn maybe when he was still fresh, but doubted they could get themselves to anywhere distant, anywhere not on foot, or that if they did, that they could get themselves back. And what if they ended up in New Jersey or something? So they chose to stay in Manhattan and after they put Curt on the pre-dawn bus to the starting line on Staten Island — "Don't call me," he admonished as he silenced his phone. "And no texts. I have to stay focused!" — they picked a couple of spots along the course in Manhattan that they could get to on foot from the hotel so they could be part of the experience on the sidelines. Thus, their first chance to see Curt was just past mile 16 after he came off the bridge into Manhattan. And then, if they hurried, they could probably get to somewhere along the east side of Central Park before he did. David said this reminded him of going to Curt's high school cross-country meets, hurrying to see him wherever they could along the course. Only this time everything was bigger. The distance. The buildings. The crowds. The noise.

After that, all they could do was hustle through the Park to wait for Curt at the exit after the finish line. It would be a long, exhausting day, and they weren't even running the marathon.

Kelly would have ignored the call except that he recognized the number. David was too focused on spotting his son to notice, but Kathy, who never missed anything, must have seen the face he made when he glanced at his phone because she nodded when he looked at her as though for permission. He'd likely miss Curt, but he couldn't miss this call.

He had to trot half a block from the raucous sideline crowd with their horns and cowbells to be able to hear. "Just a second," he'd shouted into his phone. "Just a second." And even then, he had to step into a doorway and stick a finger in his other ear to hear.

She had tried to reach him early that morning, the nurse said, but they had both turned off their phones so Curt wouldn't be disturbed as he tried to sleep before the race. There was still nearly a month to go anyway.

The news was unexpected, but it was good. Mother and baby were fine. Technically a preemie at 33 weeks, but with an Apgar score of 7, the nurse said. Aside from a little jaundice and a body full of fine hairs that would go away, everything looked fine.

Curt and Kelly had been monitoring the pregnancy from a respectful distance since the opportunity to adopt this baby had first come to them. They'd paid the considerable medical and legal bills for the young mother, and they did their best to present themselves as worthy potential parents for the child. Suitable. Stable. And most of all eager, eager to give the baby a family and a home. And that seemed to be how it was all working out. They understood, of course, that everyone's plans could change at the last moment. When the new mother first held the baby in her arms, she might change her mind. Such things happened. And she could still change for many months afterward, too. That was a risk they knew they were taking. They'd already had one close call that hadn't worked out. It could happen again. That's why they hadn't shared any details with David and Kathy this time. If it happened, then they would share their news.

The pregnancy had been by the book. Matters progressed normally, and when they got the first, fuzzy ultrasound images, they began wrapping their heads around the big revelation that they were going to be the parents of a daughter.

They would paint the spare bedroom pastel yellow, they agreed, because they did not want to begin imposing any gender norms on their little girl. They knew they would be flooded with pink gifts for her, but as much as possible, they intended to be open and supportive to however their girl chose to live her life. In Curt's experience, this would begin to manifest itself early anyway, and then her two dads could follow her lead. "She'll be who she'll be," he said. "We can maybe influence her personality but not her personhood. We can nurture her talent but not the presence of it, or her intellect, or her fast-twitch muscles."

"So you're saying essence precedes existence?"

"Don't try to misrepresent me with your English major sophistry."

When Kelly finally got back to David and Kathy, they said he hadn't missed Curt. "Unless we all did," said David. Neither made mention of the call Kelly had left them to take, which was best since he wanted Curt to be the first to hear the news.

"I see him!" shouted David above the cheers and the horns and the cowbells. "There's his green shirt!"

They leaned over the barrier to see Curt. He looked angry, as he always did when he was running hard. Exhausted, too. Sixteen miles of constant drive, and another ten still ahead of him. In a pack of people that may have pushed his pace more than he'd intended or trained for, he was in his moment, showing the grace of an athlete exerting himself to the extreme limits of his ability. Maybe he lifted a finger of acknowledgement to them. Maybe he didn't see them at all. But three people on the sidewalk felt a surge of love for him.

Kelly wanted to shout his news but knew it would distract Curt. This great challenge needed his complete attention.

Curt's green shirt merged with the other runners as they moved up First Avenue, and soon he was lost to their sight.

"Okay, so one would think it's only four blocks from First Avenue up to Fifth Avenue and Central Park," Kelly said over the noise of the crowd, doing his best to get back in spectator mode and hide his big news. "But that's not what the map on my phone shows. And we have to get an uncounted number of blocks *up* Fifth Avenue if we want to see Curt again before he turns into the Park. I think we need to get moving."

Kelly was concerned about David's feet, which still gave him pain if he walked too far or too fast. Maybe they'd splurge on a cab back to the hotel. Funny that he had become the leader of their little group. He was as provincially Midwestern as they were. It was only the few scenarios Curt had discussed with him in the days before the marathon that gave him any sense of how they should get around to where they needed to be. But he suspected David would never trust himself to navigate the streets and avenues. And Kathy was too giddy about her son running this big city marathon to focus on anything else.

Kelly watched his phone to keep a bead on Curt's location. He still had half of Manhattan to cover, and then it was into the Bronx. And then back into Manhattan to cover the same distance he'd already run there, but on a different street. Kelly was mostly sure they could station themselves on Fifth Avenue in plenty of time to see Curt again. The marathon turned into Central Park at about 85th Street, so he led them there.

"Is that the Metropolitan Museum?" Kathy said when they hurried up Fifth Avenue.

"I think so."

"I can't wait to go there this week!"

Lucky you, Kelly thought. He'd have to see it on another visit.

When they saw the masses of runners coming up Fifth Avenue and turning into the Park at the corner, he knew he'd worked it out correctly. If Kelly could trust his phone, Curt still had about fifteen minutes of running before he reached them.

They would have to change their plans and fly home the next day. Curt normally would *not* want to fly the day after a big run — there were some health risks — but this was their chance, and they had to be present for it to happen. This would leave David and Kathy on their own for a week in New York. That hadn't been the plan, but plans change. He felt confident they could figure out how to spend the remainder of their vacation without their help. He'd tell Curt the news as soon as he could, and then together they could tell Kathy and David. The hotel was paid for through the week. All the touristy things they'd talked about doing they would have to do on their own now, and the reservations at the fancy restaurants they had planned to treat themselves to would surely have to be cancelled. But they could make it work, and then Curt's parents would return to St. Louis at the end of the week to a newly expanded family and the joys that would bring.

Or Kathy might insist they fly home too. Nothing, he realized, would keep a woman like her from caring for her first grandbaby. And that was probably for the best. A couple of greenhorn dads would need all the help they could get. Okay, they'd work it out however it needed to be done. Somehow the chaos felt good.

Curt appeared just when Kelly's phone said he would, and he threw something like a smile to his family as he pounded past. He was digging deep, finding the will to keep pushing after coming so far.

He had three miles left to the finish line and then the long, slow walk to the exit, intended to help the runners cool down their overworked leg muscles. To be where Curt left the Park, they'd have to cover nearly the same distance he had left in his run. They should get a cab, Kelly thought.

Kelly led them back down Fifth Avenue to where there was traffic and then did what he'd seen in dozens of movies. He raised his arm to hail a cab. The cabbie said he could get them close, but the route there would be indirect with all the closures, so it might cost more. Were they being hustled like rubes from the hinterland? Kelly wondered. But they jumped in, and the cabbie got them close enough, so that they only had to walk a block to get to Central Park West and the march of exiting runners where they scanned the crowd for Curt.

However, nearly all of the runners staggering out of the park wore identical hooded ponchos, issued to help them stay warm in the November chill after their extreme exertion. Hundreds of identical runners, a weary army of them shuffling, limping, weaving, and wobbling on exhausted legs that had forgotten how to walk.

The race literature had cautioned that cellular signals might fail in this area from too many phones trying to connect in one place.

Kelly tried to track Curt's location but got an error. He might have passed them already.

But then they heard him call.

"Mom! Dad! KELLY!" One of the ponchos opened and there was Curt, his finisher medal bouncing against the race bib on his chest.

He weakly reached for each of them, sweating and leaning on them, struggling to stay upright.

Curt groaned, "I hurt in places I didn't even know were places."

Kathy said, "Congratulations, my running boy!"

David said, "I'm so, so proud of you, Curt!"

Kelly said, "IT'S A BOY!"

Chapter Six

Name Calling

The summer before, when it had seemed like it was going to happen this time, Curt and Kelly allowed themselves the luxury of thinking about names for the child they would adopt.

When they'd first begun talking of adopting, they'd agreed not to discuss names for a child whose arrival was so uncertain. The emotional investment, they told themselves, was too great.

But when it had finally begun to look like it would happen, they found such speculation an indulgence and no longer held back. They lay in bed together on lazy Sunday mornings, arms and legs entwined, pillows bunched under their heads, mumbling sleepy suggestions to each other. Or they took themselves to the cabin and sat before the fire with beers in hand for more earnest conversation. Curt was mostly agreeable about every suggestion, which gave Kelly the opening he sought because he wanted to be the one to name their child.

"Your mom once told me," — Kelly's words came through the heat and haze of an Ozark afternoon — "that your grandmother called your dad her little Dandelion. Because of the nimbus of blond curls he wore on his head when he was a boy."

Was that true? Curt wondered. How had he not known this? Dad was Dandelion? It seemed impossible that he could ever have been anything other than just Dad. Or David. Or Davey, as his mother usually called him. Yet Curt easily recalled the head of shaggy, curly hair his father had worn, much the way Curt had worn his own red curls until he got to high school and decided to grow up. He wished that he could have known his father as a little boy. The wish was so sudden and urgent that it surprised him.

"Dandelion," Curt whispered. "Dandelion." The name had an odd taste. It felt clumsy on his tongue, but also good. Maybe he would find such a vivid, loving nickname for his own child someday. Names did indeed have power, he thought. Curt's head was thrown back and his eyes remained closed. The fire before them crackled, as though wanting to join the conversation.

He raised the beer can to his lips but it was empty, so he set it in the gravel. "You realize, Kelly, that I have surrendered my place early in the alphabet and moved much farther down when I became a Shepherd. The things I do for love."

"A good name, nonetheless, for a doctor formerly known as Clark. Which is also a fine name, in my observation. And one I would have gladly taken."

"I was named for my mother's father," Curt said. "He died when I was little; I never really knew him. I understand he was an asshole."

"Medically speaking?"

"Metaphorically speaking. That's a metaphor, isn't it?"

"It is."

"Marry an English major. That's what I'll tell our child. You'll never lack interesting conversation."

They both laughed.

"Well, I'm glad I didn't know that about your grandfather when I met you. Imagine if my understanding of your name had been tainted with that knowledge."

"And you?"

"A maiden aunt. My mother's sister. I think my mom was sure she was going to have another girl and had the name already picked out. Nevertheless, my aunt doted on me like the child she never had."

Curt was still careful about Kelly's past. As far as he knew, Kelly no longer talked to his parents or his sisters. He'd been clear that he wanted no part of them if they wanted no part of him. He carried a deep wound, and Curt suspected that if it ever did heal, though he had no certainty about that, it would leave an ugly scar. Thus, he chose not to press Kelly about supposed virtues like forgiveness. Unless his namesake aunt had told them, he doubted Kelly's parents even knew their son was married. It was a mess, and he didn't want to make it worse by probing too deeply, or at all.

"I'm pretty sure my father thinks that's why I'm gay. Because I was given what he thought was a girl's name when I was born. That my aunt would take me shopping and buy me dresses and jewelry or something. Ha! Imagine if that was all it took! Maybe that's why he called me Fathead all the time. He must have hated my real name."

Kelly was winding up, and Curt knew he had to stop him. Maybe somewhere else he could have his release, but he knew Kelly would regret going into his dark place while at the cabin. Curt tossed pebble of gravel at him.

"I'm glad your name is Kelly. I'm glad you are who you are. I'm glad I get to spend the rest of my life with Kelly Shepherd. In fact, I intend to be a Shepherd far longer than I'd been a Clark."

His words were intended to draw Kelly back to the moment, but Curt suddenly felt grateful that he had spoken to them, that he had allowed himself to be spontaneous.

"Is that the beer talking?"

Curt looked down at his feet, resting on the stone blocks that formed the fire ring. He softly said, "No."

The chirring of the forest and the crackle of the fire filled the silence that fell between them for a while.

"I was nearly given up for adoption," Curt said after a moment. "Did I ever tell you that?"

"You hinted once." Around the fire ring where they sat. After a few beers on a warm spring night. But he'd never brought it up again, and Kelly suspected it was a matter that still troubled him. Sometimes it seemed to him that people were made more of darkness than light.

"Hard to imagine that when I see how much your parents love you."

"Hard to imagine it myself. Someday, if you're good, I'll tell you the story. But hardly a day goes by that I don't try to picture who I would be now had that happened. Had I been raised by different parents. Had a completely different childhood, a different set of influences and experiences. And certainly a different name. Would the person I am now be erased from the universe? Would some other man have this body that was supposed to be mine? Would whatever the 'I' that I am have never existed? I wonder that about this little child, too."

"Still not the beer talking?"

"What I'm saying is, I'm beginning to see what you mean, Smartass. Maybe that other boy who might have been, whatever his adoptive parents had named him, would've come to wonder what his true name was."

"So we have to somehow figure out the *true* name of our child?"

"I see it all the time at the hospital. Mothers saying they won't know the name until they see the baby. I don't know how true that is and how much is just emotion. But they certainly seem to mean it when they say it. Names are important."

"I guess her birth mother will give the baby a name."

"Yes, but it won't be legal. Or it will be, but we'll be able to change it. We can amend the birth certificate. And if we do, we could name our child Kelly. How about that?"

Kelly's thoughts rushed into the past then. He was a freshman in high school. Confused. Frightened. Unsure about everything. Pretty much his normal state. And one of the junior boys had begun calling him at home. Just to chat, it seemed. He was wary at first. Why was this upperclassman calling him? But he was also flattered. He liked having the attention of an older boy, and when he looked back, he thought that maybe this was his first real hint that he was gay. Eventually, the boy had suggested they go to a movie. Maybe hang out with some of his friends afterward. It sounded like a date to Kelly, and in his inexperienced mind, he puzzled what it meant. But it was cleared up with a fist in his face the next day at school. The boy thought he had been calling a *girl* who was also named Kelly Shepherd, and with his pre-pubertal voice, Kelly had passed for a girl over the phone. When the boy discovered his mistake, he confronted Kelly at his locker, shaking his fist and saying that if he ever said anything, he would be ground into little chunks. "Got it, faggot?" That was the first time the word had been spat at him. Long ago, but the memory was still fresh.

That campfire conversation seemed long ago to Curt now. The months had passed. November came. The leaves had fallen, and the air grew crisp. Curt had run the marathon. And they got the big surprise. The baby came to them a month early. And now it was time to announce the *boy's* name.

Kelly knew what he would name a son if they ever had one. He would return Curt's loving gesture.

Kathy was changing the boy's wet diaper, a task she had begged for the privilege of doing and that Curt was perfectly fine letting her do as often as she wanted. Kathy pulled the diaper from beneath the boy and folded it. Then she handed it to Curt who wasn't sure what to do with it. Becoming a parent had happened so quickly, despite the long months of waiting, that they hadn't fully equipped the nursery yet. He set the wet diaper carefully on the top of the dresser and hoped it wouldn't leak. If his mother noticed his clumsiness, she didn't say anything.

"Mom, you're going to have to pretend that I am not a pediatrician and talk to me as though I were a clueless first-time dad, which is what I am. I'm scared witless!" And it was true. When he was in the hospital, where he could put on his dispassionate medical persona, he knew what he was doing. And there were always nurses around who knew a lot more than he did. But this, here, now, a naked, quivering newborn on the changing table before him, left him frightened and helpless.

"Well, I don't know about this. I understand you have to keep the area under his foreskin clean. He may not like it though. Where are the wipes?"

He found an unopened packet in one of the bags of supplies they'd rushed out to get and that now lined the wall in the little yellow bedroom, waiting to be put away. He fumbled it open to give her one. His fingers pulled out three.

"It was his birth mother's decision not to circumcise him. It's getting more common."

"We had you circumcised."

"Funny, I don't remember that. But all the signs are there."

"You wouldn't believe how eager your father is to take this little fellow to the cabin, Curt."

"Oh, I can believe it. But let's wait for warmer weather."

Kathy began cleaning the boy, and he cried at the intimate intrusion.

"Hard to believe a little voice like this used to wake me in the night. It would be easier to soothe him," she said to Curt, "if I could use his name. When do you think Kelly's aunt will get here?"

They were waiting to announce the boy's name until the whole family had gathered. That meant Curt's parents, who were already there, and Kelly's aunt, who was supposed to be on her way. Kelly had told Curt to expect a lot of mayhem when she arrived. She was larger than life, he said. She spoke her mind freely and gave big hugs just as freely. Curt could hear both admiration and exasperation in Kelly's voice. And he wondered if he should have removed the breakables from their front room.

"Don't know." He watched carefully as his mother diapered his son. "She called Kelly about an hour ago and said she was on her way. She lives up in Bridgeton, so it's a long drive for her to get into the city."

Kathy finished diapering the boy. He was still fussing, so she lifted him and held the tiny thing to her chest, rubbing his back and swaying slightly in a dance she had never forgotten.

"This feels so good," she sighed. "Holding a baby boy again. Your beautiful baby boy." He could see the tears forming in her eyes, and maybe she knew this for she dropped her face onto the infant's shoulder. And then, "Thank you, Curt!"

He touched her arm and let his hand stay there. He knew he would learn how to be a father. That the behaviors and the insights and the techniques would come to him. The routines. The feelings. The delights and frustrations. Sure, the birdlike little thing, with its confused eyes and supplicating mouth. Anyone would care for it. Curt fed the boy. Changed him. Held him. Kept him warm. Saw to his needs. He wasn't a monster. But in the two days since this baby had been in their home, he hadn't felt anything close to what he could see was overwhelming his mother. When would that part come?

Kathy looked at Curt again, her face more composed now. "Babies smell so good."

So far, his baby hadn't smelled very good to Curt. The boy had produced every one of the expected smells, in abundance, but Curt did not think even one of them could be defined as good. In fact, he wondered if anyone would object if he just put the boy in his carrier and set him by the exhaust fan in the kitchen.

"I don't think I can be as good a parent as you and Dad, Mom."

Kathy didn't look up from admiring the baby in her arms. "You're being silly, Curt. Of course, you can. All you have to do is love this child with every ounce of your soul. The rest is easy."

From the front room he heard Kelly cry, "Oh, boy! Here she is!"

They reached the front room at the same time that Aunt Kelly pushed her way through the door that Nephew Kelly was holding open for her. She carried what looked like a dozen bags from Target that she promptly began shoving into Kelly's arms. "Just a few things. I couldn't help myself." Then she shed her coat, which she also gave to her nephew and topped with her cane. She surveyed the room. "Hi, everyone!" From behind the bags and coat and cane, Kelly made introductions. Everyone smiled and greeted her, and she did the same, shaking David's and Curt's hands and standing before Kathy, wanting to hug her but seeing the baby in her arms.

"If I sit myself in that big chair over there," she boomed, pointing to the recliner, which David had quickly pushed himself up from when she'd entered, "would someone put a baby in my arms?"

Everyone agreed that this sounded like an excellent idea, in part because Aunt Kelly's personality filled the room and in part because it might be a way to contain her.

She made her way to the recliner and dropped herself into it. If she was embarrassed that her descent had ended with a thud, she didn't let it show. More likely, Curt thought, she didn't care. Kathy approached her and placed the baby boy in her eager arms. "Freshly diapered."

"Such a beautiful child! Such a beautiful family!" She pawed at the blanket that swaddled the boy so she could see more of his face. "Now what is your name going to be, little fellow?" He stared back at her; he'd seen a lot of faces in his first two days of life. Kelly imagined his aunt having held *him* the same way long ago. That must have been nice. He wished he could remember it. He'd extracted himself from the bags she'd bestowed on him, hung her coat in the closet, and leaned her cane against the arm of the recliner. He glanced at Curt across the room and saw him leaning against the wall on his race-weary legs, smiling mildly, reserving his energy for the hours ahead.

"So we have cake for later," Kelly said. "And mint ice cream. No one has to wear a party hat, though I had lobbied heavily for them but was outvoted."

He was doing pretty well. They both were. As they expected, they got very little sleep the nights before and finally struck upon the clever idea of caring for the baby in shifts so one could sleep while the other rose to his calls, though Curt had the worst of it because he was still recovering from running a marathon only a few days before. Kelly had gotten family leave from work. This meant that Curt could continue his doctoring at the hospital, though he did find ways to spend more time at home. The weeks and months ahead waited for them to slog their way through, but they had to get through this one day first.

They knew they couldn't put off telling everyone the baby's name. As soon as they had the boy home, they said, and they'd both had a chance to take showers and put on some decent clothes, and maybe close their eyes for a few minutes, they would have everyone over and make the name announcement. It felt bigger to Curt than it needed to be, but Kelly was excited by it and wanted to have a party. Yet when Curt's eyes fell on his mother and his father, sitting together on the couch, being marvelously assaulted by Aunt Kelly, he understood how important the name was that Kelly had chosen for their son. The two names he had chosen. And how important they were to Kelly, still trying so hard to insert himself into a family that had already, long before, fully embraced him. He felt something like grief that Kelly still couldn't let himself feel accepted. That he didn't trust it. That he felt he had to earn it. No one should ever feel they had to earn love.

"If you would let me have this little guy," Kelly said after he had stepped before his aunt, "we can make the announcement."

Aunt Kelly reluctantly surrendered the child. "Come back to me just as soon as you can, little one," she said. With the boy in his arms, Kelly moved over to where Curt leaned. He pushed himself off the wall that was holding him up and put his arm around Kelly's shoulders. So many experienced hands here, he thought. It would be nice if he could take a nap. But instead, he smiled big and waited for Kelly to begin.

"I meant to have balloons, too, but we just ran out of time."

"Oh, I could have gotten you some," Aunt Kelly said from the recliner. "Who knows? Maybe I did. We'll go through the bags later."

Everyone chuckled.

"Okay." Kelly took a breath. "We're forming a new family. But we're already part of a larger family." He looked directly at David and Kathy. So did Curt. "Curt let me pick out the name for our son, and I knew from the start what it would be. What it *had* to be." He opened the top of the swaddle a little and propped up the boy in his hands.

But then he stopped, thought for a moment, and carried the baby over to David, putting him in his arms. He stepped back and waited before speaking.

"Everyone, the newest member of our family is named Clarkson Catalin Shepherd!"

Kathy looked at David, but David stared at the boy he held.

"Clarkson?" David Clark muttered. "Clark, Son?"

Kathy grabbed his arm. David brought one of his hands to his face to dab at the tears that had already begun falling. "Clarkson!"

"And Catalin," Kelly went on, "is a form of Kathleen."

Kathy soon used one of her hands to do the same thing as her husband.

"Hello, Clarkson Catalin Shepherd," David said through his tears. "I'm Grandpa."

Chapter Seven

You Pushed Mountains Out of Your Way

"Clarkson is not a saint's name," said Kathy's mother.

"No, Mother. It's to honor Davey's family name. It was Kelly's idea. David was in tears when they told him what his grandson was named." Even your heart would have melted a little, Mother.

"That's an unusual name. It could become a burden to the child. I don't suppose they intend to have the boy baptized."

"Clarkson. No, they haven't said."

"You haven't asked?"

"No, I haven't. It's not my business, Mother."

"And I guess they're not going to raise the child Catholic either."

"I don't think so. His middle name is Catalin, Mother. A version of my name."

"They gave the boy a girl's name? No good will come from that. He'll be bullied on the playground, Kathleen. The more I hear about all of this the more unsettling it sounds to me. I'll never understand Curtis."

"He and Kelly are good together, Mother. And they love little Clarkson. You should see Kelly's face light up when he holds his son."

"Does Curtis's face light up?"

"You know how reserved he is, Mother."

"Father McBride says I must keep my judgments to myself. But I don't mind telling you, Kathleen. All of this is against God and nature. You know how I feel."

"They've given a child a home and a family."

"Yes, I suppose that is a corporal work of mercy. I'll say a prayer for the child."

"For Clarkson."

Kathy's mother had called in the middle of the small party Kathy and David were hosting to celebrate the finalization of the adoption of their new grandson. She'd received an invitation in the mail from a name she'd claimed she didn't recognize: Kelly Shepherd. And since she didn't know who this person was, she had dismissed it, sliding the unopened envelope across her breakfast bar with the other junk mail on the way to the trash can.

It was only two days later, when Kathy had called her to see if she was coming that her mother recalled the invitation and retrieved it from the trash, a little stained with coffee grounds and orange juice. She held it by the corner with her fingertips. No, she had said, she wouldn't be able to travel to St. Louis in the middle of winter for the party — though the invitation clearly showed a date in May — but she'd send a gift. "You don't want a fussy old lady spoiling all of the young people's fun."

But then she called during the fun. No, she didn't remember that they were having the party that day. She hadn't written it on her calendar. She had just felt like talking to her daughter. What was wrong with that? And, no, she didn't need her to get Curtis on the line. She was sure he was busy with his guests. But she didn't say she would call later once she learned the party was ongoing.

Kathy could manage her mother, who, she knew, was torn between the disapproval she believed her faith required, her embarrassment at being connected to such an unconventional family, and the curiosity she couldn't stifle about the life her only grandchild was leading, now including a great-grandson for her. Kathy stayed on the line with her mother because she knew that

Clarkson was fine being passed among a small crowd of happy people, many strangers, all packed in their tiny front room to admire her six-month-old grandson and give him gifts. The guests offered loads of conflicting parenting advice and cautionary tales to Curt and Kelly. Kelly politely gave full attention to whatever disaster was being described, moving seamlessly on to giving attention to the next person and the next disaster. Curt had heard it all from his patients. It was an eclectic mix: a couple of co-workers from Kelly's office, who, he guessed, were there to show they were enlightened about their gay office mate; a few PICU nurses from the hospital where Curt worked; neighbors from up and down Sunset Avenue who remembered Curt as a boy; Kathy's friend, Darby, from the bank. People came and went, but no one from Kelly's family showed. They had invited only his Aunt Kelly — the one blood relative who still talked to him — but she had booked a vacation to the sunny Caribbean for the week of the party before receiving the invite.

Curt and David escaped to the back patio, standing in the crisp May air and struggling with cigars that Kelly had passed out, a convention of new fathers. Curt didn't mind Kelly's exuberance, especially when Kelly said he'd bought the box because he knew that smoking a cigar reminded Curt of his grandfather. Such spontaneity endeared Kelly to him, reminding him to strive to be open and alive himself.

It was the *smell* of the cigar smoke, however, not the smoking, that evoked Curt's memories, but he didn't say that, not wanting to diminish Kelly's attempt to honor what he believed was a Clark family tradition. This one family tradition, Curt thought, probably could expire.

"Is lighting a cigar like lighting a campfire?" Curt asked his father.

"How so?"

"Should I do it with only one match?"

David smiled. "I think we can ignore that challenge. I just want to get this thing fired up, smoke enough of it to be polite, and get back inside where it's warm. I'm sure it's not good for my heart."

"What's wrong with your heart, Dad?"

"Oh, nothing. Nothing at all. Just trying to stay healthy. After I finish this cigar, I'm going to brush my teeth too. Or as soon as everyone's gone, I guess."

Curt chuckled and cut the tip — Kelly had put a cutter in the box atop the cigars, a box that would find its way to the cabin and be tucked in the back of the mouse-proof cabinet to be forgotten. He handed the cutter to his father. They'd brought out a box of kitchen matches that they only used for lighting scented candles around the house, which had grown more frequent with a baby present much of the time.

"Kelly tries so hard to be thoughtful, Dad. He once gave me a box of strike-anywhere matches for lighting all the one-match fires he hopes we'll have out at the cabin. I didn't have the heart to tell him about the boxes and boxes of matches already out there in the mouse-proof cabinet."

"One of the problems of lighting one-match fires is that you don't go through matches very fast. Throw some of those old boxes on the fire when he's not looking."

Curt struck a match against the box and let it flare, then brought it to the end of his cigar and began puffing. David watched him for a moment, then did the same. Both men were silent as they worked the cigars to life, examining the glowing tips and puffing more.

"It's not as fragrant to me as woodsmoke, but I guess our clothes will smell like cigar smoke soon. I hope your mother doesn't make us strip before we go back in the house."

"I caution my older patients, the tweens and teens, about smoking and how bad it is. I'm glad none of them can see me now."

"Surely one cigar isn't harmful, especially with all of the running you do."

"None is better, but one isn't so bad in the big picture. I'm just glad I have that marathon behind me. That was tough enough as it was. I imagine even one cigar would have made it tougher."

"That was a fun trip. Especially the surprise at the finish line and the mad dash home. I liked that."

"Flying the day after running a marathon was probably more dangerous than this cigar. I'm glad I'd brought my compression socks." Curt tapped some ash into the grass. How much of it did he have to smoke to be polite?

"Kelly looked so excited when he shared the news. I think he could have run a marathon himself right then. We knew something was up after he got a call, just before you came off that bridge into Manhattan. But we never suspected what it was. Your mother could barely sleep that night. She was going to have a grandson!"

"I could barely register it, Dad. Remember, I had just run twenty-six miles."

"Twenty-six *point two* miles."

"Yeah, that point two is the hardest part. I had tunnel vision by the time I crossed that finish line! I can see how runners get lost sometimes." He pulled on his cigar and let the smoke curl from his mouth. There was a charm in quietly smoking a cigar. "I didn't even know what Kelly had said at first. But I saw Mom jumping up and down, and even in my delirium I guessed it was about more than me successfully beating my body to shreds for four hours."

"I heard what Kelly said, but I didn't make the connection. I remember you had said before that the baby wasn't due for weeks. Looks like being premature hasn't hurt Clarkson any."

They'd held off having the party until the mandated waiting period had passed and the judge decreed that the adoption was final. Those six months hadn't been easy for any of them. Waiting for certainty while they all lived in uncertainty. The possibility that they could still lose this boy they'd all come to love.

"I'm not supposed to tell you any of this, Dad, but the birth mother was a little unclear about how far along she was. She was just a kid and didn't have regular cycles, apparently, so she didn't even know she was pregnant for a couple of months. Clarkson may not have been premature at all, or not by much."

"Well, I'm just glad he's healthy. He sure seems healthy. And officially part of the family now. When the weather warms up, we need to take him out to the cabin. Dip him in the lake."

"Dip him in the lake?"

"It's a tradition, Curt. A sort of welcoming ritual. Your grandfather did it with you and apparently with me, and now it's my turn to do it with my grandson." David examined his cigar for a moment. "I'd really like to do it, Curt."

"Then we will, Dad!"

Curt had never had any worries about his parents accepting — embracing! — an adopted grandson. There was never even a hint that things like bloodlines or family genes mattered to them. Clarkson Catalin Shepherd was a part of the family, a child of his grandparents' hearts and minds, now a legal member. He always knew this would be so, that his parents would love their grandson. It was part of the reason Curt had finally yielded to Kelly's drive to adopt.

He supposed Kelly's family knew about their new grandson. They'd kept his Aunt Kelly up to date — she probably would have attended the birth if she'd been given the chance — and she probably told Kelly's family, but no word had come from any of them. They'd likely never even acknowledge they had a new family member. From what Curt could tell, they would probably rather cut Kelly off altogether, say he had defective genes, gay genes that tainted something precious in the lineage. Their purity, maybe. Their normality. Their conventionality and smallness. Curt knew that Kelly would always carry the wounds of their rejection. His husband was better off without them.

David and Kathy had some sense of this. They knew Kelly was no longer in contact with his parents or his sisters and that he'd been rejected by the Shepherd family for being gay. Curt watched his parents double their effort to welcome Kelly into their family. That would be natural for his mother. Her heart could expand to love anyone. And his father had welcomed Kelly as a second son, invited him to partake in all the things he did at the cabin, teaching him, nurturing him, and loving him in his way. He could see the effect in Kelly's smiles and in his mood and manner when he was around them. Kelly needed family, and Curt's parents had provided it.

When Curt had taken Kelly's last name, he'd done it in part to seize the Shepherd name from Kelly's rejecting family and redeem it for their new family. Kelly and Curtis Shepherd. Kelly returned the kindness by naming their boy Clarkson. It was the union of both families, Kelly would say loud and proud. Curt knew that mattered.

"I'm not sure how Dad could have liked these things," David said, examining his cigar. "My teeth feel like they're wearing sweaters."

"That's good, Dad! I'm going to use that in my hygiene talks with the kids."

"Be my guest." He put his cigar down on the edge of the table. "I'll be right back."

Inside, David saw that someone had brought wine. An empty bottle sat beside a half filled one on the kitchen counter. The clamor coming from the front room suggested the wine was being enjoyed. He glanced into the living room where Clarkson was making the rounds of eager, loving arms. His round blue eyes looked up mystified at the new faces before him. Kathy beamed at David. Kelly followed her gaze and saw his father-in-law, calling to him, "How are those cigars? I'd join you, but . . ." He gestured to the crowd. To David he looked happy.

"They're fine. Really nice."

"The man at the store said they were mild. Suitable for all tastes."

"Yeah, they're great, Son." Curt had told him how touched Kelly had been the first time David had referred to him as Son. Kelly had cried when he explained to Curt what the word meant to him.

David retreated to the kitchen and rummaged through the junk drawer. When he found what he wanted, he slipped it into his pocket and went back out to the cold where Curt waited.

"Here, let's try this." He held his cigar before his face, and using the scissors he'd snuck from the kitchen, chopped it down to a third of its length. The smoldering end fell to the ground, and David toed it into the grass where he smashed it under his shoe.

"This way, we can make it look like we smoked these all the way down. Just leave the burnt-out stubs where Kelly can see them. I hope he didn't pay too much for these."

He took another match from the box and struck it then tried re-lighting his shortened cigar.

"I hear re-lighting a cigar is supposed to make it taste worse," Curt said as he reached for the scissors.

"How can it taste any worse?"

Curt cut his cigar and puffed the stub back to life. He mused for a moment before speaking.

"It turns out you did everything right, Dad."

"What do you mean?" David pulled on the cigar, to keep it going. "Cutting the cigars?"

Neither man met the other's eyes. This kind of conversation was easier that way.

"I mean raising me. Every single step of the way."

"Is that the pediatrician talking?"

"Partly, I suppose. Or the nicotine. But mostly it's the grateful son talking. I got my first inkling of this when I went off to Mizzou. I got to see how other people had been raised. The kinds of families they came from. The stories they had to tell. All of that opened my eyes. It didn't take long for me to realize how good I had it. You and Mom are wonderful parents!"

"Your mother gets most of the credit."

"No, Dad!" Curt turned and faced his father. "You get an equal share. I know I didn't say it enough — maybe I never said it at all — but you're the best father in the world. I mean it! I see all kinds of dysfunction at the hospital every day. Things I have to report sometimes because they're so bad. It would frighten you. It frightens me! And the stuff I'm slowly learning from Kelly. The little references he lets leak out now and then." He looked across the yard and shook his head. "He has some dark days, Dad. He can stare into the campfire for what seems like hours. Sometimes I think he might benefit from therapy. Maybe I shouldn't have said that. Forget I said it."

"You know I can't."

"I know."

"But it's your business. Yours and Kelly's." Still, David knew that Curt wouldn't have said it if he hadn't intended it, at least on some level. He was a careful person about revealing himself, and if he said this specific thing, even if he tried to withdraw it quickly, he must have been seeking validation of some kind. David wasn't sure what he could do to help, though more trips to the cabin with Kelly had to be good, a kind of therapy. He *would* dip his grandson in the lake. And *both* of Clarkson's fathers would be there when he did.

Curt paused to let the tone reset. He took another draw on his cigar. It did smell nice to him. Kelly had that part figured out.

"I won the lottery when I got you for a father. I know it sounds corny, Dad, but I need to say it out loud to you."

"I did my best, Curt."

"I was hoping for a little more than that."

"More gratitude?"

"No, gratitude is *my* job, Dad. My lifelong job. No, I was hoping you could tell me how to do it. How to be a good father. I mean, I know I'll never be as good as you, but I don't want to screw up this boy's life."

"You're not going to screw up Clarkson's life. You've *saved* Clarkson's life."

"Don't exaggerate."

"You said just a second ago that sometimes things need to be said out loud. Well, now I'm going to say it out loud, Curt. You went through all the expense and waiting and disappointment and sadness. The frustration. The lawyer fees. The hospital fees. I don't even know what else. Never certain it would ever happen or if it did that it would stick. I was watching you, Curt. Watching closely. You did all of this because you *want* to be a father. I got my perfect son the old-fashioned way. But you pushed mountains out of your way to have a son. Don't tell me you won't be a good father! You're a nurturer. That's your nature. And that's all you need. Love that boy and he'll be okay. I didn't have any guidebook, no rules or studies except seeing what my father did for me. If I did one or two things right raising you, then take your lesson from that. And I'm sure I did more things wrong than right. We all figure it out as we go. That's the big parenting secret. Anyone who tells you otherwise hasn't been there." He reached up and caressed his son's freckled cheek. Curt's eyes closed so he could absorb the moment fully.

Curt turned to his father with tears in his eyes. He was smiling. "Let's snuff out these nasty cigars so we can hug, then go inside where it's not so chilly."

In the front room Curt was met by a smile from Kelly.

"Just in time," Kelly said. "Your son needs his diaper changed."

Chapter Eight

A Tree Grows in the Forest

The job was bigger than Kelly had imagined. The rocky Ozark ground in the clearing was not yielding easily to his shovel, no matter the number and quality of his swear words. Soon after Clarkson was born, Kelly had said that they should plant a tree in the forest in honor of his birth, a tree they could visit every season and photograph the boy beside. "The winter snow in the background. Clarkson in a bright red parka," he enthused. "And the bright green of spring. Darker green in summer. Then the fall colors. Clarkson growing through it all! Getting bigger each season. Wouldn't that be wonderful?" They would feed the tree, and water it, just as they were feeding and watering the boy. Both would grow and thrive, and somehow it could help forge a bond that would keep their son coming back to the forest.

"It needs to be unique," Kelly had said at the table in David's back yard on a warmish day the previous November. The baby was in the house with Kathy.

"We have plenty of oaks and hickories. Too many cedars. We need to select a tree that is different. One that will stand out."

His enthusiasm had caught David off guard, but he withheld his objections. It had always been his intent to be a steward of his land, to plant and nurture only what would normally be found in a Missouri forest. Fooling with the natural balance might somehow loosen the grip the place had on them. But the growth of his grandson was also something he wanted to nurture in his forest. If Kelly's choice to plant non-native trees brought Clarkson closer to David's hundred forested acres, he'd support the idea.

Curt was letting Kelly make the case for it. He smiled as Kelly spoke, nodding his head throughout. He'd obviously coached Kelly on some of the points. It pleased David to see his two sons' interaction. He pulled on his beer, though it was a little chilly for drinking beer this November afternoon. Kelly wasn't working very hard on his beer, and Curt had demurred saying he would be driving them home later, more important than ever now that he had a son. This pleased David too.

What to plant and where to plant it? Kelly had said he'd seen a clearing just up the hill from the cabin that would be a good place. David cautioned that when there is a natural clearing in a forest, a place where even the scrub wouldn't grow, there's usually a reason for it.

"Maybe the reason is because Mother Nature has reserved it for Clarkson's tree."

Or maybe the reason is because there is just a thin layer of soil on top of bedrock. Or the clearing was where some past owner had a burn pile. Or a trash dump. Those can affect the soil for decades. David kept these thoughts to himself. Maybe Kelly was right. Maybe the spot had been reserved by the universe for a tree to grow along with the boy. But maybe more than one tree in case that one doesn't make it. Why not a small grove of trees? If half of them fail in the sketchy soil, half might survive, and half of those might even thrive. Clarkson could be photographed, a little boy beside his own little forest in the bigger forest.

"Kelly, I'd like your idea. I really do, and I wish I had thought of it when Curt was a baby. But I'd like to suggest a modification."

Curt turned to look at his father, expecting the wet blanket of wisdom to fall. His dad *did* know this forest.

"Or maybe an expansion. Instead of just one tree, why not plant a whole little grove of trees in that clearing. I mean, you have to expect some not to survive, and it would be a shame for Clarkson's single tree to be that one. But if you planted a dozen in that clearing, all the same kind of tree, not only are you improving your chances of success, but maybe you'd be giving my grandson his own little forest of trees. Maybe it could become his special place at our special place. Where he takes you to tell you his little secrets. Or where he takes his friends when he brings them to the cabin. Or just where he goes when he wants to be alone. But anyway, I think if you want to try this, you should hedge your bets. Put in a bunch of trees and you'll have a better chance of at least some surviving."

Kelly looked at Curt. Was David's advice just what he needed to hear? Curt smiled mildly and nodded. He trusted his dad's advice, especially about their forest.

"It's just that," Kelly said, and then tried again. "Well, I've already done a little research. Trees aren't cheap. One, maybe two. Okay. But when you're talking a dozen, that's a big chunk of change to gamble with."

"I guess I painted too bleak a picture. And, actually, trees are cheap if you know where to buy them." He took another sip of his beer for dramatic pause. "You can order seedlings from the Conservation Department. Real cheap. A buck or two a tree. I've done this. Remember those pecans we planted below the dam, Curt? I got those from the Conservation Department."

"I *do* remember that! But I don't think any of them survived."

"That's because I didn't protect them from those vandal deer who browsed them and then thrashed the velvet off their antlers on any that grew tall enough. Actually, I think a few made it." He turned to Kelly. "*There's* where you'll be spending your money. On fencing and posts to put around Clarkson's trees for the first ten years."

"Conservation Department?"

"Yeah. Go on their webpage and browse their listing. You gotta take whatever they have available each year, but that will still leave you with dozens of choices. And now's the time to do it. Trees sell out fast. They'll deliver them in the spring right to your door if you want. And then we can plan an overnight to the cabin to put them all in the ground and say kind words over them."

He could see Kelly's mental gears working.

"Keep in mind, Kelly. They're just twigs with some roots at the bottom and some tiny leaves at the top, if that much. Not much more than a foot long. But if I were doing this, that's exactly what I'd want. A tiny tree to take the picture of a tiny boy beside. They could grow together in the photos over the years. Wow!" His voice suddenly became a little husky. "I really wish I'd done this with you, Curt!"

David circled the rim of his beer can with his finger for a moment.

"Anyway, look into it, Kelly. Pick out some tree you think is suitable. Not only what you have in mind, but if it says what kind of setting it will thrive in. That's south-facing, dry, ridgetop land where you want to do it, so see what will grow in those conditions. And you'll probably have to order a minimum of twenty or so, but whatever doesn't fit sensibly in the clearing we can scatter through the forest to survive as they will. Depending on what you pick out, maybe we can do something now to prepare the soil."

He paused a moment, folded his hands on his lap, and then added. "This is your idea, Kelly. I'm talking as though I've got it all figured out for you. I'm sorry. I'll just say this much more. I support the idea. I like it. And if you want my help, I'll gladly give it. Now can we go inside? I'm getting cold."

Kelly remembered David's encouraging words when he stood in the May air at the clearing with the new shovel his father-in-law had just given him. It had a long, narrow blade, which David said would be perfect for the job of the day. "Drive it into the ground at least a foot, wiggle it back and forth enough to create a space we can drop the roots in, stomp the ground to close it, and move on to the next. Simple!"

They were planting the trees — two dozen blue spruce saplings — in the best grid the rocky ground would allow. It became clear to Kelly early that if they continued the grid, with the spacing recommended between the trees, they would have more trees than the little clearing could hold. A big part of him was glad of that because it meant he could see an end to this planting chore.

Nearly every time he jabbed his shovel in the ground, he struck a rock that threw sparks. Or if he didn't hit a rock right away, he did an inch or two below the ground when he stomped on the shovel to drive it deeper. He'd move over a little and try again and try not to count in his head how many of these holes he had yet to dig.

But he reminded himself they were barely holes. Just thin wedges in the soil when he could manage them. What if he'd stuck with his original idea? What if he'd bought a more mature tree with a real root ball. The hole he'd have to dig for that single tree in this evil Ozark soil would cost him far more time and swear words than the dozen wedges still before him.

Curt and David had joined him. And at first they felt that Clarkson needed to be present too. But after they took a few photos of themselves with their new shovels, they decided it was still a little cold for the baby — now seven months old, and when did that happen? — so Kelly sent him back to the cabin with Curt. It was his crazy idea, Kelly said, so he should stay and dig.

But David remained, pausing and resting his hands on the top of his shovel. He looked downhill from the clearing. Kelly could see the lake glinting through the trees. No skinny-dipping today, but David suggested they haul some buckets of water up from the lake to pour on the trees once they planted them but before they fenced them. Another chore along with pounding a fence post into the evil soil beside each tree, then cutting some chicken wire to encircle the tree, zip tying it to the post. Another reason Kelly was glad the clearing wouldn't fit all the trees he'd bought.

"What do you see?" Kelly called, using the chance of a conversation to take a break.

"I see a pignut hickory. I see a tree that is not so much right now but will probably grow into something later. Not much competition around it. Probably gets a good flow of rainwater runoff from this clearing. Ought to do well in its setting."

"And that's a good thing, right?"

"Normally. But it won't be long before it towers over Clarkson's spruce and steals their sunlight. That won't help with their growth. I think that hickory and I have a date with destiny. Someday, one of us is going down."

David turned back to Kelly.

"So what I did before with those pecans was slide the roots into the wedge in the ground. Maybe you could open this one a little more with your shovel — try to shake the roots open as much as possible. Pour in some root stimulator, then press the soil closed with the toe of your boot. Say a blessing."

Once David showed him how to do it, Kelly got to work on his own. He teased a half dozen twigs from the tangle and then planted each one, more or less successfully, he thought. Most of them even pointed straight up. Soon they'd filled all the holes they'd prepared.

The actual planting went so fast that Kelly found a vigor in himself he didn't realize he had. It would be nothing to cut the wedges for the remaining twigs in the bucket, what they could fit in the space left. David said he knew some places on the other side of the lake where he could plug the others, maybe tomorrow, so Kelly didn't feel bad about not using them all. He fought with the soil as he had all morning, and he followed the erratic lines of the grid. They were planting them a little closer than the instructions recommended, but David said they would grow to fill the space. And a dense stand might offer more protection for the wildlife. "We're nurturers," David said as he stabbed the ground. "We're a family of nurturers." And Kelly thought the man didn't know how true that was.

About the time they had finished planting all the trees they could fit in the clearing, they smelled the lunch fire that Curt had started. Both Kelly and David imagined Curt patiently explaining to their seven-month-old how to build it with only one match.

"Lunch call," said Kelly.

"Yep. You go. I'll be there in a minute. I'm going to take this bucket down to the lake and get some water to pour on the trees. Ought to help a little. Say a prayer or do a rain dance if you know either one. A man and a bucket can do only so much. A wet spring is what we really need."

The plan was to take Clarkson up to the clearing after lunch and snap his first photos beside the trees there. He couldn't stand on his own yet, so each of them would take a turn crouching beside him, propping him up and keeping him from grabbing the twig beside him.

But they were going to save the fencing work for the next morning. It required a different set of tools, a different set of swears, and rested muscles. David had already been caching fence posts, but once they knew how many posts they had compared to how many seedlings, one of them was going to have to take the truck into Osceola to get more. And probably another roll of chicken wire to be safe. Everyone would surely need a candy bar by then. And whoever got the job would have to check the beer in the cooler first.

Throughout the afternoon, after the photo session, each wandered up to the plantings on his own to admire the new grove. Curt came back and pronounced it a work of art, possibly even better work than his prodigious effort changing Clarkson's many diapers while they were digging and planting. Kelly looked at it with a kind of wonder. He carried Clarkson up there with him, and whispered in his ear that this grove was Poppa's way to sink more roots into this family and it was for Clarkson to grow tall and strong in the love of that family. The baby touched the tears on Kelly's cheeks.

David lingered the longest on his solo visit. He'd taken another bucket of water with him because "it can't hurt." When he was done pouring the water, he overturned the bucket and rested on it, studying the plantings. Two dozen or so hopes they'd sunk in that uncooperative soil. Then he carried the bucket to the other side of the clearing and sat again, studying it from there. How would the sun touch these little trees in the morning? Through the day? Was that hickory going to be a problem? Which of the forest trees around the perimeter needed to have their branches trimmed back? That sunlight now belonged to Clarkson's trees, he thought. Then he moved the bucket and sat again, collecting more thoughts.

David and Kelly had cleaned the shovels after they'd recovered from their lunch stupors.

"Won't they just get dirty again tomorrow when we put the posts in?"

David suppressed a chuckle. "No, we're going to be a lot more serious tomorrow." He put down his shovel and walked into the cabin. When he came back, he was carrying a long red cylinder, which he dropped into Kelly's waiting hands, so heavy it nearly knocked Kelly over.

"This is a post driver. It's going to do all the hard work for us. You set the fence post in place where you want it, then you slide this beast on top of it and slam away. Thick gloves, of course. And you might want ear protection too. But it'll sink a post into the ground, even that rocky ground up in the clearing, in no time. And you'll know what satisfaction means, for the first ten anyway. After that you'll probably be having different kinds of thoughts."

David moved the post driver to where they'd see it in the morning before their trek up to the clearing for the work of the day.

They sat around the fire, each holding the baby by turns. Clarkson was interested in the flickering flames and tried to reach for them. David and Curt told tales of the adventures they shared at the cabin, and Kelly sat in awe and envy, wishing he'd been with them.

"I was thinking," said Curt, "that if every time we crossed the gravel to the cabin or the truck or the fire, we picked out one weed, we'd have this whole area weed free in no time. Makes sense, doesn't it."

They agreed, though when they got up to go inside, it was too dark to see the weeds.

None of them wanted to get up to go to bed, and when Clarkson finally drifted off in David's arms, that was where he remained. This was the way they had wanted their boy to fall asleep, held in loving arms, lullabied by a forest, warmed by a campfire. Yes, exactly this.

But they were also wondering if they would hear a whippoorwill. David thought it probably wasn't too early in the season and in the trees beyond the firelight the first whippoorwill call of the evening came as though a gift for them. It was answered from across the lake. Each man savored the sound.

After their good day of work and play, they went to bed, Clarkson nestled warmly between his two fathers.

Kelly was the first to wake in the morning. The woodstove was still warm, and he thought he could add some sticks to renew the flame and put a pot of coffee on, but as this was David's turf, he left it alone. He changed Clarkson's wet diaper and snuggled the child next to Curt. Then he slipped his bare feet into his boots and stumbled up the hill in his boxers and flannel shirt to the clearing.

David had already tied short strips of red tape to each of the plantings.

And while he stood in the pale dawn light, as the birds tuned up for the day, Kelly added his voice to the chorus. He spoke a blessing. He didn't know any proper words for this kind of thing, but he thanked the sun and the clouds and even the rocky Ozark soil for the chance to plant this little grove for his boy. He hoped they looked favorably on his effort and that the trees and the child could grow strong together. Then he rejoined his family in the warm cabin.

Chapter Nine

STOP! STOP! STOP!

By the time the police arrived, the man was finished with Kelly and had left the playground. Most of the other parents had hurried off as well, yanking their children from an afternoon of innocent play that had erupted into violence. They drove away as quickly as they could, though a few stayed to watch from their locked cars.

Kelly lay crumpled on the ground beside the baby swings, wood chips and mud pressing into his face, his shirt torn, his nose bleeding. His arm was bent at an ugly angle. Three-year-old Clarkson was kneeling in the mud beside him, tugging on his shirt, screaming for his Poppa to wake up. No one knew what to do for the child. No one wanted to get involved.

Curt sat in the chair beside Kelly's hospital bed, speaking quietly into his phone, relating to his father what he had learned from the police and the EMTs. Kelly was still mostly unconscious and what little he'd mumbled hadn't been coherent. He was breathing on his own though, Curt said. That was good.

"From what the witnesses told the police, some ape at the playground had been striking his child. With his fists. Quite violently, from the sound of it. And they said that Kelly had *exploded* from the bench nearby, shouting at the man to stop hitting the boy. The man did stop, Dad, and he began hitting Kelly instead. When it was over, Kelly had a broken arm, a bloody nose, his two top incisors were gone, and he was unconscious. He's being kept overnight for monitoring in case he has any internal injuries. The police said the man had been kicking him too, so internal damage is possible." Curt heard himself saying these words like he was someone else.

The man had been loud and brutal — something about the boy getting his shoes muddy. No one could have missed seeing the man hitting his boy, but they felt helpless to intervene as they called their own children close. Kelly's response had been quick and unexpected, so most of the other parents missed what had happened until Kelly was on the ground, being kicked in the stomach.

One mother, who had called the police when the man had first begun battering his child, said that Kelly had run up to him, shouting "STOP! STOP! STOP!" The man had ignored him — she thought that maybe he hadn't even heard Kelly because he was in such a rage. He continued to strike the cowering boy until Kelly grabbed his arm. The man then turned his fury on Kelly.

The police had told Curt that by the time Kelly was on the ground and curled into a ball, he was heard crying, "No, Dad! Stop, Dad!" Curt didn't share that part with his parents.

The man gave Kelly one last kick to the head — this was probably when he lost the two teeth — then grabbed his own kid and ran to his car. The mother who called the police had stayed with Kelly, asking him if he was okay but getting no response, while her own terrified children huddled nearby.

The EMTs arrived soon after. A policewoman did what she could to calm Clarkson. The little boy had caused some confusion when they were trying to sort out the details, especially when they continued to ask Clarkson how they could reach his mommy.

None of the adults lingering at the muddy playground knew Kelly, though one woman volunteered to the police that she'd seen him hanging around there before and had watched him closely. A man at a playground, without a wife or girlfriend, sitting alone on a bench, looking at the playing children was creepy to her, felt wrong! Her assertions contributed to the initial confusion.

It was a lucky coincidence that Kelly had been taken to the hospital where Curt worked. When they had gone through his wallet and identified him, one of the ER nurses wondered if he might be "that nice Dr. Shepherd's" husband and summoned Curt, who frantically notified his mother to collect little Clarkson, who had been crying ceaselessly in police custody, begging for his Poppa. Everything was confused he told her as he rushed down the hospital halls and leapt down the stairwells.

She took Clarkson to her house where she did nothing for an hour but sit on the couch with the mud-caked boy in her arms, stroking his long blond hair and telling him everything would be okay. Eventually, Curt texted that Kelly was stabilized and sleeping.

Clarkson smiled when Grandpa David rushed in the front door and lifted him from Kathy's lap, hugging him close.

"Your Poppa's going to be fine, Sprout. He's just a little hurt right now." Kathy nodded to confirm David's words though neither knew if this was true. "He'll get better."

"The bad man hit Poppa."

"I know, Sprout, but that's over. The bad man is gone. Dad is with Poppa now. No one is going to hurt Poppa anymore."

He decided to divert the boy.

"Maybe you need a bath, Sprout." He stroked Clarkson's cheek where splashes of mud clung. "How about a bath?"

"Will you stay with me?"

"We'll both stay with you," said Kathy.

David sat on the toilet and Kathy on the edge of the tub, while slowly Clarkson got clean, dried off, and dressed in pajamas. He would spend the night with his grandparents, sleeping between them in their bed.

Unless there were internal injuries, the ER doctor had told Curt, Kelly's condition did not appear to be serious. The bone would take time to knit, of course. "He'll still be able to pitch for the Cardinals," she assured Curt with a smile. He could probably get implants to replace his missing teeth as there was no fracture of his jaw. The bruises would fade. The facial swelling would subside. He'd need a lot of TLC for a while, but he could expect to recover fully in time. Likely they'd discharge him in the morning. "Any idea what happened?" she had asked, but Curt knew little more than she did.

Curt sat quietly in Kelly's room, a trained medical man in a modern, urban hospital, helpless. The monitor beeped. The IV dripped. Shoes squeaked as people passed in the hallway, and nurses came and went, giving Curt a sudden smile of recognition when they saw that one of their own was sitting bedside in the darkened room. Except he wasn't one of their own. Not then. He'd become a frightened and worried husband, and he listened carefully when the nurses spoke to him, as though all his medical knowledge had suddenly left him, and he was no more than a turbulent snarl of worry and fear.

When Kelly finally began to come around, opening one swollen eye and seeing Curt's anxious face before him, he whispered, "Clarkson?"

"He's with my mother. He's safe."

"Am I in heaven? Because I'm looking at an angel."

Curt let out a breath he hadn't realized he'd been holding in.

"I'm glad to see your humor is undamaged."

"Fighting back the darkness, Dr. Shepherd. Any chance I can get a sandwich?"

"Nil by mouth, Mr. Shepherd."

Kelly snaked his tongue through the new gap in his mouth, touched the holes in his gums. "Hmm. Probably hard to eat without teeth anyway."

Kelly lifted his arm slowly and saw the cast on it. It took him a moment to understand.

"I guess I'm going to reach my deductible this year. Lucky it's my left arm. I can still write checks to the hospital."

"What happened, Kelly?"

He let his head fall back on the pillow. He closed his eyes.

"He was hitting that little boy, Curt. He wouldn't stop." Tears welled in Kelly's swollen eyes and rolled down his bruised face.

"Okay. We can talk in a bit. Quiet now. Your job is to rest. Just rest and heal."

Kelly shook his head, though he winced. "You don't understand, Curt. There is no rest. Not for me. I'll always be on my guard." The tears continued. "I thought it was over," he mumbled. "I thought I'd never go back there."

Curt knew where this was coming from. Some children were reared by animals, like the man at the playground that morning. Kelly had spoken about darkness in his childhood, about his father always bullying and hitting him, his mother and sisters ridiculing him. Fights at school. Humiliation in the locker room. Hints he let slip after a few beers at the cabin. Curt was trained to listen for these kinds of things, but from children, not adults. Not from a grown man who was his husband and father of their son. When Kelly would utter those vague references over the campfire flames, they startled Curt so much that he had no response. He'd seen some horrible things with the children he treated at the hospital, and he'd worked hard to remain the clinical practitioner his patients needed. Yet here it was in *his* life.

But they weren't at the cabin now. They were in the hospital. Where Kelly had been brought because he had been beaten savagely by a man who ought to be locked up, kept away from civilized people. Kept away from children.

"I don't know what to say, Kelly. You're safe with me. You can talk to me."

"There is too much to say, Curt. What about Clarkson?"

Patients sometimes repeated themselves because they were confused when they woke and found themselves in a hospital bed.

"He's with my mother. He's fine."

"You said that. What did he see? Did he see all of it?"

"I don't know, Kelly. The police didn't say."

"He did. He must've. How could he not have seen it all?" He paused for a moment, taking in a few breaths through his mouth, and threw his head back on the pillow. "I let him down, Curt. Because I did something stupid, he saw something horrible!"

What Curt had heard from the police didn't sound stupid. It sounded heroic.

"He's just three, Kelly. He probably won't even remember it in a few years."

"You don't forget violence." He fixed Curt with his one working eye. "You don't ever forget violence. You remember it on some level, deep inside you. You're not allowed to forget it." He closed his eye and turned his head. "Nor should you."

"The police said a mother heard you saying 'Stop, Dad!'"

"This isn't the first time I've gotten into a fight on the playground," Kelly said with an attempt at a laugh. But then his tone changed. "It's just the latest time."

"Kelly, don't dodge me. There's more to this than you're letting on."

"Let's go to the cabin this weekend, Curt. Just you and me."

"We're going to get you home as soon as we can and let you rest. That's what we're going to do. We're going to gather our little family close, and we're going to heal together. Clarkson needs to see you recovering. There's plenty of time to go to the cabin later, after you heal up some."

"We can't let this harm Clarkson. No more than it has anyway. We have to put this behind us as quickly as we can. Not talk about it. Pretend it never happened. A child shouldn't brood on the violence in his life."

Was he speaking about Clarkson or about himself?

"You said 'Stop, Dad.'"

"So what if I did?" he snapped. "Drop it, okay?"

The heart monitor seemed to beep more quickly. In a moment a nurse would run into the room to see why her patient was agitated.

"How are we supposed to get this behind us if you keep denying it?"

"Denying *what*, Curt? Just leave it!"

"The fact that your father used to hit you, Kelly."

"Oh, you got that all wrong, Curt. My father never hit me. No, he never hit me." His voice sounded strange, coming through the gap in his front teeth. "He *beat* me, Curt. He beat me with his fists until I collapsed to the floor, and then he kicked me. All for whatever unforgiveable sins a ten-year-old boy could commit. Is that what you want to hear?"

Kelly's heart was racing, and a nurse soon hurried in.

"It's okay," Kelly lisped to her. "My impossibly handsome husband over there was just suggesting that he and I should have a romantic weekend. Gave me palpitations!" He fluttered his good hand.

The nurse threw a scowl at Curt as she checked Kelly's IV, fussed with the machines a little, and then made a quick, huffing exit.

"Maybe I could become the hospital's stand-up comic. Go room to room with my swollen face and broken arm and missing teeth to cheer up patients."

"Listen, Kelly, my love. We all have secrets. If you don't want to talk to me about this, maybe you should think of talking to someone else. Professionally. I mean, people share their secrets with their besties all the time. Their barbers and bartenders. Their priests. Why not share yours with someone who is actually trained to help? Maybe begin exorcising your demons. You take such good care of me and Clarkson. It's time to take care of yourself. You deserve this, Kelly. Do you hear me? I don't want something like this to stand between us. You're the most important person in the world to me."

"And Clarkson?"

"Yes, Clarkson, too."

"Ever the healer, Curt." There was conciliation in his voice. Maybe even concession. Maybe it was time. Maybe there were finally enough good things in his life that he should protect himself for them. Kelly smiled.

"Life is not fair. I learned that lesson early. It was beaten into me. You're the best thing that's ever happened to me, Curtis David Shepherd. You know that, don't you?" He sniffled then reached for Curt's hand with his working hand. "I guess if you want me to try, I'll try."

And so it happened that after a few weeks of rest at home, doing his best to be jolly around Clarkson and as affectionate as he could with Curt, Kelly began seeing a psychologist connected to the hospital. His intake session lasted an uncommonly long and generous three hours, Kelly being the husband of one of the doctors in the hospital and Curt pulling every string he could behind the scenes. Clarkson was already in bed when Kelly got home after his first session.

He'd come through the garage and into the kitchen. Curt watched him from across the room, ready to reach for him if he gave even the slightest sign that's what he wanted. Or willing to hold back and wait to be invited, however long that might take.

"How'd it go?"

"About what I expected. She's smart, this one. But it will take some time before I'm comfortable spilling my guts to her. I think I will, though. I can maybe see a reason to." He didn't smile. He'd done a lot less smiling since he'd lost the two teeth. He hoped he would smile more once he received the implants.

"They say she's the best."

Kelly walked into their front room. He spoke without looking at Curt.

"My witch doctor thinks I should go back to the playground with Clarkson," he said, his back turned to Curt. "Reclaim it. Not sure Clarkson is ready for that. Not sure I'm ready for that. Though maybe I could find my teeth in the wood chips."

"Maybe a change in the seasons will make the place feel different."

"She also said I should share with you what I shared with her. About my uproarious, fun-filled childhood. At least some of it, some sanitized parts. She says it's unfair to you and harmful to our marriage for me to keep this kind of poison bottled up and hidden from you. She says you have as much at stake as I do. And maybe if I share it more, I can relieve myself of some of the burden."

"Clever doctor." Curt had asked around about her, even visited her in her office once, though both knew she would never be able to speak of any specifics.

"We're family, Kelly. Supporting each other is what we do."

"Yes, you're right, of course. But let's keep Clarkson unburdened by the messy details as much as we can."

"Agreed."

"And you have to understand that I've been hiding these messy details all of my life." He stood alone in their dark front room. "I've gotten very good at suppressing them. Shoving them down. Locking them away. It's not easy for me to expose them to the light. Relive them. Speak about them. I don't know where to start."

Kelly dropped onto the couch, grabbed a pillow, and held it to his chest. Standing in the kitchen doorway, Curt could see how weary Kelly was. Healing took exertion.

Kelly rose, tossed the pillow on the couch, and crossed the room to Curt.

"Please give me one of your fabulous hugs, Curt. Hold me like it's the last time you can. Because I'm afraid that after I tell you about myself, you're going to think I'm too messed up and you'll never want to touch me again."

The first time Curt had ever seen him, when Kelly was out on the trail trying to make himself into a runner and doing it all wrong, he had seen in his face that he carried some hurt. It was unmistakable, and Curt could not forget it. He found himself returning to the same bit of trail at the same time each day just to see the wounded man again. Kelly's barely hidden pain had unexpectedly opened a part of Curt's heart, a part that needed to be opened, and their life together had flowed from that first encounter. The hurt, he understood now, would always be there no matter how many hugs he gave.

Curt took Kelly's hand and led him back to the couch. He sat and pulled Kelly to him so they both sprawled across it. Curt tugged a quilt off the back of the couch and spread it over them, then he wrapped his arms around Kelly.

"Like this?"

Kelly sighed. "Exactly like this."

Curt could feel Kelly's body begin to shudder and soon he was sobbing. Curt held him.

When the tears stopped, the words began to flow. At first they came in stammered fits and starts, then in torrents. Harsh words that made Curt wince and want to cry. Ugly words from deep inside the man he loved. Words about a father too absent sometimes and too present others. And about a son who was always a disappointment, always in the wrong place at the wrong time. About innocence and innocence lost.

Kelly talked for a long time. And Curt listened.

"And that's why my witch doctor thinks I jumped from the bench and confronted that monster at the playground. She thinks it's PTSD. That I must have had a flashback to my own father beating me like that little boy was being beaten, and I acted without thinking, became the adult I needed in my childhood. I honestly don't have any memory of what I did. I have to rely on what the witnesses told the police. All I can remember is feeling very, very angry. Like *insanely* angry. And waking up in the hospital."

As Curt adjusted the quilt around them, he felt the cast on Kelly's arm. Curt had written the word LEFT on the cast with a marker to normalize the thing for Clarkson and teach him left from right. Clarkson colored it.

"They never caught him."

"No, he left before the police arrived." And then Curt realized that Kelly wasn't talking about the man on the playground.

"Well, you're here now, Kelly. You're here and you're safe and you're loved. And together we're going to move ahead with our lives, and wherever that takes us, we're going to walk together. And be the best fathers Clarkson could ever have, too. We're better together."

"I'm going to have bad days, Curt."

"It's okay. I'll still be here."

He kissed Kelly's forehead and they both closed their eyes.

In the morning, Clarkson found them there asleep, and they only awoke because they heard him miss his bowl and pour an entire box of cereal onto the table and the kitchen floor.

Chapter Ten

A Multitude of Sins

Clarkson was with Grandpa and Poppa at the hardware store. They were getting drop cloths and painter's tape and rollers and trays and brushes. David had those things at home, but Curt thought they needed their own set now. They were also getting a gallon of paint for the front room at their house, and Clarkson was going to help. "Paint hides a multitude of sins," David had said.

David had wiggled the boy into the seat of the cart — which was a bit of a chore because his long legs didn't want to slide into place easily. "You're certainly feeding this boy right," David had joked as he struggled to get the boy situated. Clarkson reached for everything he could and asked about the everything he couldn't reach.

"Take your time," Curt had said. "We still have plenty of crayon to clean off the walls." He hoped there was a lilt in his voice, a benign tone suggesting that Clarkson's use of their walls as his crayon canvas was just one of those things life throws at you when you have a scamp for a son. Part of why Curt had insisted they take the boy with them was so he might appreciate at some small boy level that his mischief was causing them a good deal of trouble. It was harmless enough, really, coloring on the walls. Even Curt could admit that. He could tell himself it was an age-appropriate if lingering developmental benchmark. Increasing dexterity. Thinking in a new dimension. Coordinating colors. He would sometimes draw a rainbow now, though mostly at Kelly's urging, and occasionally an orange dog; left on his own he drew brown lines. Lots of them. He had even begun showing a degree of independent problem solving.

"Dad, will you color with me?" And when Curt had begged off a few times with this or that excuse, Clarkson had solved his problem by taking to the walls. Whether or not this was an act of defiance, Curt wasn't sure.

Still, it annoyed him. One more bit of chaos in a house full of chaos. This was the cost of living with a man he loved who also happened to be a casual housekeeper. Sometimes, he claimed jokingly, he had to clear a path to the couch so he could clear a space on the couch so he could sit on the couch with his husband and son at the end of the day and eat a bowl of ice cream with them. But ice cream on the couch! Who did that? Messy treats like ice cream belonged at the table. Yet if he squirmed with discomfort in his place on the couch, he'd hear the crunch of chips down in the cushions, and he'd know if he didn't like it, well, he could do more of the housework himself. And sitting with his family, in the quiet at the end of the day, spooning ice cream into each other's mouths, had a charm that seemed more worthwhile anyway.

So it ought to be with the crayon drawings on the wall, he wanted to believe, though they did also disturb him a little. They weren't drawings of cats or clouds or flowers or stick people like he might expect. They were lines. Long, parallel lines that ran around the room. Interrupted by the doorway here and the bookcase there. But lines. As straight and level as Clarkson's little hands could make them. Parallel to the floor, and soon enough parallel to the ceiling if they let him.

"I don't understand the lines, Mom. Is he just drawing something that's easy for him? Building his base for greater creativity to come?" Curt squirted a little solvent on the wall and began rubbing with the cloth.

"What do his teachers say?"

Curt worked the cloth for a moment before he spoke.

"I wouldn't say this to anyone else, but since you can see right through me, maybe you can tell me if I'm wrong." He stopped and sat back on his feet. "This will sound arrogant, but sometimes I think they're intimidated by me. The hospital pediatrician who must know so much more than they do about children. I think they're afraid to say anything to me that they fear I don't want to hear. Or that I might contradict them as though they are uninformed, not up to date. That's why I asked Kelly to go to these school conferences."

Kathy thought about this for a moment. "Well, what do they tell Kelly?"

"As you can imagine, Kelly's not as concerned about this as I am. He doesn't see anything to worry about. And maybe he's right. He's a creative, like you, Mom, and I think this sort of cheers him to have a son who loves to draw. They tell him to indulge Clarkson's creativity for now."

"Well, I think most kids do this, Curt. My friend Darby told me her daughter had been drawing on the walls inside her closet well into her teen years. Not just with crayons but permanent markers, too. Quite a big project. She said they couldn't bring themselves to paint over it."

"Did I draw on the walls when I was little?" He resumed scrubbing.

"You? Never! You were such a neat and tidy boy that I made your father take you to the cabin just so you'd get dirty, tear your clothes, occasionally skin your knee. Not that I had any complaints from Davey about that. I loved seeing you come back from those cabin trips all messy and stinky and needing me to put a bandage on your knee, kiss it to make it better."

Curt knew he had been a boy who had to be induced to be boisterous. To be compelled to get dirty. Who needed a booster shot

A Multitude of Sins

of wild periodically. And now he was the neat and tidy man who still needed that kind of nudge.

"Kelly's the best thing that has ever happened to me, Mom." Kathy remained silent, hoping her son would keep talking. "He opens my heart. I can be myself with him."

She kept up her work on the crayon marks and waited for him to say more.

"Kelly's so much better with Clarkson than I am, Mom. He's more patient, that's for sure. More tolerant of the child being a child. He seems *attuned* to him. Like he can anticipate what's about to happen and head it off. Indulge or defuse it. He *knows* Clarkson, Mom. He's got insight and connection I don't have."

"That's because he gets to spend more time with him, Curt. He got to be a full-time father for Clarkson's first year when he had that time off. Just like I was with you. You pick up things, little things that don't seem to mean much at the time but then turn out to be lifelong qualities. I remember you used to line up your dolls in your crib before you would go to sleep. It was so adorable, Curt, watching you do this. Sitting before them and babbling to them in your baby talk. Getting everything just right before you closed your eyes. I could have worried about that. Might it be the sign of some disorder? But I just went along and watched you become an orderly adult, strong, healthy, and successful." She kept at her work. "Kelly has just had more of a chance to do this with Clarkson than you have. It doesn't mean you don't have your own connection or that you can't develop what you have more deeply. It's just a matter of being present when you can be."

He was right about sending Clarkson to the store with Davey and Kelly. Kathy knew this. It was important that the boy begin making connections between his actions and their consequences. But Kelly could have just as easily been the one to stay behind and clean. Curt could have gone with his son instead. They could have brought color swatches back for Kelly to choose from, gone out for a second run. She would have been comfortable chatting with Kelly as they worked together on the wall. Probably got more done too. And yes, leaving Clarkson behind would have made no sense for their cleaning effort either. Whatever progress they would make in the front room he'd probably being undoing in his bedroom. So he needed to go with them.

No, it wasn't Curt's insistence that the boy go. It was that *he* remain that concerned her. Early on she had dismissed the signs she was seeing. Just coincidences that she happened to notice and persuaded herself surely weren't indications of Curt's way all the time. But Curt had a too easy readiness to pass off Clarkson to any willing hands whenever he could, and she had noticed. "Take him," he'd say, pushing up from the couch and putting the baby in her arms. "I'll go help Dad with the burgers." Or "Can you go check on the boy and see if he's awake from his nap?" Or "Someone needs his pants changed!" he'd say in a joshing manner as he juggled the boy into Kelly's hands. Even calling him "the boy" rather than using his name. Those kinds of thing. The kinds of little things that seemed to mean nothing in the moment, and yet that she kept seeing and then began watching for.

Kelly had told her one day a few months before that he was saving his nickels and dimes to buy a treadmill for Curt's birthday. "Last winter, he ran a lot of his miles on the one they have in the hospital gym. I get it. He wants to stay fit. I certainly have no problem with that! And he needs his alone time. But it keeps him away from home so much. Suiting up to run. Then maybe waiting for the machine to be free. Then showering at the gym afterward because he says he doesn't want to come home to my big, sloppy hugs all sweaty and disgusting. I wouldn't mind a sweaty hug from

A Multitude of Sins

him. He could sit here and stink up the place and I wouldn't mind at all because I'd rather he be here, full of endorphins, or whatever the magic chemicals are, and be full of chatter too. We'll either put his birthday treadmill in the front room, although I know that will bother his need for order, or we'll squeeze into the garage. It will be a lot closer than the hospital gym. And maybe I'll use it too."

Kathy told him she liked his plan. But she saw something else behind it, something she suspected Kelly was beginning to see too. Curt was finding ways to avoid being home. And she didn't like thinking that. She looked at Curt, distracted for a moment.

"We'd better apply ourselves if we're going to have enough wall cleaned for painting when they get back."

"Oh, you know Dad. He'll have to walk back and forth before it. Look at it from every angle possible. Turn on all the lights. Open the blinds. Think about it. Sit and study the wall. Stand and study the wall. Then he'll have to apply the masking tape to the trim exactly right. And tear half of it away and do it again to make sure it's perfect. Lay out the drop cloths just right. He'll clear his throat when he says he doesn't need any help. It will be hours before a drop of paint touches the wall, Mom."

"You know who that sounds like."

"Yes. I am my father's son. I'm just glad Dad's willing to do the painting. I can't get that nice finish he always does. So smooth and even. No brush marks. He's an artist. Like you and Kelly in his way. I just hope we're not just preparing a new canvas for the boy."

"We'll keep Clarkson occupied while they do the work. You and I. It'll be fun. We could bake a cake or something. He'd probably like the mess in all of that."

"Oh, then we'll be agitating Kelly. Being in his kitchen. Doing things the way he wouldn't do them. He'll be at our elbows watching, a wet rag in his grip, peeking over our shoulders. He'll be checking the temperature of the oven. Fretting. Wanting to stay back and wanting to help."

Kathy kept working the wall. She was trying to apply longer swipes, to see if that might take off more at once than the concentrated rubbing she'd been doing.

"I hope it's okay to ask." She paused. "Tell me if I'm out of line, Curt. But how's Kelly doing? He talks to me about some of what he's coping with, but not much."

"He's embarrassed, Mom." Curt continued his work on the wall. "When you and Dad welcomed him into the family, he didn't believe it. He was on guard the whole time, almost literally, waiting for something bad to happen. For the ugliness he expected, the only thing he'd ever known. He couldn't trust himself to believe that families might actually be places of care and love. I'm not sure he's ready to trust it now either. Not yet. Not fully. He had a pretty bad childhood, Mom."

He stopped working and turned to his mother. "I'm going to spend the rest of my life giving that man a good family, Mom. I'm going to do it and not stop doing it until he surrenders." He could feel the tears coming. "I don't know if I ever told you, but one of the reasons I took the Shepherd name when I got married was to wrest it from his family, to redeem it, to give Kelly a good Shepherd family to be a part of. Maybe that sounds strange, but it was important to me, and I think it's meaningful to him."

She'd guessed that after the incident at the playground, and from the bits of ugly backstory about it that began to filter to her. It made her heart swell, the depth of her son's compassion and the means he'd chosen to express it. He truly was his father's son, finding his own ways to speak his love that he couldn't always manage with words.

"Going to that therapist," Curt went on, "has made a lot of difference. He says he's learning some tools to cope. Working

A Multitude of Sins 115

through some of his issues. Coming to accept that he was not to blame for the things that happened to him. I don't even know the whole story. I may never know. I probably don't want to know." Curt sprayed the wall and rubbed vigorously, angrily with the cloth.

"He comes back from his sessions — he schedules them in the evening so Clarkson is asleep when he gets home — and he's really down. He says they just validate that he's screwed-up, that he can't dismiss it all and walk away from it. He repeats some quote from Faulkner about the past not being past. He spends an hour facing down his demons with his therapist, waging his battles and skirmishes as he calls them, and discovers he's still a mess in the end. So he comes home and just sits on the couch in the dark to decompress. Sometimes he wants me beside him. Sometimes not. He's actually told me, Mom, that he's unworthy of my love. He's said that! Used those words!"

She tried to keep a calm face.

"That's when the darkness is on him. But then the next morning, he's a new man. He's had some time to process. And he's found a way to be appreciative. I see it, Mom. He practically sings the morning after his sessions. He dances around in the kitchen while he's fixing us breakfast. Preparing our lunches. Laying out our clothes for the day. Going over our schedules. He's full of kisses and hugs, and I can't help but dance with him, because I know he's turned a corner. Clarkson laughs at us, but I think he understands. Kelly chatters about whatever book he's reading or some show on television. He speaks about the future. In these moments, I think he understands this life he's in, and maybe he feels that if he embraces it, despite all his doubts, it *can* be his new life. His better life. The Shepherd life he deserved."

"I'm glad, Curt. He's always so jolly around me. But I know it's a mask. I can sense something, some reservation in him. Still, you can see from all of this, I'm sure, why he's forged a close bond with Clarkson, can't you?"

"Because he is grasping fiercely for the life he wants to have. The life where he can try to be the kind of good father he didn't have growing up. The kind of father I *did* have growing up. I get it. And I want to do everything I can to make that work for him. For both of us."

"For all three of you."

"Yes, the boy too."

"When they get back, will Clarkson need a nap?"

"Lunch, at least. But he'll probably be too stimulated to go down for a nap. All of you here. All the activity."

"Okay, so here's what you're going to do, Curt." She pointed her spray bottle directly at him in case he raised an objection. When she'd arrived that morning, she had her long hair drawn back and tied with a bandana. She was in cleaning mom mode, and there was a don't-mess-with-me menace about her. "After lunch you and Clarkson are going to go to the art supply store. And you're going to get him a shiny new box of crayons."

Curt's eyes flashed. His mouth dropped open. He dared to glance at the colored wall but quickly turned his eyes to his mother, afraid she was about to grab his chin and snap him back to attention.

"Listen to me." And she brandished the spray bottle again. "You're going to get him a brand-new box of crayons, full of lots of color and lots of promise. The biggest one they have. You're going to get down on your knees in front of everyone in that store and hug Clarkson tightly and tell him that you love, love, love his artistic skill and that you want to see more of it. Then you're going to buy a half dozen pads of drawing paper and a roll or two of tape. You're going come home, and together you're going to tape the drawing paper to the wall in his bedroom at just the right height for him.

Cover the length of the wall. And you're going to encourage him to draw on the paper and not the wall. With his new crayons. And — listen to me, Curt — you're going to *sit* with him as he does this! Maybe he'll draw more of his lines. Maybe you can ask for that orange dog or something. But you'll sit with him, and you'll watch him, and you'll say encouraging things to him. You'll ask him about his drawings. And then you're going to praise his drawings, and you'd better find it in yourself to *mean* what you say, too. Because you have to cherish this part of him, Curt!"

She paused, and he thought maybe she was finished, but she rounded on him.

"He's going to mess up. He's going to find some unprotected bit of wall and think it needs embellishing. You have to expect that, Curt. You can tell him what you want, and maybe he'll listen. But then he'll forget. Or he won't be able to help himself. So you'll tell him again. And again. Tell him he can do drawings like this for his grandmother's walls, that they have to be done on the drawing paper so he can bring them to me. I'll tape them up. I'll cover every surface I have with them if you draw them with him. Because you know what, Curt?" And she jabbed the cleaning bottle at him one more time. "You're going to spend the rest of your life giving your *son*, this magical little boy whose name is Clarkson, a good family too!"

Her words continued. He heard them or half heard them, but what he really heard was the love within her words. Keep talking, he thought. Tell me again. Teach me how to be a good father. Something has to stick. Kathy was thinking the same thing.

Chapter Eleven

Battles and Skirmishes

Curt suspected the evening before what the coming day would hold. Kelly was withdrawing. Without reason or warning, his darkness was settling upon him again. He barely spoke through dinner. The few words he did speak sounded forced and superficial. His mind was somewhere else. He washed their dinner dishes in silence. He had his back turned to them at the sink and didn't chatter as he usually did. Long moments passed while he held a plate in one hand and the dishcloth in the other, without bringing them together. Later he moved through the front room as though he was a ghost, his eyes down, his movements lifeless. He announced that he was tired and going to bed.

Curt helped Clarkson with his homework. They watched television. Clarkson showed Curt some things on his tablet, the games he was playing and the progress he was making in them. Curt immersed himself as much as he could while wondering how Kelly would be when he came back to them.

He'd seen it many times as a doctor and knew how bad depressive episodes could be. As Kelly's husband, he knew how bad they could be for Kelly and for their family. Early on, he'd tried to reason with Kelly, to remind him that he had a good life now, that he'd escaped his past and was in a safe and loving place. But he quickly learned that depression didn't yield to reason. Its darkness was too dark. Its depth too deep. Its reach too vast.

After he got Clarkson showered and into bed, Curt stepped into their darkened bedroom. Kelly was an unmoving lump on the bed, the blanket pulled over his head. Curt undressed quietly, collecting his clothes and Kelly's, which he had left where they fell. He decided to wash a load of laundry so that Kelly wouldn't have that to do later. Little things sometimes helped.

When he crawled into bed later, he touched Kelly's back — touch was important — and told him he loved him. And to himself he said, "Come back to me, Kelly. Find your way back as soon as you can."

In the morning, Kelly had not found his way back. He was still curled into the ball he'd presented the night before, the sheet gripped in his fist. Curt read the signs.

"I'll take Clarkson to school today. And I'll call your office and tell them you're not going to be in."

Kelly might have grunted an assent.

"Try to get something to eat today. Maybe take a shower."

Curt never forgot an incident early in their relationship, when he'd first seen the really deep darkness descend on Kelly.

"A shower?" he had said wearily when Curt had tried to use good sense. "A shower? Do you have any idea how much effort it would take for me to have a shower? You don't know, Curt!" There was more exasperation than anger in his words, but Curt had stepped back with surprise.

"But you'd feel much better," the naively reasonable part of Curt asserted.

"For a few minutes, maybe. And exhausted for the rest of the day. You want me to feel better? Just leave me alone."

It made no sense, and it took Curt a long time to realize that it never would. When the darkness gripped Kelly, for an hour or a day or a week, common sense, even the gentle persuasions of love, did not work. Kelly was lost — was that why he was always so fearful of getting lost in the forest at the cabin? — and would have to find his own way home.

Yet Kelly was also brave. He dutifully went to his therapist each month, though he often returned from the sessions seemingly more destroyed than when he left. He tried various pills to keep the darkness away, enduring the predicted side effects, which were the only influence they had on him in the end: the tremors in his hands, the hours when he could not concentrate, the brain fog, the sleepless nights, the frightening episodes when his mind seemed to leave his body and he eerily watched himself go through his daily motions. Despite his attempts at treatment, the darkness returned whenever it wished.

Curt had to accept his helplessness. His medical training, his rational mind, his will to solve problems, his love for Kelly — none of that was enough. It wasn't even the right way to think, he came to see. "YOU CAN'T FIX ME!" Kelly had once shouted, and Curt recognized his limits. He could be present. He could do the big and little things to make Kelly's day-to-day easier. He could step back and allow him to fight his battles and skirmishes. He could wait for him to recover and return. But, no, he couldn't fix him.

And this day had to begin without Kelly's help. Clarkson hadn't appeared in the kitchen, and Curt worried that the boy would be late getting to school if he didn't get the morning in motion. Curt felt uncertain of the routine because of the fuller parenting role Kelly took on. He went to his son's room, knocked on the door, and waited a moment before he pushed it open. The room was dark. Clarkson was still in his bed. Did their son share Kelly's affliction despite not sharing his genes? Had he somehow inherited depression from his Poppa? Inheritance was one of the risk factors for serious depression and Curt had been grateful that Clarkson couldn't inherit it, not biologically.

He walked over to the boy's bed and sat on the edge. He touched his son gently on the shoulder. Clarkson stirred and rolled over, looking at Curt with surprise; it was Kelly who normally woke him on school days.

"Poppa's sick, isn't he?"

Curt had hoped he could finesse the morning somehow. That he could get the boy dressed and fed and off to school without his Poppa's episode intruding. But the routine was already broken.

"Yes, he's having a bad day. We're going to let him sleep."

"The darkness has him."

How did his boy know such things? Why did he have to learn about the ugly things so soon? Sometimes Clarkson seemed wise beyond his years. But as Kelly had reminded Curt once, if he were fighting cancer, it wouldn't be something to hide from their son. Depression, he stated flatly, was a disease like any other, and not talking about it, trying to hide it, just gave the disease more power.

"Yes. He's fighting the darkness. I'm going to get you to school today. Can you get dressed and come down for breakfast? I can fix you eggs and bacon if you want."

No, it would be a bowl of cereal. The idea that *Dad* could fix him a cooked meal was foreign to Clarkson. That was something Poppa did.

"Poppa picks out my clothes, Dad."

"I think I can manage that," Curt said in a cheerful voice, rising from the bed and stepping toward the closet. The simple task, however, proved more difficult than Curt expected. Whatever mad science or alchemy Kelly used for organizing Clarkson's clothes in his dresser and closet escaped Curt. The boy giggled from his bed while Dad poked around to find him a complete set of clothes: underwear, socks, a pair of jeans, an undershirt, and a shirt with buttons. He found one sneaker but not the other. "I'll find it," his son said after Curt looked around for a bit. "I think it's under my bed. Or in the garage."

"And for breakfast?"

"Just cereal."

"And toast?" Something warm at least.

"Okay."

"Be sure to brush your hair and teeth. Then hurry downstairs. We don't want to be late."

Curt left the boy to dress himself and went to the kitchen, passing the closed door to their bedroom, fighting the urge to look in.

He put four pieces of bread in the toaster and two bowls and spoons on the table. There were six boxes of cereal in the pantry, and he arranged them on the table for Clarkson to make his choice. He set out butter and plum jam for their toast and poured them each a glass of orange juice.

Clarkson hadn't brushed his hair; Curt hoped he'd brushed his teeth. Was he too worried about his Poppa?

"Breakfast of champions!" Curt said, waving his arm at what he'd prepared.

"Thanks, Dad." Clarkson sat at the table.

"Which cereal would you like?" He hoped the boy would pick the bran flakes, though he expected him to want the Froot Loops, which he did. They should stop buying such junk, but that was Kelly's territory, and it wasn't worth the fight. Curt poured the cereal in his bowl.

"Pop lets me to that myself. I'm not a baby, Dad."

"I know. But I guess it warms my heart a little to do this for you, Clarkson."

The boy thought for a moment, and then a smile bloomed on his face, which did warm Curt's troubled heart.

"Thanks, Dad."

"And your school things?" Curt said, pouring himself a bowl of bran flakes.

Battles and Skirmishes

"Oh yeah."

"Okay, we'll get that together next. And then it will be about time to get you to school." He poured milk over his own bowl of cereal.

Clarkson was quiet for a moment, but then he spoke.

"Why is Poppa sick?"

He could explain the medical etiology of major depressive disorder, the scientific explanations for this elusive affliction. Or he could tell the boy about his Poppa's childhood, about the fractures left in his soul, and how something as horrible as his dark, depressive episodes made perfect sense as a reaction. Or he could say that even with his medical training and his love for Kelly, he just didn't know.

"Some people have this problem, Clarkson. It has different names, but it makes them very sad, even if it doesn't seem to have a cause. And they have to fight it. Poppa always comes back, Clarkson. You've seen that. He always finds his way back to us. We just have to let him win his fight and be here waiting to love him when he gets back."

Why did it have to come to him right then, in this close moment with his son? Might there be a time when Kelly *didn't* win the fight? He had to put his spoon down and grip the edge of the table until that thought passed.

"Are you okay, Dad?"

Curt popped back into the moment. He reached across and tousled Clarkson's unbrushed hair.

"I have a family, and we love each other, Clarkson. As long as I have that, I'm okay. Now drink your juice. It's good for you."

"I wish Poppa didn't get sick like this."

"Me too. He's fighting it very hard. And what we can do to help is go on doing our best."

"I hate it!"

"I hate it, too, Clarkson. But I love your Poppa. So do you. And I think that makes a difference in him getting better."

"Can I go in and give him a kiss before I go to school?"

"Let's give it a try."

And so, after breakfast, and after collecting Clarkson's school things in his backpack, the two of them stood before the closed door of the bedroom and the boy knocked softly.

"Yeah. Come on in," came Kelly's weary voice from behind the door.

The room was dark, and Curt knew not to turn on the light. Kelly was sitting on the edge of the bed. When they approached him, it was clear to Curt that if he had slept, he hadn't gotten any rest. He looked exhausted. His eyes were distant. His skin was wan. His face, drawn and expressionless. And this was the best show he could put on for Clarkson.

"We're about to head off to school," Curt said. "But we couldn't leave without giving you a kiss."

Kelly held out his arms and Clarkson fell into them.

"Please get better, Poppa," he said before kissing him on the lips. Kelly didn't let him go for what may have been a moment but felt to both like it needed to be a lifetime. Curt leaned in and wrapped his own arms around them. He kissed Kelly on the forehead, the only part of his face available.

"Yes, please get better, Kelly, my love."

"I'll try," came his response, but the words were lifeless. "I'll try."

When they left, he fell back on the bed.

Curt didn't know where to drop off Clarkson in front of his school and the boy had to instruct him. After he left the car, Curt rolled down his window and called to him.

"What about lunch? I didn't pack you a lunch."

Battles and Skirmishes

"Oh yeah."

"Can you buy it? Is five dollars enough?"

"Ten would be better."

Curt tugged his wallet out of his pocket and then fished out a ten. "What time should I be here to pick you up?"

"I don't know. I think 3:30."

"Okay, I'll be here waiting for you. Have a good day." He reminded himself to call the school to confirm the time.

After Clarkson left, Curt found a parking space in a fast-food restaurant. He turned off the engine and let the silence wrap around him. He needed to become a better father for his son.

It would play out as it usually did. He knew that. Or he hoped that. Kelly would have a day or two where he would be lost. His pills wouldn't make a difference; his doctor needed to come up with a new cocktail. He was weeks away from his next witch doctor session. The mundane would have to heal him, the routine of their lives, which included two people who loved him.

At times like this Curt wanted to scream awful curses at Kelly's family for doing what they'd done to him. To blame them and accuse them and convict them of the crime of not loving their son. Worse, of abusing their son in ways he didn't know and didn't want to know. Of emotionally starving this very good person into half of the man he could have been. Of beating hope out of him.

It would do no good, he knew. They would deny or dismiss the accusations. They would say whatever wrong that may have been done was Kelly's fault, not theirs. That they were glad to be shed of him. And anyway, Curt thought, it was far too late for them to beg forgiveness. The damage was done. Kelly would be afflicted for the rest of his life by the crimes of their parenting. All he could do, all he and Clarkson could do, was help Kelly move on. Be the reason he carried on. Support him in his fight. Guide him when they could and follow him when they must. Make a new family for him and acknowledge that his fight was real, just as real as the love waiting for him when he was finished with each battle and skirmish.

Curt sent a few texts to Kelly during the day, but they went unanswered. FEELING BETTER? and WHAT CAN I BRING HOME FOR DINNER? and LEAVE THE LAUNDRY FOR ME. Maybe they helped?

He collected Clarkson successfully after school and suggested they stop and get a big bag of fast-food burgers and fries — "And onion rings for Poppa," Clarkson said. "He likes onion rings." — to take home for dinner. Every doctoring instinct told Curt he shouldn't be feeding his family junk food, but a wiser part of him told him that comfort was the kind of nutrition they needed then.

When they got home the house was silent and dark. Before Curt could stop him, Clarkson ran up the stairs to the bedroom where they had left Kelly that morning. Curt ran behind him.

The door was ajar, but the space beyond was dark. The smell of a sick room met their noses. The curtains had been drawn sometime during the day. Kelly was in the bed, but on the bedside table was a half-eaten bowl of cereal. So he had gotten up, Curt saw. He'd tried, but it must have been too much, because he'd retreated to his bed.

"Hi, Poppa," Clarkson said with hesitation.

Kelly pulled the sheet down from his head and opened his eyes. In the gloom before him he saw Clarkson and Curt. Had they not left for school yet? Or, came his next thought, had he spent the whole day in bed? He hated himself for doing the very thing that he could not have done differently.

"Hey, Clarkson." His eyes wandered to Curt's face, and Curt saw defeat in them.

"We have burgers for dinner, Poppa. And we got you some onion rings!"

"That sounds too good to miss," he mumbled. But he didn't move.

Clarkson leaned over and stroked his shoulder. "Burgers will make you feel better, Poppa. We can pretend we're at the cabin."

Kelly smiled. "That's great, Clarkson. Just give me a minute to pull myself together." The apathy in his voice suggested this would take a long time.

"C'mon, Kelly. Take my hand." Curt reached past their son and offered his open hand. In what felt like a miracle, Kelly's hand emerged from the sheets and took Curt's. Curt hoisted him up from the bed. "Help me, Clarkson," he said as they steadied Kelly, who stood on uncertain legs before them. His face was full of stubble. With the sheets thrown back and Kelly standing in his underwear, Curt knew that he hadn't found the energy or the will to take himself to the bathroom when he'd needed to. He smelled like urine. He was sorry Clarkson had to see his Poppa like this.

"Kelly, I know it will take some effort, but I'm going to get you into the shower and then into some clean clothes. Don't try to argue with me about this because the prize of onion rings waits for you at the end."

Kelly smiled weakly, still holding Curt's hand. "You seduce me with your wicked words, Dr. Shepherd."

"Prize of onion rings. Is that a metaphor?"

"I don't think so. But keep trying."

As Kelly stood, Curt pulled his tee shirt over his head and then his boxers down to his ankles. "Step out."

Clarkson had seen these episodes before, but none had been as dark as this, never with the indignity of Kelly wetting himself. The boy left the room and went downstairs to begin his homework without being asked. He thought it was how he could do something right for his Poppa, something that would hurry normal back.

Curt led Kelly to the bathroom and sat him on the toilet. He turned on the shower and adjusted the temperature. "I don't know what our utility bill is like, but if you need to stand in there until the hot water runs out, that's fine. I'll wash your back if you want. I'll wash every inch of you, Kelly, if that will help you get better." He lifted his husband's head from where it drooped onto his chest and looked him in the eyes. "Understand?"

"Where's Clarkson?"

"Downstairs."

"I've been in a really bad place, Curt."

"I know."

"If you want to get rid of me, I'll understand."

"That's *never* going to happen, Kelly."

"You and Clarkson are the best things that ever happened to me, Curt. Is it okay if I cry in the shower?"

"It's encouraged. Doctor's orders." He helped Kelly into the shower and pulled the curtain.

While Kelly stood under the hot water, Curt checked on Clarkson, pleased to see him attempting his homework. "Poppa will be better after his shower. Let me know if you need any help." He returned to their room to strip the sheets off their bed and muscled on clean sheets to make it as crisp and fresh as he could. If Kelly needed to return to bed, he would find it ready and welcoming. Curt rolled the soiled sheets and Kelly's undershirt and boxers into a ball to put in the washing machine after dinner.

The water was still running when Curt went back to the bathroom.

"How are you doing?"

"Do I have to use shampoo like an adult?" he said over the hiss of the water.

"Only if you want to. Or do you want me to?"

"I think I can manage. Are there really onion rings waiting for me?"

"Really and truly. Clarkson insisted."

"He's a good boy."

"I put a fresh towel here by the sink, Kelly. And there are clean clothes set out for you on the bed. Let me know if you need me to help you get dressed."

Curt had pulled on his doctor persona and was making decisions, acting in charge. But underneath he was terrified. What if one time Kelly didn't win? What if he came home one day and found that the darkness had won? What if the good life they had created for each other wasn't enough? He didn't know what he could do.

"Actually," Kelly said after he turned off the water and, a few seconds later, pulled back the curtain. "Would you mind helping me a little?"

"Whatever you need!"

"I know it sounds silly, but could you maybe dry me with that fresh towel and then help me into my clothes? Maybe it would do me good to have a little personal care. Just this once."

"Sure." Whatever you want! As much as you want!

He helped Kelly out of the shower and dried his body as though he were a baby. He wanted this because he'd never had much personal attention as a child. Of that Curt was certain. He helped Kelly into his clothes and held him close and kissed him.

"Whatever else is going on, Kelly, Clarkson needs to see you up and about. This is tough for him. Can you manage it?"

"Yeah. The shower helped." He still sounded weary. "You two are the reasons I keep fighting."

"I know."

"And maybe onion rings."

They both laughed, and when Clarkson heard them, he bolted

up the stairs and came rushing into the room with his eyes wide to join their hug.

"Hi, Poppa! Hi, Poppa!"

Kelly held the boy's head against his stomach. After a quiet eternity he said, "Let's go eat some burgers."

"And onion rings!"

Although they never kept an accounting of such things, their procession to the kitchen was the best one of their lives. Kelly sat at the table, happy to be served a fast-food meal in his own kitchen. Happy to see the unsteady smiles on the faces of his husband and son. Happy to feel something like happy. He didn't trust it, but it would suffice for now.

He listened as Clarkson told him about his unremarkable day at school. He smiled when Curt suggested a trip to the cabin the coming weekend. That would be nice. He ate half of a burger and most of his onion rings. This moment was enough, and he could feel himself turning a corner. He was going to win this time.

"Well, I stared into the abyss, as they say, and the abyss stared back into me. Then it got bored and left. So here I am!"

Chapter Twelve

How to Really Make a Mess of Things with Your Son

"I really made a mess of things, Kathy. I think Curt's going to be mad at me for a long time."

David had come into the house after they'd dropped him off and immediately fell into the recliner. He hadn't even taken off his boots, which he always left outside the door when he came back from the cabin.

He was home earlier than Kathy expected for a day trip to the cabin. She was in the kitchen, peeling apples for a pie, when she heard him come through the front door. When he didn't appear around the corner with a kiss and a hug — which she would always pretend to fend off until he'd had a shower and changed into fresh clothes — she walked into the front room and found him sitting there, boots on his feet and head in his hands. Whatever it was he'd made a mess of, it looked to be serious.

"He may never talk to me again, Kathy."

"Of course, he will, Davey. Whatever happened will get resolved and he'll talk to you again." She seated herself on the couch. "Now tell me what happened?"

Everyone seemed to be alive. There didn't appear to be any broken bones or as much as a torn fingernail because she would have heard about it from Curt already. But she'd rather hear from David what was wrong than from Curt. David was less filtered, once he got going. Curt would probably try to dismiss whatever it was, keep it to himself and manage it on his own rather than see it build into an emotional blowout. She'd only get selected details from Curt, and it would seethe unaddressed inside him. Patience, she'd found, was one of the keys to a healthy relationship with a man, whether husband or son. She didn't think she'd have to wait long given David's state.

David began to give her an account of his day.

Curt and Kelly had come by to collect him before dawn that morning while she was still asleep. He'd been sitting on the front porch step — boots on and a mug of coffee in his hand — so that the sound of him leaving wouldn't wake Kathy. When he slid into the back seat, he found Clarkson slumped over in his booster there. "Just as well," Curt had whispered. "The long drive bores him. No new water towers for him to inventory. He's always too eager to get there and start messing around." David recalled Curt being the same way.

Once they were out of the city, they stopped for gas then settled in. They had to stop again soon when Clarkson woke and said he had to go to the bathroom, but his ploy to get a Snicker's bar didn't work. The rest of the drive was unremarkable, each person mostly quiet inside his own early morning mind. Curt and Kelly occasionally exchanged words, but then Kelly would glance back to make sure they didn't wake the boy. Soon after they turned off the paved road he did awaken. He didn't want to miss splashing through the stream they had to cross, sticking his hand out the window, hoping to catch a drop or two, even get splashed in the face, then peering into the tall trees around them, maybe to spot a deer or turkey. He was beginning to develop his own routines at the cabin, his own ways to love the place, which heartened David.

They unloaded their things with the ease of long practice, and Clarkson had gone down to the dock to look across the lake. Each of them kept an eye on the boy, though he'd grown up with the forest, and they felt safe with him on his own.

There were chores they could do. Or shirk. It wasn't warm enough for a swim, but they could hike or build a fire or clear cedars or take a nap or any number of pursuits perfectly fitted to a long day at the cabin. Each of them bustled about with some activity.

David paused, somewhere in the middle of it, and eased himself into a chair on the porch. He too had grown up with the forest, and each tree, each bird call, each knothole in the dirty siding of the cabin could evoke a memory he might live in for a while. He knew Curt had a similar warehouse of memories, and he hoped Kelly was actively stocking one of his own. Now it was Clarkson's turn. This, David thought as he closed his eyes and soaked in a moment of rest, was what he wanted the cabin to mean to them. It was Curt's cabin now. David had passed it on, just as his father had before him, and he was pleased that Curt loved the place equally in his way. If he'd done nothing else well with his life, he'd done this right.

When it was time to build the lunch fire, David and Curt conferred that duty to Kelly, who was still practicing the art. Clarkson hadn't shown much enthusiasm for learning how to build a one-match fire — Curt said he thought the boy knew how but just didn't care — and would rather poke holes in the ash with a stick while someone else lit the fire, which was better than grabbing handfuls of ash and smearing it on his clothes and in his hair like he had when he was a toddler. Curt made certain the child was current on his vaccinations.

Kelly knelt before the ring, carefully assembling each stage. Glancing at him often as though for confirmation. David noted that he was doing it right.

He lit the fire with a single match and gave a little cheer. Clarkson cheered with his Poppa. When the coals were ready, Kelly spread their burgers on the grill to reach some approximation of cooked so they could devour them with appetites that were always heightened at the cabin. "Chips are really bad for you," Curt said to no one in particular as he shoved a handful in his mouth.

It had been a routine morning. To David that meant idyllic. He and Clarkson practiced whittling with their pocketknives, David remaining beside him to ensure his grandson was safe. Kelly had used their shavings to start the lunch fire. They tried to split some logs, but the sledgehammer was too heavy for the boy. David pointed out bird calls, and together they filled the feeder. When he suggested throwing lines in the lake to catch some fish, Clarkson mutely shook his head. He wasn't going to be a fisherman, which was fine. There were plenty of ways to love their forest.

After lunch around the campfire, Curt proposed a hike to the four corners of their property. "To check out what's going on there." Defining boundaries had been a part of his nature since he was a boy. Kelly was eager to see parts of their forest that he hadn't yet seen. David said he was content to sit by the fire and tend it till it burned out. They shouldn't leave it alone anyway, he cautioned. And Clarkson, they all knew, was more of a sitter, preferring to see and hear what the forest brought to him when he waited silently. He'd just slow them down if he went with them and would need to be brought back too soon. Clarkson's preference to stay at the cabin with Grandpa pleased them all.

"Since we have a sitter," Curt said to Kelly, "let's go on a date."

The two took off, loppers in their hands and daypacks on their backs, while David watched the fire die and Clarkson poked in the ash.

"I see rusty nails."

"Yes. Those are from an old fence that used to be around the backyard. Before you were born. It was rotten, so I brought pieces of it here to burn. You can find other stuff, too. When it's time to retire a worn-out pair of gloves, we toss them in the fire."

"Poppa says that's one of our family rituals."

"I guess your Poppa is right." He liked Clarkson's use of the word "our."

"The ash is gray until you pour water on it. Then it turns black."

"Yes, it does."

Eventually, Clarkson rose from the gravel and crawled onto his grandfather's lap, resting his head on his shoulder. He wasn't little anymore, but he still fit in his grandfather's arms. As a boy Curt had done the same many times. David's arms remembered. Had their adopted grandson learned this comfort from his father or was the nature of the place, the warmth and safety of their cabin, that led little boys into the arms of their fathers and grandfathers? David supposed he'd nestled in his father's arms many times long ago. He wished he could remember.

Holding his grandson, David tried rocking in the camp chair. He brushed away a curious fly with his free hand. His other hand, at the end of the arm that was cradling the boy, was going numb. And where Clarkson's hip pressed, his leg was beginning to tingle. Maybe the boy would rest better on the soft mattress of the bed in the cabin. David knew his own limbs would appreciate the mattress.

"How about a nap, Clarkson? Up in the cabin."

"I'm not sleepy," the boy murmured, but his eyes remained closed.

David rose from the chair, gave a parting glance to the mostly dead embers in the ring, and turned toward the cabin. He carried Clarkson there — the boy was getting heavy, he observed as he mounted the porch steps. They passed through the door and David laid him on the bed. He opened his eyes and looked at his grandfather.

"You sleep too," he said, and David lay down beside the child, pulling the quilt over them as he had done hundreds of times with Curt. He hoped he might do this hundreds more times with his son's son.

But Clarkson was now awake.

"Did you have a cabin when you were a boy, Grandpa?" he asked, staring wide-eyed at the ceiling.

David chuckled. Curt hadn't filled him in on some of the family lore yet, it seemed. There were so many things waiting for the boy to learn. Had Curt deliberately left some of it for David to pass down?

"This was my cabin too, Sprout." He bunched the pillow beneath his head. "My dad built this cabin when I was a little boy. He was your great-grandfather."

"You came here when you were a boy?" Clarkson's words were somewhere between disbelief and awe.

"Yes, I did. My daddy brought me here when I was a boy, and I brought your daddy here when he was a boy. Poppa came along a little later when he was a man."

Clarkson sat himself cross-legged on the bed beside David. "Wow! This cabin is really old!"

There were days when David *did* feel really old. He was older than the cabin, though only by a year or two. But the place and this forest didn't seem old to him. Old wasn't the right word. Maybe eternal, always there. In his heart they had been here yesterday, today, and would be here tomorrow.

"I remember when my mom and dad would bring me out here for whole weekends. We'd swim and fish. We'd cut logs. We'd rake leaves away from the cabin. We'd have a fire that I got to light. I'd get really dirty. One time I saw a fox, across the lake."

"I see a fox here all the time."

David doubted that. Maybe a coyote. Maybe. Or a brownish

raccoon passing through the scrub. Even an armadillo. More likely, Clarkson's "fox" was a product of his active imagination and his wish to fill the forest with magical creatures.

"Foxes are very clever. He must like you if he let you see him."

"It's not a boy. It's a girl fox."

Clarkson's imagination was also precise.

"My dad taught me the names of all the birds and the trees. He showed me how to saw a log. How to whittle a stick. We looked at the stars. Listened to the coyotes across the ridge at night. Swam in the lake." It would be nice, David thought, to lie there in the bed, close his eyes, and just drift along with these old memories. It would be a long journey, this drifting, because he had lived a long journey.

"Did you cook hamburgers on the fire when you were a boy? Like we do?"

"Hundreds and hundreds of them, Sprout. The ash in the ring grew more than a foot deep. We had to rebuild the block wall more than once to make it tall enough to contain the ash."

Half the meals of his life, it seemed to him, had been cooked over those flames, although he knew that wasn't literally true. Maybe the most nutritious meals came from there. The most savored and remembered. The best ones.

He wanted to remain in the bed, to continue drifting, but he also wanted to share his childhood with his grandson. David threw off the quilt and pushed himself onto his feet.

"I'll be right back, Sprout. Don't go anywhere."

David stepped across the room to the mouse-proof cabinet and poked around inside it for a moment, returning with a stack of his old Superman comics.

"My daddy used to surprise me with a new copy sometimes when we came to the cabin. I had to do a chore first, or light the fire all by myself. Some big-boy thing like that. But if I did, he'd make one of these appear like magic. It was my reward for being a good boy." He plopped the stack of comic books on the bed and then plopped himself beside them. The old bed springs squeaked. Clarkson bounced a bit, righted himself, and smiled.

As most parents do, Curt held ambitious hopes of raising his son with a kind of purity, so he mostly disdained pop culture and its influence, but he knew that would be a lost cause. Kelly was trying to foster an appreciation of the classics and would read to Clarkson from books of fairy tales most nights, which Kelly admitted was the pop culture of its day. Curt supposed it was better than the modern stuff. If pressed, Curt might acknowledge that his father's Superman comics stood somewhere between the ephemera of pop culture and the honored longevity of folk tales. What Curt would not hesitate to acknowledge was that his father's Superman comics had earned their own honored longevity in the family lore, and he wouldn't mind his boy sharing that with his grandfather.

David watched as Clarkson flipped through the raspy pages of the comic books and paused over the full-page action panels. He sounded out the larger words he didn't know. He traced his fingers across the drawings and followed the lines that enclosed each panel. He was appreciating the artistry, David realized.

"Superman fights the bad guys. He keeps the world safe. But it's only pretend."

"The land of make believe."

"Yes. And it's fun. I used to lie on the floor of the porch and read these comics over and over. Imagine I was Superman. That I could fly and was really strong."

"You *are* really strong, Grandpa. You can lift the sledgehammer."

"Not as strong as Superman, Sprout. He came from a different planet. He's adopted, just like you."

Later, describing the moment to Kathy, David untied his boots and tugged them off, standing to put them outside on the porch. He returned and sat next to Kathy on the couch. If she worried about his buggy clothes rubbing against her, she didn't say.

"That was it, Kathy. Sprout didn't look up from the comic book, but he did say, 'I'm not adopted.' And I knew then that Curt hadn't told him yet. But I just did."

Curt and Kelly had said many times that they would explain to their son that he was adopted "when he was old enough to understand all that it meant," and everyone seemed fine with that. It never came up, and eventually the boy had seemed old enough, so David had assumed he had been told. He was still a child with no interest yet in where babies came from or that there had to be a mommy in his background somewhere. Kelly and Curt had done an excellent job giving Clarkson the normalcy of a family. Having two dads was not common among his classmates, but it didn't seem strange to him. It was just one of the many kinds of families kids had.

"I shut up about it then, Kathy. Instead, we talked about Superman's cape and his Fortress of Solitude and his dog. I hoped what I had said just floated out of his mind. We flipped through the comic books for a little while, but he lost interest, which was fine with me. We went outside and raked some leaves together. The crows were calling so we talked about them. I showed him the turkey vultures circling over the south ridge across the lake, and we talked about them. He drew his lines in the gravel with a stick. We both peed on the remaining coals. All the stuff we normally do, and I kept wondering if what I said had stuck with him."

"I didn't have to wonder long. When Curt and Kelly came back from their hike, looking tired and irritated — it's a long way around the whole hundred acres, and some of it's pretty rough — the first thing Clarkson said was, 'Dad, am I adopted? Grandpa says I'm adopted.'"

"Curt gave me a look that I thought would stop my heart! I think maybe it did stop for a second."

He had glared at David, his green eyes afire, but only for the moment it took to compose himself. Then he smiled at Clarkson and tousled his hair, saying, "No, you're not adopted, Clarkson. You're my son."

The boy seemed fine with that, and whether he saw that his grandfather had been directly contradicted or if it was all just part of the confusing, mysterious world that adults lived in, no one knew. David knew, however, that the boy had just been lied to by his father. That wasn't right. What they told Clarkson about his past was Curt and Kelly's business. It wasn't his right or duty to tell the boy he was adopted, and if his slip was dismissed and forgotten, well, he supposed that was good. But you don't lie to your son.

Soon after this, Curt said he thought it was time to head back home. They had a long drive, and he wanted to stop for gas again because it was cheaper in the sticks, and there were some work things he needed to get done at home. Kelly could read Curt's mood as well as David could. His day at the cabin had been ruined by David's slip. Better to get away before it ruined all of their times at the cabin. David felt horrible.

And so they packed quickly and were soon on the road. Clarkson held his hand out the window when they splashed through the stream, and when they stopped for gas, Curt bought him a Snickers bar to eat in the back seat as they drove. He'd also handed some treat to Kelly, but he had nothing for David. There wasn't much conversation on the drive. David never caught Curt's eyes looking at him in the mirror because he avoided looking up. When they dropped David off before his house, Curt had started to pull away before David had closed the door.

"I don't know what to do, Kathy. I know it wasn't my place to tell Sprout he's adopted. But I hated to hear Curt lie to Clarkson. I don't think I've ever heard Curt tell a lie in his life."

"He was caught off guard, Davey." Kathy had been holding his hand and now began to stroke it. "He had to act quickly. And maybe it's a good thing. What you did. Maybe it will motivate them to have that talk with Clarkson now. Honestly, I thought they'd already told him too. It could have been me who slipped up just as easily as you. At least he learned it at the cabin."

He rested his free hand on hers. He knew she was trying to put the best spin on his mistake and loved her for doing so. He knew she'd defend him to Curt, if it came to that, because it seemed like she'd been doing that for a long time. And he was right. Kathy was already thinking of what she would say to Curt, her surprise that he hadn't yet told his son this important thing, and her concern that he had lied to him.

"Why don't you get out of those buggy clothes and into the shower, Davey. When you're done, I can wash them. And then later we can have some pie." She rose from the couch, signaling an end to their conversation. He'd had three hours in the car to brood; it was time for him to move away from his self-doubt.

Being in the shower, David didn't hear the doorbell ring. When he shut off the water, he heard voices and clearly heard Kelly saying, "Let me help with that."

David dried himself and pushed a brush through his hair. His fresh clothes were set out on the bed, about three steps from the bathroom door, so he wrapped his towel around his waist, opened the door, peered out, and dashed into the bedroom. Kelly had seen him naked when they skinny-dipped at the cabin. And Kathy, of course, had seen him naked. But if Kelly was here, was Curt also here? Did he want to face his angry son with nothing but a towel around his waist? But maybe Curt hadn't come because he didn't want to see his father at all.

When David emerged from the bedroom in sweatpants and a tee shirt, his hair still wet and his feet bare, he saw Kelly and Kathy working on the pie. Kathy smiled and nodded toward the front room, indicating that a guest was waiting there for him.

Curt sat in the recliner with Clarkson on his lap, holding him much the same way David had held the boy at the cabin. They stopped talking when they saw David. They were still wearing their cabin clothes.

"Remember what we talked about," Curt whispered into his son's ear. He set Clarkson on his feet, rising from the chair to stand behind him.

"Curt," David began, but Curt held up his hand.

"Before you start, Dad, I want to apologize. I want to apologize to you for how I acted at the cabin. That was cold and unfair. It was the part of me I've been trying to put behind me for a long time. And it was certainly no way to behave in front of my son. Or to behave at the cabin. Or toward my father." He rested his hand on Clarkson's shoulder. "And I want to apologize for putting you in an impossible situation. Yes, we should have spoken to Clarkson about this sooner, but I should have at least had the sense to let you know that we still hadn't. I guess everyone assumed we had. We've been meaning to, but we keep putting it off. It's a tough conversation. So that was my fault, and I'm sorry. But as always, Dad, you led me to do the right thing."

His words sounded sincere. Unexpected, but sincere. Maybe he had to practice what he wanted to say, rehearse it a few dozen times on the drive over.

David was about to speak, to make his apologies, but Curt continued.

"Clarkson has something he wants to say, too."

David heard Kathy and Kelly crowding in the kitchen doorway behind him.

"Grandpa, you were right. I am like Superman. I am adopted. Daddy and Poppa told me about it when we got home. Adopted means my first parents couldn't take care of me. So Daddy and Poppa got to. That's how come we're a family. They wanted to be my new parents. And Daddy said he wanted *you* to be my Grandpa most of all."

David had to sit. He felt lightheaded. He didn't know if his heart could take what he was hearing. He lowered himself to the couch, and Clarkson crawled up beside him.

"I'm glad you get to be my Grandpa."

The boy buried his face in David's chest, and David felt his arms enfolding him. Curt smiled at him from across the room. David felt like he was flying. Like he was Superman.

Chapter Thirteen

Hush Arbor

A marble. Odd to see in the gravel around the cabin. David reached down to retrieve it — one of Clarkson's surely — and saw another nearby. And another. Had the boy dropped his entire bag of marbles? Marbles and a weekend overnight at the cabin with Grandpa were the only birthday gifts he'd asked for that year.

Was this a spill, or were they laid down deliberately? They were spaced in a line more or less evenly and appeared to be pressed into the gravel. Had Clarkson placed them here in a magical arrangement to remain, or was the boy going to collect them later? Whichever, David liked this splash of color in the gray gravel.

Clarkson was off in the woods on his own. The boy knew their hundred acres and carried his walkie-talkie as David required. Dinner and birthday dump cake would lure him back, but David didn't want to start the fire without him. David's instructions from Curt were to encourage Clarkson's interest in building one-match fires. He decided to walk the woods himself hoping to cross paths with Clarkson.

The boy was easy to follow. The forest told tales that David had long before learned to read. Clarkson's feet had kicked an obvious trail through the fallen oak and hickory leaves going downhill, and David would follow this as far as it took him then look for other signs. Clarkson's red parka stood out ahead among the grays and browns and muted greens of the November forest. David could see it through the low branches of a clump of cedars down near the dry streambed. David's father had wanted to rid the forest of all the cedars, but, though he had made a pretty good start, some required too much effort, and he'd begrudgingly allowed them their place in his woods. David respected these old timers as survivors that had earned their tenure.

Clarkson appeared amidst a small congregation of these old timers.

"Hi, Grandpa," Clarkson said as David approached in the crunching leaf litter.

"Can't sneak up on you, can I?"

David didn't see an obvious entrance to the clutch of cedars. "How do I get in there?"

"You have to crawl. By the marble tree."

The marble tree turned out to be a blackjack oak into whose rough bark the boy had wedged two red marbles.

Opposite the marble tree was a low break in the cedar branches that David had missed, and he dropped to the ground and crawled through, the carpet of the cedar duff being kind to his knees.

Inside he found a small chamber that Clarkson had created by cutting away branches. At the center was the bleached log of a long-fallen oak where his grandson sat. David had to sit cross-legged and hunched over to fit.

"This is my secret place, Grandpa," he whispered. "Don't tell my dads, okay?"

"Okay. It's a nice place." It smelled vaguely of Christmas. "Just where a forest sprite might live."

"And a fox. Please don't cut down these cedars, Grandpa."

"Never, Sprout." But if he were going to join his grandson there again, he might snap off some of the inner branches to give himself a little more space. Already needles had fallen down the back of his shirt.

"I guess you come here a lot."

"I keep my treasures here." He whispered, as though someone might be listening.

For a short time as a boy David had had a treasure box, one of his father's old cigar boxes that he hid under his bed. But aside from a couple of old silver dollars, a few cubes of calcite he'd found in the cabin gravel, a Blue Jay feather, and a pocketknife, he'd never accumulated much. What treasures, he wondered, would Clarkson have?

"I'll show them to you, but you have to keep them a secret," the boy said. Clarkson slid from the log and knelt beside the end where the core had rotted. There a boy could hide important things. He reached in and plucked something out that he showed to David. A three-point deer antler. David sometimes came upon these in his rambles through the woods, though critters had usually gnawed them into rough shapelessness by the time he happened along. Clarkson's was whole and unmarred. David ran his fingers along the smooth surface.

"A pretty good treasure."

Clarkson held out a fragment of an orange-red brick. "I found it up on the ridge, near the old road."

As far as David knew, no one had ever actually lived on the hundred acres. No pioneers or settlers had sunk their roots here, only passing through to hunt and take timber. He indulged in the possibility that there might have been an earlier cabin.

"Look at these." Clarkson handed David two shards of pottery. Glazed and painted with flowers, they may have come from a teacup or plate. Evidence of a household?

"I like this one," the boy said as he reached into the tree cavity again. "I remember you said your dad used to smoke cigars on the cabin porch."

Clarkson produced a long, slender catalpa seedpod and handed it to David.

In the decades he had been stomping around the hundred acres, David had thought he knew most everything there was to know about his forest. Yet he had never found a catalpa tree among the oaks and hickories and cedars. Not a mature one that was producing seeds. David rattled the pod.

"Where did you find this, Sprout?"

"Near the east fence. They're on the ground there sometimes."

"Maybe tomorrow you can take me over there and show me."

Clarkson didn't agree or disagree but reached again into the log, stretching farther and closing his eyes in concentration. Only by touch could he find what he sought. When he pulled his arm out, he held something curled in his fingers that David couldn't see. He studied it for a moment before opening his hand. On Clarkson's palm rested two tiny arrowheads, each not much bigger than his thumbnail. What David's father had sought in his own rambles through the forest but had never found. One was made of gray stone, but the other was black and glossy, like a piece of glass. It was unlike any rock he had ever seen in his forest, and he knew it came from far away. True treasures indeed, David thought. From people who *had* once lived on this very land. They were here all along, Dad, David thought.

"Those are *really* special, Sprout!"

"I was following the two crows one day, and when they stopped, I saw them on the ground in the sunlight."

"Two crows?"

"I follow them a lot. They showed me the cigar tree too."

David's own boy had always been serious and analytical; even at Clarkson's age he rarely strayed into imaginary play. Nor could David remember being this imaginative in his own boyhood. Yet here he was in his grandson's secret place, seeing his secret treasures, and he knew the moment itself was a treasure.

Clarkson had not handed over the arrowheads, and though David dearly wanted to touch them, he didn't reach for them. The boy's fingers soon closed over the arrowheads, and he returned them to their hiding place deep inside the log. He collected his other treasures and methodically returned them too.

"Promise you won't tell my dads."

"Cross my heart, Sprout." David drew an X on his chest. There was nothing about any of this that he thought needed to be kept secret, but a promise was a promise.

Clarkson returned to his seat on the log.

"Do you ever find treasures in the forest, Grandpa?"

Did he? Did he ever look? David thought the forest itself was the treasure. The forest and the lake and the cabin, the hugs his father would give him. The lessons he taught him. The memories from his lifetime here. This secret place his grandson had crafted for himself was the biggest discovery David could recall.

"You know what, Sprout? It's *all* a treasure to me."

"Do you ever find anything strange in the forest?"

"Strange, Sprout?"

"Things that don't make sense. Surprises."

"Well, let me think about it." The forest was familiar to him, he supposed, in nearly every aspect. Sure, he learned new specifics — he had a catalpa tree, for example — but was he ever surprised?

"Sometimes, when I'm hiking in the forest, I see a rock sitting on top of the fallen leaves. Now how did the rock get on *top* of the leaves? I didn't put it there."

"The raccoons do that, Grandpa."

"The raccoons? How do you know that?"

"Scrapefoot told me. She says they're rascals."

Hush Arbor 151

Something felt wrong to David then.

"Who is Scrapefoot?"

"She's a fox that lives in your forest."

"Is that from a book your Poppa read to you?"

"No. Sometimes when I sit here, Scrapefoot comes and talks to me."

A wild animal approaching a human is almost never a good thing. He'd seen a rabid raccoon in the forest once, and it had shown none of the aversion to humans that it typically would. A fox approaching the boy, talking to him or not, could be dangerous.

"Clarkson, wild animals don't come up to people. They're afraid of us. If you saw a fox like this, it was probably very sick, and you should stay away from it."

"She *isn't* sick, Grandpa. She sits here just like you are, and we talk about stuff."

"Was it a dog maybe? Did it have a collar?"

"She's a fox!" He dropped his hands into his lap and stared ahead. "I thought *you* would believe me."

David was too far outside of his understanding to know what to believe. Was the boy having hallucinations — was that the right word? Or had he fallen asleep in his little arbor and had dreams he was confusing with reality? What was he supposed to say? Or do? Or not do? He didn't want to frighten his grandson and end this private confession in his secret place. He remembered then the arrangement of marbles near the cabin. Did it all serve some magical purpose in the boy's mind?

David felt alone suddenly, much as he had when Curt began to outpace him in understanding the world, running ahead and leaving him behind. Was Clarkson off on his own journey? And was it to a bad place? As much as David wished there *were* talking foxes in his forest, the boy's story was unsettling.

"What else do you and Scrapefoot talk about?"

Clarkson eyed him. David was afraid that the boy could see that he didn't believe, that he was indulging him. Or, worse, was going to betray him to his parents.

"Does Scrapefoot like the cabin? Does she mind us coming here?"

"Sometimes she doesn't say anything. She just sits there. Sometimes she talks about you."

"Me?"

"She says she's been watching you for a long time. She thinks you're one of the good humans, Grandpa."

"Good humans?"

"Because you don't hurt the animals. You do things to help them. Like when you showed me that salt block for the deer. And that time you scattered corn in the woods."

Only once had David done that, and it was long before Clarkson had been born. He'd bought the bag of dried corn impulsively at the hardware store in Osceola and then placed the cobs on logs and rocks in the forest. But he'd never told anyone that he'd done this. How could Clarkson have known?

"Would Scrapefoot ever talk to me?"

"Oh, no. She only watches you. She won't come if you're here. She only talks to me."

A silence fell between them, and David could feel the November chill reaching him from not moving for too long.

"Don't tell my dads about Scrapefoot, okay, Grandpa?"

"No? Don't you think they'd like to know, Sprout?"

"Dad wouldn't. And Poppa would just laugh and mess my hair."

His Dad, the analytical and sometimes impatient doctor. He would take this seriously. His Poppa was the more imaginative of the pair, but for some reason Clarkson wasn't comfortable sharing this with him either. Maybe because Kelly *wouldn't* take it seriously?

David had to meet the boy on his terms. Had Clarkson lured him into this hidden place because he needed to talk about it? Chosen him as his confessor? Was he seeking help of some kind? An adult to confirm what he thinks he sees is real? How old is too old for a child to still have an imaginary friend? And why does he want it to remain a secret from his dads? Was it because he was adopted? Was there some trust issue lingering in that? But he was adopted as an infant then. His dads are all the family he has ever known.

David concluded he would believe that the *boy* believed Scapefoot was real.

"We need to get started on the fire before it gets darker and colder, don't you think?" Would they ever come back to Clarkson's special place?

The boy rose from the log and looked at the end the cavity that held his treasures. He turned to his grandfather. David crawled out of the secret arbor first, and Clarkson followed.

They marched up the hill to the cabin, built a fire, and burned some burgers. Later they would horse around in the cabin and fall into bed where the boy would sleep curled in David's arms. In the morning they would stand on the edge of the porch together and pee, then hurry inside where their clothes were kept warm by the wood stove. They'd eat their oatmeal and bananas, rake fallen leaves away from the wooden cabin, cut more firewood, find that catalpa tree, pack up, and go home.

All the while David would ponder and worry. And listen for the boy to tell him more.

And watch for Scapefoot in the trees. Just as the fox might be watching him.

Chapter Fourteen

Motherlove

"He's afraid you're going to leave him, Curt." She stood at the kitchen counter, facing away from her son because that was the easiest way to start the conversation.

Curt rose from his chair abruptly, knocking it over behind him. She didn't turn.

"He said that?"

"Yes. And he says he's told you that."

"He tells me that at least once a month. And I tell him how wrong that is." He righted the chair and then sat in it again. "That's supposed to be private. But now he's told you. I will never leave him, Mom!"

"I know that. But Kelly isn't certain. He needs to feel certain, Curt. Here's your slice of cake."

She brought over two plates with chocolate cake, and then two mugs, which she filled with coffee. "Now eat."

The secrets of the confessional. As a little girl in catechism class, Kathy had been told they were inviolable. That whatever sins she confessed were between herself, the priest, and God alone. Maybe that was true. And Curt, of course, had his obligations about patient confidentiality. How Curt and Kelly chose to pursue the privacy of their marriage mattered just as much.

But Kelly was her son-in-law, Curt's husband, their mutual family member, and he sought love from both of them.

Kelly had been friendly with Kathy nearly from the start. Even relaxed, once he'd let his guard down. "He can't believe people are nice to him just to be nice," Curt had told her once. "He still says that to me sometimes." Often Curt would stop whatever he was doing and hold Kelly in his arms for however long it took for him to understand he was loved. Late to work, late getting Clarkson to school, late to brunch — too bad. This was more important.

She thought Kelly had come to accept, at least tentatively, that she loved him for who he was and that she didn't have an agenda for him. No requirements or expectations. Nor did David. And she understood this kind of family must feel strange to him.

Over the years, he'd never really confided in her. He never told her about his past. Whatever darkness he experienced there, which seemed to return regularly to his present, he never shared with her.

He came by the house often, sometimes with real errands but just as often on some pretense, to sit and talk with her. Maybe they'd bake a cake or cookies he'd take home to Clarkson later. Or he'd tell her about the novel he was reading that he thought she'd like. He'd bring over some of Clarkson's drawings to hang on her crowded refrigerator. They'd chat about innocuous things: his old car that needed some work, Clarkson's grades that needed some work, their latest trip to the cabin, which always needed work. Davey might happen upon them at the kitchen table or on the patio out back and join the conversation that was all about safe stuff.

Early one Saturday morning, when Clarkson was sleeping in and Curt was caring for him, Kelly arrived. She saw immediately that something was wrong. He trudged in the front door, his eyes searching beyond the room, his skin gray. She got Kelly seated at the kitchen table with a mug of tea and told Davey to go to the store and take a long time.

Kathy sat opposite Kelly and waited.

"My mother died," he mumbled into the mug he held in his hands. But then he looked up. "No. Let me correct that. My *birth* mother died. My aunt called me this morning while Curt was in the shower. When he got out, I told him I was coming over here for a visit, and he seemed to understand because he sent me on my way and said he'd look after Clarkson for as long as I needed."

"Curt doesn't know?" That might not have been the best response she could give, but she was trying to read Kelly. What she understood then was that his previous visits had been testing her, seeing if she was safe, not so much that she could keep his secrets as that she could *bear* his secrets.

"No. Not yet. I'm still trying to figure out what I feel and don't feel."

"Kelly, I'm so sorry."

"Don't be. I'm not."

Now Kathy felt she was in a strange land. For a son to say such a thing about his mother . . . she didn't know what to think. Except to realize that she knew little of the darkness in his life.

"One of my earliest memories," he said, turning sideways in the chair to face away from her, slouching a little, "was going to my mother and telling her that my dad had hit me. And do you know what she said? She said, 'Well, what did you do to make him angry?'"

He laughed. A laugh of disbelief and disgust. "What kind of crime can a five-year-old boy commit that he deserves to be hit, Kathy?"

His right hand kneaded his left arm. He turned to her with something like a smile. "That's the first bruise I can remember, Kathy. One of my earliest childhood memories. Isn't that nice?"

She thought of her own father. He'd never been a physically violent man. He'd never so much as spanked her or her sister. But he had treated Davey horribly. That was a kind of violence.

Motherlove 157

"My mother made me wear a long-sleeved shirt to kindergarten the next day to hide the bruise. That and all the bruises that followed. She said that no one should ever know about it. That it was family business. She hid the violence and never did anything about it."

She recalled that he always wore long-sleeved shirts. Even on the hottest days. He was wearing one now. Did Curt understand this? Surely, he must.

"My dad got better about it though."

Should she smile? She wanted to reach across the little table and rest her hand on his arm but kept still.

"He stopped hitting me where the bruises would show. He didn't give me shiners or black and blue arms any longer. His fists found my torso. And his feet too when he kicked me. The thing is, Kathy. My mother let it happen. Never once did she try to stop him. Never once did she comfort me or tell me I was a good boy. She was what my witch doctor calls an enabler."

"Your witch doctor?"

His smile lasted only a moment. "My therapist. She said it's okay if I call her that."

It was nice to see him smile.

"Will you go to the funeral?"

His face fell. He brought the mug to his lips but didn't take a drink. He took a while to find his words.

"No. I don't think I would want to anyway, but the funeral was last week. I wasn't notified until it was over."

So the abuse continued beyond the grave. Kathy could not stop her arms from reaching across the table to touch the back of his hand. He did not flinch.

"Aunt Kelly said she wanted to let me know, but my father had forbidden it. It's like I'm in a Victorian novel and they're trying to cheat me out of my inheritance or something."

When Curt was a baby and they lived with Davey's parents, she'd do her best when Curt cried, but sometimes she couldn't figure out what he needed. She changed him. She nursed him. She sang to him. She gave him baths. Still, he cried, and he felt beyond her reach. That was how she felt with Kelly this Saturday morning. Was her love for him enough?

Yet he had chosen to speak to her about a pain he had never shared before. His mother had died, and even in death had rejected him. Or had his father spoken for her? She couldn't imagine a mother not loving her son.

"You see how ugly my life is. You see the mess I am. My therapist tells me not to think that way, not to talk to myself that way, but after twenty years, it's hard to turn it off that recording. I haven't told Curt yet because I think this might be the last straw. He's been kind to me. He says he loves me, and I try hard every day to believe that. But everybody has a limit. I've kept a lot of stuff from him, but I figure I have to tell him this. That my mother is dead and that I feel nothing. And when I tell him, the rest of it will probably spill out. And then he'll see the mistake he made."

"Curt would *never* do that!"

"Part of me knows that. Part of me isn't sure."

"*I'm* sure, Kelly."

"My father left me at a gas station once." He was staring at the floor, dodging eye contact. Kathy wondered if this was how he spoke with his witch doctor. "I don't remember where we were going. I must have been in second or third grade. They took off without me. I saw our car pull away when I came out of the restroom. The funny thing is, I didn't cry. I remember thinking they did it because I hadn't washed my hands. I guess I was already figuring out that they didn't want me. Even before I came out, they hadn't wanted me."

Motherlove 159

Kathy didn't move. What could she say in the face of such cruelty?

"They came back eventually. The attendant invited me inside and gave me candy. I don't know how long I was there. I saw the car pull up outside, and my father honked the horn and shouted that I should hurry up. When I got in my mother said she hoped I had thanked the attendant for the candy and that I should share it with my sisters."

Curt must never leave this man!

"I wanted so much to adopt Clarkson so I could give him a home where he could grow up with love and without violence and neglect. It doesn't seem like a hard thing to do."

It had never been hard for Kathy.

"That woman was my mother. And now she's gone. But I found a new mother. I feel as though you have always been my mother, even before I knew it. That's what I want to think. If you'll have me."

He wouldn't meet her eyes, and she knew he was afraid she would reject him too.

She rose from her chair and stepped around the table, pressing Kelly's head to her breasts and holding him until they both finished crying.

Chapter Fifteen

The Journey is the Destination

"He learned how to swim at the Y, Mom!"

Kathy had turned away for a pair of scissors, to snip off a stray thread she found, and Curt took the chance to snatch Clarkson's tee shirt that she had folded the wrong way. He flapped it open and quickly refolded it the "correct" way. Kathy pretended not to notice and decided to let him fold the remainder of the tee shirts.

"He's afraid of the fish, so he won't go in the lake." Curt rooted in the basket for the match to a sock he held.

"I'm the one who should stay out of the lake. The fish always go for my freckles. All of my coaxing couldn't get Clarkson to dip a single toe in after Dad caught that fish. It frightened him, so Kelly took him to the Y pool where there were no fish. Kelly thought was doing me a favor. I had to pretend I was grateful, but I was supposed to teach him, Mom. In the lake. Like Dad taught me. And Grandpa taught him."

"So now Clarkson can swim? He's confident in the water?"

"He's getting there. He's graduated from tadpole to goldfish to dolphin, which doesn't make any taxonomic sense. Next stop is shark. Maybe then he'll be confident enough to swim in the lake next summer. I'll tell him the fish will be afraid of a shark! I want us to go skinny-dipping in the lake, Mom. It's a family tradition!"

She rested her hand on his.

"Your Grandfather used to say that a man's life is the accumulation of all the little confidences he achieves along the way. He gave Dad little tasks and challenges, disguised as fun and games

— or chores — and didn't tell him they were to help him grow up strong, caring, and authentic. Davey did the same with you. And I'd say it worked. Look at you, my beautiful son!"

Curt blushed.

Blushing, along with his curly hair, came from his father. Kathy could easily make David blush. It was one of the ways she read him. Curt was more guarded, so if he blushed for her, she hoped it meant he was opening a little, briefly.

Clarkson and Kelly would soon be back from their dash to the hardware store to get leaf bags. Their activity for the day was raking the leaves that had fallen from the three maples in Kathy's backyard that they'd planted when they moved there the summer before Curt's freshman year in high school. One for each of them, and they'd grown large in the years since then.

"I don't disagree with you, Mom. About how Dad raised me." He continued to dig through the basket, looking for the missing sock. "But sometimes I think Dad stepped out of the way and let me find my own achievements rather than setting them up for me."

Kathy selected a pair of Clarkson's jeans. Surely, she could fold jeans correctly. They were fraying at the cuffs, and she could feel the patch Kelly had sewn on to reinforce one of the threadbare knees. Clarkson was an active boy, despite his withdrawn ways. He lived much of his young life inside his head. Did Curt recognize how similar his son was to him? If he did, did the similarity encourage or concern him?

"I don't think it's here, Mom."

"What?"

"The other sock. I don't think Clarkson's other sock made it into the laundry basket. It could be anywhere. He's just a child. I know. But Kelly lets him off too easily. We're forever scrambling to find things that Clarkson has lost, or Kelly hasn't put away properly.

We found my car keys in the kitchen junk drawer the other day. No reason for them to be there. And a half-finished bag of M&Ms in one of Clarkson's running shoes. I mean, first of all, who leaves a bag of M&Ms *half* finished?"

Curt smiled. "I still can't entice him to run with me. Even when it's just to run to the playground." After the incident at their neighborhood playground years before, which they still could not get him to talk about, Clarkson wouldn't return there. So they had to visit a playground farther from their condo, requiring a longer run and decreasing Clarkson's interest. "Kelly said he would lace up and run too, but no way Clarkson would agree." Clarkson was afraid of the fish in their lake and the playground in their neighborhood. Curt wondered whether he was giving Clarkson a happy life.

"Maybe he'd run with me. Around my neighborhood."

"You're still running, Mom?"

She arched an eyebrow and glared at him. "One of the things children have difficulty understanding is that their parents have full lives of their own once their kids are grown and flown. Yes, I still run. Sometimes I can even get your father to go with me. Maybe that's how I could get Clarkson to run a little. Go with his grandparents."

"And end at the ice cream store?"

"Grandparents are entitled to indulge their grandchildren, Curt. It's the law. Plus, I keep ice cream in the freezer. Whether or not Clarkson takes up running, he'll always get treats from me."

Curt tried to recall being taken to the ice cream store as a child. Back in his Kansas City life. Money was tight — even as the little boy he'd understood that. Still, there always seemed to be a carton of ice cream in the freezer at home. Usually mint, which his dad liked. Mint had become his favorite too.

"When's your new washing machine going to be delivered?" Kathy asked.

"Wednesday. Kelly's taking a half day to be home for the delivery. Then we can stop coming over and using your machine." He pulled another tee shirt from the basket and began folding it to his liking.

"Never stop coming over, Curt. Find some other excuse to come. Find a sudden need for some obscure tool. Paw through Davey's workbench until you find it. Then sit and have coffee with us and forget that's why you came over. Watch some dumb show on television with us. Just don't stop coming over because if you do, we'll come to you."

"You'll need to give me a little warning. Kelly's not the tidiest housekeeper."

This was not news to Kathy. She'd noted the general chaos of her son's home and knew how it chafed him. But she also saw their good health, their happy and ready smiles, and the laughter and warmth that greeted her there. She knew Clarkson drawing on the walls had really bugged Curt. But when Clarkson drew a little orange dog and a tiny door above the baseboard in their bedroom, behind her nightstand, she'd cautioned Davey to *never* paint over it.

Curt's frustration with Kelly's casual housekeeping had sometimes led him to bark words he later regretted. He shouldn't be harsh with Kelly, and, anyway, his words rarely made a difference. It was his house too; he could help more.

"There's not a room in that house I can pass through, Mom, that doesn't need something done to it. A door closed or a chair pushed in. A toy to step on in the night that wasn't put away. Marbles to slip on. Shoes left wherever they came off. Smelly socks. Probably the match for this sock. Clothes draped everywhere. Clean or dirty. The TV running when no one's in the room. Cups on the counter. *Stuck* to the counter half the time. Milk left out to turn sour. Kelly's books all over the place. Clarkson's tablet missing. Or its battery dead again. Every horizontal surface becomes the resting place for something that never seems to find a better home. I can't find the scissors when I need them and then sit on them when I don't. I don't think we have two matching spoons in the house. How is that even possible, Mom?" He paused to let his words relax. "Kelly gets it. He knows how frustrated it makes me sometimes. And I try not to be too fussy. Or at least not rag him about it so much. He says I'm waging a one-man battle against the forces of entropy. Had to look that one up."

Kathy listened to his litany.

"I don't like . . . living this way, Mom!" He didn't look at her when he said it, and his words were hesitant. Maybe he was embarrassed by his thoughts, or ashamed of them.

She grabbed a piece of laundry from the basket and shook it in his face.

"What is this, Curt?" Her words came at him abruptly and almost sternly. They caught him off guard.

"Kelly's boxers?"

"Wrong! Guess again."

Curt squinted at the bunched-up boxers in her hand. He'd given them to Kelly as a joke. They had alligators on them, and he cautioned Kelly about getting bitten. That conversation had quickly descended into playful naughtiness, and he smiled remembering it.

"I'm pretty sure that's Kelly's underwear you're holding, Mom."

"It's life, Curt." And then to be clear, "It's life."

Either his mother was having a senior moment, or he was about to be schooled.

She tossed the boxers in his face, and he took them off his head.

"Sure, people go on immersive trips around the world. Or jump out of perfectly good airplanes. Or ski down mountains. Or cheer on the sidelines at the big game. Or at the cross-country meets. All kinds of exciting, thrilling stuff."

She snatched one of Clarkson's tee shirts from the basket and snapped it in the air before she began deliberately folding it the wrong way. Curt wasn't about to correct her.

"But this is where life is really lived, Curt. Right here. Right now. Just like this. In the quiet moments. This is when *most* of life happens. When you're folding clothes or shopping for groceries or raking leaves in the yard. Having a bowl of ice cream at the end of the day with your family in your messy house. Or sitting on the porch at the cabin and just taking in deep breaths. *These* are the moments when you do most of your living, Curtis. When you're most yourself. When you can appreciate your contentment. And you can't be looking the other way and miss them when they're happening."

She placed the tee shirt on the stack with the ones Curt had folded. Then she pressed her palm on it as though daring him to refold it.

"It's not about having a tidy house, Curt, but a happy one. Are you going to look back someday and say, 'at least my floors were always gleaming'? That you kept control of all the messy details of living?"

"Your floors gleam."

"Yes, you were always a fastidious child. You kept your room tidy. You showered regularly and dressed neatly. Took care of your things. Every pencil was in its place on your desk. All your books lined up on the edge of your bookshelf. Your shoes lined up in your closet. Your bed always made. You were a mother's dream. But then you'd come back from a weekend at the cabin with Davey, all muddy and crawling with ticks. Stinky and needing a bath. I'd load the washing machine — remember? Down in the basement of that apartment on The Paseo? — while you, my feral little boy, sat on the dryer beside me in your underwear and breathlessly told me all about your adventures. About a salamander you saw or a rock you found that I had to put on the windowsill with the others. Clearing cedar trees with your dad. Catching fish. Swimming. There was a green fire in your eyes then, Curt. You were living your life, the messy, glorious thing we call being alive. That's where the true excitement lies, Curt."

They heard Clarkson and Kelly bumping through the door upstairs. "Anybody home?" the boy yelled. "We got the bags!"

"We don't get the lives we want, Curt. We get something much better! Now here's what you do, my son," she said quickly. She took Kelly's boxers from him. "You go tell Kelly that you're uncomfortable with your mother handling his underpants. Tell him you'd like him to finish folding your laundry. And you go outside with your precious boy and start raking leaves together. I don't care if you only fill one bag. Make a big pile and jump in it. Throw leaves at each other. Get more down your shirts than in the bags. Rip out the knees in your jeans. Get dirty. Get itchy. Just be with your boy and live in the moment with him. Don't lose this moment!"

Chapter Sixteen

Catch and Release

The point was not to catch a fish. Not really. Not for Curt certainly, and he suspected not for his father They would release any fish they caught back into the lake, only a little shaken up by its strange misadventure.

At least that's what they had told themselves for a long time. When Clarkson was little more than a toddler and first witnessed his grandfather catch a fish, it had been exciting for him. They'd talked it up with the boy, how they'd go fishing, and Grandpa would show them how it was done. Curt guessed later that the boy hadn't really understood what was happening. But when David pulled the fish from the water, a nice, dinner-sized bass that flopped around on the end of the line, hanging by a sharp hook in its mouth, Clarkson was suddenly horrified. He had cried and begged Grandpa to put the fish back in the water, back in its house. And Grandpa quickly did so. Their fishing adventure was over for that morning. Back in the cabin, Kelly consoled the child and Curt was a little mystified. It wasn't that he wanted his son to become a fisherman. Curt had never been very good at catching fish either. Nor was he bothered that his boy showed compassion for living things, which he thought was a good sign.

He was just surprised by the horror his son had felt in that sunlit moment, at this place where everything should be happy and peaceful. It was as though they had a list of things you shouldn't feel when you were at the cabin, and they had walked him right into one, revealed one of life's ugly realities to the unsuspecting boy without thinking first how he might be affected.

It needn't be a trauma, Curt said. Yes, they should acknowledge the boy's response. It was valid because it was *his* response, coming from all the influences that made Clarkson who he was, including his inherent nature. They should try to treat the incident as just one more misstep in a life that would inevitably be full of them. Revisit it if he needed to talk but try to move on to other things. Still, they never again brought out the fishing poles when Clarkson was at the cabin. And the boy refused to swim in the lake for a long time, which disappointed Curt because father and son skinny-dipping had been such a fun way to bond, and Curt wanted to experience it with his boy just as his father had with him.

Clarkson wasn't with them on this day. He'd stayed in St. Louis with Kelly while Curt and David made a day trip. As long as they were going, David proposed they take down a tree near the cabin that was old and losing branches and might fall onto the extension they'd built. What did Curt think?

Curt looked at the old tree. He didn't know what kind it was. Pointy-lobed leaves. One of the black oaks? He supposed that affected any decision to take it down. Some black oaks are hollow, and he knew that made them less stable, especially when they begin the long process of dying. But he didn't know how he knew that except that he'd picked it up by osmosis some time in his past. While they stood, hollow trees also made them good homes for wild things. It was the kind of forest knowledge his father had, and asking Curt's advice was just a pretense. They both knew that. The point was to get the two of them out to their forest for a day and talk about familiar things. To spend unguarded time together in this nurturing place. What mattered was that they were there together, father and son.

"I suppose some owl lives in it," David concluded after they circled the old tree a few times. "I'd hate to destroy its home."

Curt had suggested they hike to The Old Man of the Forest, where he and his father had had many good conversations, but David wasn't up to hiking that far.

Their feet led them to the dock, picking up their fishing tackle on the way. They stood in the sun with their caps pulled low and tossed lines in the water then reeled them back in. David could cast twice the distance Curt could. He kept his line taut, his fingertips aware of every tremble of the rod. He examined his lure, seeing things Curt couldn't. He made it all look graceful and effortless, which Curt knew came from decades of practice. So many times he had watched his father as he drew his arm back and then swung it forward, releasing the line at just the right moment. How did he judge that? And he had watched David get a strike, a small smile creeping onto his face. He worked the fish as the line zigged and zagged on the surface, sometimes reeling it in, sometimes not. When he landed the fish he spoke to it, thanked it for the good fight, gripped its lip between his thumb and forefinger, worked out the hook, and then carefully eased the fish back in the water. "Go tell all your friends," he'd say. Curt imagined his dad would speak to the fish even if he were alone.

If he watched his father carefully enough, if he studied each motion, could he figure out how to be a fisherman? There had to be a science to it. A formula. An equation showing the ratio between effort and result, the physics of the force of the cast and the flight of the lure, even the psychology of the fish in the water. If he could master all of that, repeat it exactly, he could be a success like his father.

David knew it bothered his son that he couldn't do this thing as well as he could. But Curt was a doctor, he saved lives every day.

"No, Dad. It's never as dramatic as that!" He'd said this every time David made the claim.

But he'd sensed that Curt wanted to talk. It had been his suggestion that they go to the cabin that day and that they throw some lines in the water. They didn't have to make eye contact. They could be alone, just the two of them. On the dock with poles in hand, they had a ready distraction if the wrong thing was said or if they verged into uncomfortable territory. They could be there for hours if necessary, let their words ramble and find their way to the point, or close to it, and maybe reach a conclusion or find an answer or just let off some steam.

"So there's this syndrome that sometimes happens with new mothers at the hospital," Curt spoke to the murky water before them. "Where they don't bond with their baby. Where they don't have that instantaneous attachment to the child they've just given birth to."

"Hmm," David said.

"There are a number of reasons for it. Chiefly, it's seen to be due to post-partum depression in the mother, which is a complex issue on its own. Sadly, too common. But there can be other contributing factors. Poor family life growing up. Bad relationships with their own mothers. With their partners. Usually, it passes after a time. It rarely persists more than six months."

David cranked his line idly as his boy talked. He watched dragonflies cruising above the surface of the water. The turkey vultures were back, circling over the south ridge. Their shadows raced across the ripples. A glossy pair of crows perched in a dead tree across the lake.

"Sometimes it's seen in fathers, too. I can understand how that happens. A woman carries the child for nine months. And when the baby is born, she can finally hold it in her arms. A father doesn't have that direct, intimate experience with the baby. Nine times out of ten, the father is thrilled to be a parent, but when that doesn't happen, and I see it every day, it's beyond sad. If it isn't fixed, the child senses it and it's a mess for all concerned."

"That does sound sad." David reeled in his line and then cast again. Curt saw the grace of an artist. He'd never be as good as his father.

"And the reason I'm telling you this, Dad, is to ask your advice."

"*My* advice? I don't know anything about medicine, Curt. Or psychology. Or family dynamics."

"Except you're the best father I know. I want to know how you did it. So I can know how to advise this unfortunate father I know how to bond with his child."

David considered his son's words. He'd fumbled along and tried to do whatever made sense in the moment. Followed his own father's example when he could and made it up when it couldn't. If Curt turned out smart, caring, and successful, it was *despite* his fathering. Kathy was the reason.

"Dad, you never let me think I wasn't wanted or that I was a mistake. Even those dark, teenage years when I was being such a dick to you, you always let me know you loved me. How were you able to keep doing that?"

David knew that Curt had figured out he was a "surprise," an unexpected pregnancy between a pair of kids too young to be parents.

"That cabin up the hill there." David nodded behind them while he kept his eyes on the lake. "How do I say this? That's where you were . . . conceived. I'm sure it makes you squirm to hear your father talking this way, but it warms my heart to think you have been part of this place from your very beginning."

"No, I like knowing that, Dad."

"We weren't ready to be parents. We were still in high school! I was terrified. But the first moment I knew about you, Curt, the very first moment, I also knew that I loved you. That I had bonded with you, as you call it. Boy or girl, there was someone waiting to meet me and to call me Dad. Your mother felt that way too. You were a most wanted child. I don't know how or why. It just was, and that was enough." He paused to recover himself. "I'm sorry if I'm not being very helpful for your patient."

Curt felt a tug on his line, but he ignored it.

"You didn't feel hooked like a fish? Even a little? Talked into being a parent when you weren't sure you wanted that?"

"I don't know if your mother ever told you, Curt, but her parents wanted you to be given up for adoption."

"She told me. And she told me you fought to keep me. When I wake up every morning that's the first thought that comes into my head, Dad. That you fought to keep me."

The glare off the lake hurt David's eyes. He suddenly felt tired. He wished they had brought chairs with them because he wanted to sit. "If I hadn't succeeded, if I had lost you, Curt, I don't know what I would be today other than broken and forever sad. I don't like to think about it."

Curt had never considered what his *father's* life might have been. His vigorous father, who an hour before had proposed cutting down a tree, now looked old and weak. He wondered how he would feel if Clarkson were somehow taken from him. He'd feel he had failed. But would he feel broken and forever sad?

"Let's go up to the cabin, Dad. Nothing's biting anyway. We can sit on the porch and have some lunch. See what surprise Kelly packed for us."

"I don't know how much use you can make of me, Curt. For your patient. I don't know in my head about how to bond. It's all in my heart."

"I'll find some way to help this man come to love his son, Dad."

David suddenly understood what Curt was talking about. He couldn't look at him in that moment, feeling fear. He turned and started for the cabin. Curt collected their tackle and followed. To Curt, his father seemed to have aged twenty years while they were on the dock fishing.

And in a way, Curt was right. David had learned that Curt didn't love Clarkson. He hadn't bonded with him. Wasn't that what Curt was trying to tell him? It was impossible for David to understand how a father could not love his son. Or how anyone could not love Clarkson, the sweetest, most interesting boy he'd ever met. What went wrong?

Curt had to be in pieces about this. He'd proposed this day trip to the cabin to talk to his father about how to be a father, his way of asking for help. He'd failed at one of the best things in life. So he was pleading with his father in the only way he knew for a solution, a fix. To learn the words. Anything.

David recalled moments that were beginning to make a different sense now, given what Curt had hinted at. His early doubts about adopting. He'd seen the signs and hadn't recognized them.

They got to the porch, and David dropped into a chair in the shade.

"Let me get you a bottle of water, Dad."

"You have to keep trying, Curt," David whispered. "You have to keep trying," he called to his son who had entered the cabin. He felt that he needed to say these words while he could. "You have to keep coming back, showing up, doing what's needed." David remembered the times Curt had been cold to him, even cruel. He'd been hurt badly, but he also knew that he loved his son regardless. His heart had been big enough to take the blows and never give up. Sometimes love seemed so simple and other times it felt impossible.

"You just keep trying, Curt. It's the only way you're going to make it happen. That's what I'd tell your patient."

Curt drove them home that day. David had tossed him the keys while they were loading their gear. "I never get to see the scenery when I drive." David had stared mutely out the window most of the way.

Curt drove in silence, and David napped. Curt feared his father had figured him out and understood that Curt's unfortunate patient was Curt himself. Was his father so disgusted with him that he couldn't speak to him? Had Curt finally broken the bond he had with his father?

David's advice was to keep trying? That's all he'd been doing since they adopted Clarkson. He'd kept trying, hoping he would eventually feel actual love for the boy. That love seemed to come naturally to Kelly. Clarkson and Kelly were growing closer every day while Curt watched from the fringe, envious, helpless. You can't make someone love you, his mother had once told him. Neither, Curt learned, can you make yourself love someone.

David had slept until the last half hour of the drive. Or maybe he pretended to, Curt thought, to avoid talking. "Good trip, Dad," Curt said when he parked in front of his condo and turned off the engine. "Can you get yourself home from here?"

David rubbed his eyes and stretched. "Yeah. Sure. That went by fast."

Innocuous, generic talk, Curt thought. I'm a son who has known nothing but love all my life, but I can't love my own son. We may never talk of this again now that Dad has seen this ugly part of me.

But David didn't move. He stared out the front window.

"Mom once said something about my dad's older brother. I guess my mother told her about him. I don't think your Grandmother Peg wanted me to know. But I guess I have an uncle out there somewhere, though I suppose he's passed on by now. Maybe I have cousins I know nothing about and who know nothing about me. Blood relatives that I've managed to live without knowing all my life. That tells me that blood isn't what holds people together, Curt. Look at your mother. My sun rises and sets with her. I love her so much it hurts sometimes. I'm pretty sure there's something like that with you and Kelly, a bond you built, not something you inherited or were told magically exists. It's something you make happen because you *want* it to happen."

David turned in his seat and looked squarely at Curt. "I hope your patient finds an answer to his problem. I think I am right. You just never give up. I don't know much about anything, Son, but if you ever want to ask my advice about this, or anything else, I'm always ready to talk." He unbuckled his seatbelt, opened his door, and slid out so he could walk around the truck and climb into the driver's seat.

"Right now, I'm going home, taking a long shower, eating some of your mother's wonderful cooking, and maybe sitting on the couch for a while to watch something stupid on television before I go to bed. You know if you want to call me, anytime, day or night, you do it!" He took his son's head in his hands and kissed him gently on the forehead. "You understand, Curt? Day or night!"

Curt stood on the porch watching his father drive off. When he could no longer see the truck in the twilight, he stood there a little longer.

Can I do it? Can I be the man my father tells me I need to be?

Chapter Seventeen

Three Small Words

Three small words.

"Don't tell Mom."

Words calling for trust and, in the same breath, betrayal.

"Don't tell Mom," David had said, leaning toward Curt, his voice barely above a whisper. They had stopped at a noisy intersection, near where the old DX station had once stood across from the hospital. "Not a word. It's just, I've been having this pain in the right side of my chest sometimes. When I run. Then it goes away. It's probably nothing. I'm seeing the doctor next month to get it checked. So don't worry."

Curt had urged David to join him on a run around the old neighborhood to see how things had changed since he'd moved away. David had declined, suggesting they walk instead.

"Does it hurt now?"

David paused their steps and took a deep breath of the cold air. "No, not now."

Curt, whose work often called for him to read between the lines, decided not to analyze his father's words at that time, but he didn't forget them either. For years his father had loaded trucks for a living and had the physique of a man twenty years younger. But he had chest pains? Angina? When had Dad become mortal?

It's easy to believe that your parents are static, but Curt knew that as long as they lived, they'd be changing. It's only when you're gone that you become fixed.

Three Small Words

"It's not right to keep this from Mom."

"I know. I'll talk to her after I see the doctor."

Curt had learned the toxic consequences of secrets and unspoken truths when he'd come out to his father much later than he should have and found his father's love unfaltering. But too many years of guarded silence from Curt and gnawing doubt in David had left a chasm that still strained their intimacy. That his father had shared even this much had surprised him. Was he scared; was that why he told his doctor son? Was it more than "probably nothing" but he didn't know how to say it?

Opening that door led to more words during their walk.

"I don't feel old. I don't know what that even means, really. I feel like I'm the same person living in my skin that I was yesterday, and last year, and even fifty years ago."

They walked on in reflective silence. Curt hoped his father would continue talking, which he did.

"But I have noticed something lately. My *memories* are old, if that makes sense. I was thinking about a conversation I had with my buddy Jon. *It was more than twenty years ago.* I can't be sure if what I remember about my life is true or if I'm just remembering it the way I want it to be. There are a lot more years behind me than in front of me, and I won't be able to do all the things I imagined doing. There isn't enough time. I probably won't ever go to Italy with Mom, though we talk about it as though we could any time. I won't read all those books Kelly is so eager to talk about. I mean, that old beater could be the last truck I ever own. Does that make any sense?"

"Sure," Curt conceded, focused as he was on people at the beginnings of their lives, pausing not only at such unexpected musings about this other end of life but that such musings had come from his father, a man Curt sometimes had to remind himself was more complex than he seemed behind the simple facade he never fully shed before his son.

Up ahead the bells of St. Luke's tolled the late afternoon hour. When they first moved to Richmond Heights, Kathy had dragged young Curt there — even David on rare Sundays — but only often enough to assure her far-away mother that she was still "practicing." David waited for the bells' resonance to fade before speaking.

"There's going to be a last trip to the cabin. I'll come home one time, put away the gear, wash off the grit, scratch the chigger bites, and it will be the last time; I won't make it back. I won't know it when it happens, but I know it *will* happen. I never used to think this way. I guess that's hard for a young person to understand." He was silent for a few steps before continuing. "I have to make choices now. I see that. I can't do all the things that before always seemed available. There just isn't enough time left to do everything. I need to start being selective."

Their feet had taken them as far as the bridge over the interstate, a demarcation neither man felt inclined to cross that Christmas afternoon.

But something uneasy stirred within Curt, something visceral that predated his medical training and the protective sarcasm he had cultivated for as long as he could remember. Why had his father mentioned the cabin? Or rather, the unpleasant concept — yes, the reality — of a *final* visit, of an unthinkable time when David Clark would never again return to his cabin? If there was anything holy in Curt's universe, it was the cabin and his father's presence there.

He had no words. Nothing glib or clinical or comforting to offer his father. Curt suddenly found that it was he who needed comforting as they took turns kicking the same stone down a sidewalk in the neighborhood where he had grown up.

"Not soon, certainly," Curt mustered.

David let the words lie between them, unclear what his boy's reference was.

"You're going to wear those new chainsaw chaps Santa brought a bunch of times when you cut firewood at the cabin, Dad."

"And these fancy new gloves Sprout gave me." David held out his hands. "That sure is a bright orange! Didn't get the new chainsaw I was hoping for though."

"Mom said you have to pick that out for yourself."

"My birthday's coming in March."

They arrived back at the warm house on Sunset where Kathy had been indulging Clarkson with treats and unstinting attention. She had extracted from him a promise to send her at least one postcard from his upcoming trip to the Bahamas with his dads. Curt hoped he could retreat for a time from the unwelcome, discomfiting thoughts of his father's mortality.

David spoke no more of his mortality, instead steering their conversation to an upcoming trip to Kansas City to see Kathy's mother and his intention to skip out and spend the weekend at the cabin after dropping her off. "They'll be more relaxed without me around," he'd said. Curt knew that Kathy's mother had never fully accepted his dad.

That alone, Curt thought, could be enough to cause heartache in a hale, stoic man. His clinical side was already hectoring him, urging him to discover what ailment his father had that made his chest hurt sometimes on a run, because if he knew, he could make it right. Maybe his dad had mentioned it because he really *wanted* medical advice. Why else share such a personal concern with his son, which too rarely happened, when he hadn't even told his wife? Better to tell a doctor about something that might be nothing than to alarm the woman who loved him? Except that the doctor also loved him.

What was Curt's next move? He wasn't a gerontologist; he was a pediatrician. What did he really know of his father's physical life? He didn't even know the name of his dad's doctor. If he dared to speak to his mother, wouldn't he be violating Dad's trust? How could he begin to make a diagnosis based on a few whispered and then dismissed words?

Because it was asked of him, Curt didn't speak of it again during his visit. Christmas gifts were marveled at, including the bag of marbles Clarkson treasured most. How delighted his son was with the swim mask and snorkel his grandmother gave him for his upcoming trip. Old stories were laughingly shared with Clarkson.

Curt saw with startled eyes that his father had given the boy a stethoscope and was urging him to listen to the family heartbeats. Was this an admission? Curt witnessed no shortness of breath. No hand to chest or sudden grimace. No lapses in conversation, beyond the reticence he had always known in his father. There were no cryptic glances between David and Kathy, but then, she didn't know.

When Christmas day ended, Curt made himself say "I love you" into David's shoulder as they hugged briefly at the door. Sprout and Kelly were already in the car with their holiday loot. It was the best he could summon, but those three small words felt inadequate.

Curt did, however, have a place to begin whatever it was he needed to do. Long before he had discovered an old photograph of his father as an infant. Scribbled on the back were the words "Our Davey. Healthy again!" Some affliction in Dad's infancy, from a time when those who could have remembered were long gone, might be playing its hand now. It gave Curt the pediatrician something to work with.

It could have been anything, of course. Or nothing. He'd seen plenty of children present with ailments both common and surprising. Most were treatable, and most children would fully recover. Have healthy lives with no memory of their little bout, just as his father had no memory. What ailment of infancy might creep up on his father more than half a century later? Myocarditis from a lung infection? Pneumonia? Whooping cough? A host of other, more exotic assaults on the infant's body in the darker days of medicine? Think horses, Curt, not zebras. Surely they had vaccinated the boy and saw to it he got regular medical care. He wanted to find *something* in the past that could be attacked and conquered rather than admit that his father had been mortal all along and had a finite number of days as all men do. That he wouldn't be around for Curt forever.

His father's childhood medical records would have long since been shredded or carted off to the dump. And his grandparents might not have even known how severe it was, whatever it was.

His only additional resource might be in David's tidy, whitewashed basement, with an entire wall of metal shelves holding neatly labeled storage boxes. Curt had long understood that his own neatness sprang from his father's careful ordering of the details in his life. It was another way he was like his father. Was it possible that in those boxes, salvaged from his grandfather's lifetime accumulations, was a thin, brittle envelope containing little Davey's medical records?

But if what he sought was there, did he have any right to see it? Here he was with a new secret he had to keep, one Dad had only vaguely shared with him, one that he knew could easily fester like an infected wound.

By the time they got home, Curt had dismissed his doubts about the legitimacy of his interference. What he felt instead was urgency. Little time, less information, a reluctant patient, a doctor outside of his field, and a son desperately wanting into his father's life while there was still time.

The car wasn't even fully unloaded before Curt had worked out his plan. He would return to his father's basement when he knew no one would be home and search the boxes.

And if his meticulous father noticed a slight shifting of his boxes, Curt would explain his trespass by saying that he was looking for his old race medals to show Clarkson.

He needed to enact his plan soon. How could he revel on a faraway beach, indulge his son and his husband and himself in mild hedonism, with such a question nagging him? More importantly, how could he allow his life to go on without first doing everything he could to ensure that his father's own life would go on? Whether his obligation was to himself or to his father, Curt didn't know and didn't pause to analyze.

His opportunity came only days after Christmas when he knew his parents were away. He took a cab so his car wouldn't be parked out front if they returned early. He walked silently through the house, not turning on any lights or touching anything, descending the basement steps carefully so they didn't creak and be heard by people who weren't even there.

In the farthest, deepest corner of the little house, he pulled the chain for the bare-bulbed ceiling light. The mechanical click seemed to thunder throughout the house.

Were there a hundred boxes before him? Where in all of this might a single fact be, a single fact that could explain everything or explain nothing, or that might not be there at all? Worse, what *else* might be waiting for him in the boxes? What other things might he not want to know?

Curt studied the boxes, labeled with neat, hand-written words, and organized, he soon found, in sensible groupings. Three boxes marked TAXES with successive years bulleted beneath. INSURANCE

PAPERS. HOUSE REPAIRS. MOM'S ART SUPPLIES, which gave him a pang, understanding that she'd never really had the chance to pursue her talent. A box labeled SWITCHES AND SOCKETS AND STUFF. Then came a series of boxes about him. CURT'S SCHOOL PAPERS. CURT'S TEXTBOOKS. CURT'S AWARDS. CURT'S TOYS. Even several boxes labeled CURT'S BABY CLOTHES.

Soon he was among boxes simply labeled DAD, and while this seemed more likely territory, the number of them gave him pause. His search of just these couldn't be completed in a single visit unless he stumbled upon whatever he sought in the first box.

And he quickly saw his misconception. This DAD in the first box was not his father, David, but his grandfather, Joe. Curt thought that all of this, or at least much of this, had been lost in the move, when they had yanked his grandfather from his tiny but familiar house and put him in an even tinier, less familiar apartment, which hastened his decline, though none of them was ever willing to acknowledge this. It had been during that culling that Curt had come upon the photo of his infant father. "Our Davey. Healthy Again!" The haunting photo that had steered him into medical school then and taunted him now as a problem he might never be able to fix.

He surveyed the dozens of remaining boxes. "C'mon. Give me one that says DAVID'S COMPREHENSIVE MEDICAL HISTORY — FROM BIRTH TO PRESENT. ALL IN PROPER ORDER AND EASILY SEARCHED." No such box awaited him. But nor were there any that suggested they were close to what he was after. Nothing labeled DAVID or MEDICAL PAPERS or even DAVID'S STUFF.

He might never find what he wanted or worse, he might not want what he found. Why couldn't he just discuss this with his father, outright, instead of sneaking behind his back? A father and a son who loved each other should be able to this.

"It's not there."

Curt froze. His father's voice was behind him, but he didn't dare turn. He was caught with his hand in a box, and he felt five years old.

"Are you sure?"

"Yes, I am."

Curt turned to face his father. "Then tell me."

"Tell you what, Curt? That the medical records from my childhood are gone or that I have no idea what it was that nearly killed me as a baby?"

"I'm that transparent?"

"You're my son. I guess I understand a few things about you."

So it was not to be had. That thing in the past he wanted to throttle and defeat.

"I don't want you to die, Dad."

"I know, Curt." He smiled then. "I don't either."

And with those three words, the man who was never good with words, spoke exactly the right ones. Curt threw himself on his father and cried, "I love you," before dissolving in his embrace until the two of them felt for a while like one person.

Chapter Eighteen

Forest Succession

David woke in the night and reached for Kathy, but she wasn't there. He remained still in a darkness that seemed too dark, then remembered that she was in Kansas City for the weekend with her mother and he was at his Ozark cabin. The cold outside of the quilt touched his shoulder; he guessed that the fire in the potbelly had died. And so he faced the choice of rising from the bed in only his briefs to stoke the stove again or remaining wound in the quilt where he could keep warm enough to reach the dawn. He chose the bed and let his thoughts drift until he fell asleep again.

At first light, which seemed too bright, he found himself more tired than he expected. Outside the cabin, snow had fallen in the night. He should have known snow was coming, but that would have made no difference to his need to escape from a polite, girls' weekend of salads and forced smiles. The cabin was a place where he could arrive with just the shirt on his back and feel reborn.

The day before him bore no specific chores, other than what could always be undertaken at a neglected cabin in the woods to keep it standing in the face of entropy and the relentless, reclaiming force of nature, a nature that always wins in the end. For this visit he had decided to finally take down a pignut hickory that was crowding Clarkson's small plantation of blue spruce trees. Of the original planting, about a dozen now remained, sinking roots in the thin Ozark soil and reaching, as all young trees in this old forest must, for their share of the sunlight.

Spruce were not native to the Ozarks, and it had always been David's plan, his land ethic as Kelly called it, to cultivate only native plants in his forest. Yet Kelly had been so on fire about these particular trees — something different for their forest — that David had muted his objection and supported the plan. He had begun to acknowledge then, though only to himself, that it would not always be his forest, that it was becoming Curt's and Kelly's, and eventually, he hoped, it would be Clarkson's. That the spruce thrived suggested that the clearing had been waiting for these very trees, just as Kelly had believed. That Clarkson had soon claimed them as his own made David love the little grove.

A dozen years later a single hickory, a little way down the hillside sloping to the lake, was spreading its crown, its own bid for the light, and shading the spruce. David had long thought he'd remove the hickory to allow Clarkson's grove more sunlight and a better chance to thrive. Well-practiced in this woodcraft, David felt he could take down the tree easily himself. This would be that day.

Breakfast of instant oatmeal — once he had resurrected the fire in the stove — followed by collecting and checking the gear he would need filled the morning. There was no hurry in his movements but no waste either. Once the sun had advanced above the south ridge to begin giving what chilled warmth it could this January morning, David prepared to set out for the spruce grove.

He'd wished to receive a new chainsaw at Christmas, but that didn't happen — Kathy explained that such a purchase needed to be made by him so he got exactly what he wanted — but he hoped to be surprised with one at his birthday in March. Thus he was left with the latest in the long succession of chainsaws they had been brought to the cabin over the decades. A perfectly fine machine, older, but one he judged still sufficiently matched to the task.

When he stepped onto the porch and the cold light, the silence of the forest washed over him. No birdsong, no chirring insects. Even the air was still. He stood for the moment listening to this absence under the vast blue sky until it was finally broken by the calls of two crows on the south ridge. He watched as they flew across the frozen lake, on whatever mission was before them, then hefted his gear to take to the hickory.

The crunch of his boots in the crust of snow set the rhythm for his walk. The snow was not deep enough to hinder his work or his drive home the next day, but for now its white shroud robbed his forest of color, broken by the dark verticals of the tree trunks and the blue gray of their slanting shadows. Branches around him were limned with snow that made his familiar look unfamiliar.

Ahead David could see the pale blue green of the spruce. In the old days this part of the forest had been peppered with cedars, which stayed green all year. But it had been his father's mission to remove all the cedars near the cabin, a mission David took up, and then later Curt and Kelly. The canopy of oaks and hickories had thickened in the many years they'd been coming here, shading the forest floor, and starving the upstart cedars of light. David had half believed his father's ambition was hopeless, and yet here it was, successful. David's words, the only he would speak aloud that weekend, broke the silence around him. "You were right, Dad."

David often spoke to his father, though the man was gone for nearly twenty years. He'd never stopped missing him and still felt like an apprentice in his father's forest. He let himself think of his father as just far away and not seen for a while. A comforting pretense. It was easy to do in this place where the two had shared so many important moments and where David continued to feel his presence.

Walking in the snow, carrying the chainsaw and gasoline, warmed him though he could see the white plumes of his breath. His breathing came harder in the cold air. He set down the equipment a few steps from the hickory and studied the tree. He removed his gloves — the bright orange pair that Clarkson had given him that Christmas — and ran his fingers down the bark. It felt like cork and was not cold to his touch. The sloping ground favored his plan, but he wasn't sure he'd get a clean fall to the forest floor given the dense trees on the hillside below. Still, if he could get it most of the way down, the spring storms would likely finish the job and return it to the earth as everything must. Or it might hang dead in the embrace of the other trees for years. Either outcome was fine if its sacrifice meant more space and light for Clarkson's trees.

Three cuts would do the job. Make the wedge and then start the back cut. Step away when the tree began to lean and then listen as it fell, grasping desperately at the trees around it, fighting its premature end. A task David had done countless times and a skill he still hoped to teach Clarkson, his own son having never been much interested.

And yet, in his way Curt *had* been interested. He'd paid close attention to David's early lessons with tools and fire, becoming competent, but he acted as though his father's practical wisdom was a joke. And later, after his rotation in the ER and especially once he had a son of his own, Curt's interest evolved into an abiding concern for doing such work safely. He had given his father that Christmas a pair of chaps to wear when using the chainsaw. In all their years of cutting firewood there had never been a single mishap, and David knew this was due to his diligent and patient method. The chaps fit perfectly with this intent.

But David had forgotten the chaps back at the cabin.

Below him the lake boomed as the morning sun warmed the ice. David, alone in his frozen forest, supposed he was the only one to hear it. It was a rare sound since he visited the cabin less often in the winter than the rest of the year. A serious, portentous sound. He wished Clarkson were with him to hear the booming, but the boy and his fathers were at some Caribbean island for the week, taking in different sensations. There would be other chances.

On his walk back to fetch the chaps, David steered his crunching steps to the hillside above the cabin where half a century before he had buried his dog, Buddy. His father had raised a sandstone slab over the grave and scratched the dog's name into it with a nail. The slab had fallen many times, and David reset it whenever he found it on the ground. Yet on this winter morning he could not find the grave. Even this deeply familiar was made unfamiliar, not just with the blanket of snow but with the decades of growth and change that altered the landscape from what had been seared into his boyhood memory of the day. He realized he was the only person alive who even knew of Buddy's grave, and he vowed to return in the spring to reset the slab and preserve his memory. As he sat on a stump to rest for a moment, he could feel his heart pounding. The air felt cold and hostile in his lungs.

The track of his footprints in the crusty snow had wandered widely on his way. This warty oak still holding its browned leaves. That ancient chunk of ruddy sandstone dusted white. The cleft in the hillside where water sometimes flowed. The view of the glinting, ice-shrouded lake through the trees. The spot where Clarkson had, amazingly, once found a rusty horseshoe half buried in the soil, a remnant of even older, long-gone tenants on this land. All memories he savored, no rush for any of it.

His steps did finally reach the cabin, and he welcomed its warmth. He'd not worn the orange chaps since Christmas morning when he had pulled them on over his pajamas to everyone's delight, so he spent some time making sure he had them snapped and buckled correctly. They would certainly add color to the forest.

Though David wanted to linger and rest, he also wanted to face what was before him. The hickory waited. He poked a couple sticks of kindling into the stove so the fire wouldn't die and the cabin would be warm when he returned, then passed through the door.

A breeze stirred the dried leaves hanging from a tall oak nearby. Soon the crunch of his boots was all David could hear. Above, the two crows watched from their perch in an oak, then rose and flew before him in the direction of the hickory. David followed.

Not long after, the whine of the chainsaw filled the forest, but no one was around to hear it. And no one was around to hear when it stopped. Still, the lake boomed.

Chapter Nineteen

to love that well which thou must leave ere long

Suddenly, Kelly understood that he would need to take charge.

He had been in the surf with Clarkson, watching the boy's sinuous body, one with the lapping waves, his long hair like blond seaweed as he peered through the mask his grandmother had given him for Christmas and searched the sand for shells and bits of coral that he would pass to Kelly.

Curt sat on the blanket. His pale, freckled skin was slathered with mineral sunblock, and his Cardinals cap was pulled low over his face. He had already done his hour in the surf with Clarkson, holding the boy's found treasures and impressed by his devotion to finding them. When Clarkson's hand had reached out and his fingers touched Curt's ankle for quick reassurance that his father was near, Curt had felt loved.

The boy adored the island. He marveled at being able to walk out of their room directly onto the beach. How the sand felt between his toes. Wearing shorts and tee shirts and sandals in January. He could spend the entire day in his swimming suit, enjoy his first ocean wave, which tumbled him in the surf, and the taste of the salty water on his lips. He liked his big, floppy straw hat Dad had bought for him in the airport gift shop. And the three of them wearing matching sunglasses, each father holding one of his hands as they walked through the airport, through the town, down the beach. The funny Christmas decorations were still up, Santa with sunglasses and sandals. He could eat anything he wanted, as much as he wanted, whenever he wanted. No school, no homework, no bullies. Sweeping the oceanic horizon with his arms, Curt had said to him, "Our only job is to relax and have fun."

Curt had said they ought to turn off their phones. Or at least leave them in their room so any calls would go to voice mail. But then he hadn't. He carried his wherever they went, checked it often, set it on the table before him at meals. He even had it in his lap when they sat on the hotel veranda watching for the green flash at sunset, which they hadn't seen yet. Kelly guessed that Curt was waiting for some news. Something work related. Being on vacation could never be his only job. Curt had seemed off balance for days. Was it a difficult patient, or a test result he'd need to act on? He hadn't discussed anything like that with Kelly, but it was private, and they were on vacation.

When the call came, Kelly was in the surf with Clarkson. He watched as Curt frowned at his phone before answering it. Watched as Curt sat upright and then suddenly stood, the phone pressed to his ear. His free hand rose to his face, fingers rubbing his eyes beneath his sunglasses. Suddenly Curt dropped his phone on the blanket and began walking down the beach.

"Sprout, I think we need to get back now," Kelly said. The boy knew something was wrong. Only Grandpa called him Sprout. Kelly wasn't sure why he'd used that name. He would think about that moment often.

Clarkson pushed his mask and snorkel up on his head, wiped the salty water off his face, and looked at his Poppa, trying to understand the sudden shift, but Kelly was watching Curt walk down the beach.

"Where's Dad going?"

"I don't know. I think he got some bad news on the phone."

"One of his patients?"

"I don't know. Maybe. He looks sad. Let's go to the blanket and wait for him to come back. Maybe he'll tell us."

They walked across the warm sand, weaving through other beachgoers, to their blanket. Clarkson dropped his shells into the plastic bucket they had bought for him. Kelly picked up Curt's phone from the blanket but resisted looking at his call log. If it was his business, Curt would tell him.

Curt was far down the beach. Was he distancing himself from the news, Kelly wondered, from his husband and son, or from himself? Curt kept an emotional detachment from nearly everyone, starting long ago with his father. That seemed to have resolved itself, and David and Curt had forged a deeper bond, but it was something Curt had to work on, to keep from sliding back into isolation. Curt's mother had told Kelly how surprised and happy she was that Curt had opened his heart to his father. She said Kelly had a big responsibility to keep Curt from cocooning. Human contact was what everyone needed, she said, and she was glad Kelly was there to help Curt experience it. Her words had drawn Kelly out of himself a little too.

This didn't seem like the way Curt would react to bad news about a patient; he always said that he tried to keep abstracted and clinical in his professional life because sometimes the outcomes weren't good, and he still had to do his job, no matter how hard it got. Kelly tried not to let himself speculate. Curt would tell him when he was ready.

Clarkson watched the waves come in, glancing once or twice toward his dad far down the beach, identified by his red cap. He liked the repetition, the regular lines they formed, and the brief lull between each. He looked for patterns in everything. "It's a human survival instinct," Curt had said, dismissing the suggestion that their boy might have a touch of autism. "We are pattern-seeking animals." Kelly took some comfort from Curt's unofficial diagnosis of their son, who seemed engaged in most parts of his life. What scraps of family medical history they had didn't indicate any lurking problems.

to love that well which thou must leave ere long

"When Dad comes back," Kelly said, "we have to be extra nice to him, Clarkson. Something is wrong, and I think he's sad. Let's just be quiet and let him have his space." Kelly was already calculating the possible implications of Curt's news. Likely they would need to pack up, change their flights, settle with the hotel, and end their vacation early. Life intruded, even in paradise.

Curt had stopped far down the beach and seated himself at the waterline. Through the sunlight glinting off the water, Kelly could just make out Curt removing his sunglasses and rubbing his face again. Clarkson was arranging his shells on the blanket in even rows. But every minute or so, his fingers grazed Kelly's ankle.

Kelly felt powerless. Curt was out of reach, at least for now, and would probably withdraw into himself when he got back. And what awaited them back home? Even if it only affected Curt directly, it would ripple through their lives.

He thought he could check flight schedules on his phone, but that would be easier to do on the tablet back in their room when he knew what Curt needed to do. Clarkson was going to need some dinner regardless. Maybe doing laundry would keep the two of them occupied a while and give Curt some solitude. He smeared sunblock on his son's shoulders and back.

When Kelly looked up again, he saw Curt was walking with certainty, coming directly toward them.

"Maybe it's time to put your shells in the bucket, Clarkson. Here comes Dad."

Clarkson looked up and waved to his dad. To Kelly's surprise, Curt waved back.

"Let's get out of the sun," Curt said. "Okay if we all go back to our room?" He accepted his phone from Kelly and bent to collect his towel.

"Sure. C'mon, Clarkson.

They moved in silence, collecting their things. Kelly shook out the blanket and grabbed their bag, and then they all walked back to the room. Curt slid the door open for them after each had rubbed off sand from his feet. Kelly sat on the end of the bed, Clarkson cross legged on one of the towels on the floor. Both watched Curt.

He took off his sunglasses and rubbed his eyes again. Kelly saw that they were red, certainly from crying. He could almost guess the words that came next.

"There's no easy way to say this." He paused and looked at the two looking at him. He reached behind himself and gripped the chair before sitting in it. "My mother just called to tell me . . . to tell me that my father has died."

"Grandpa has died?"

Curt nodded his head.

The boy went to him, and Curt opened his arms, wrapped them around his son, feeling the boy's swimming suit wet on his legs. Clarkson's tears flowed. "No . . . no . . . no," he said between sobs. Kelly watched from the edge of the bed. Among all of them, David Clark had the deepest bond with their son. Kathy loved him completely and indulged him shamelessly, but David had bonded with him in a special way. Kelly knew it went both ways. Clarkson needed a special friend and confidant that he'd found in David, and David needed Clarkson, to forge a bond with him that he had missed with his son.

Curt, sitting stoically in the chair, stroking the bare back of their son as Clarkson cried into his shoulder, was working hard to rein in his grief. Kelly knew from their years together that withdrawal was always Curt's sanctuary whenever big emotions threatened him. He would emerge eventually, possibly in some overwrought but cathartic way. And Kelly would be there to help Curt when that happened.

to love that well which thou must leave ere long

Kelly knew he had to take charge and set aside his own grief to get the family home and help them navigate the difficult days and weeks ahead. Curt would move through the time, seeming emotionless and unaffected, but he would be a shell of himself. He wouldn't be able to make decisions and might remain silent in the face of questions. He would be a husk, and Kelly knew he must step up and carry the full burden for a while.

"I am so sorry, Curt," Kelly said. The words sounded like throwaways.

"It's quite a shock," Curt answered in the clinical voice Kelly imagined he used when delivering bad news to the families of his patients. "We'll need to get home so I can be with my mother. I think she's in shock herself."

Curt didn't have many details. His father had apparently died while at the cabin. "He must have been alone because Mom was in Kansas City visiting Grandma. I don't know who found him. I guess it was Jimmy." Arrangements were already being made, he said, and they needed to get home so they could be a part of that, to relieve Kathy. Curt spoke to the space before him, not making eye contact with Kelly. He continued to rub Clarkson's back.

"I'll get us on the next flight home," Kelly said. "Do you want me to pack your bag?"

Curt barely nodded. "I need to make some phone calls." But he made no move to remove Clarkson from his lap.

Kelly rose. "C'mon, Clarkson. Come with me."

The boy let himself be lifted from Curt's lap and led to the bathroom. "You need to have a shower and wash the salt off your skin. I'll get you some dinner from room service. What do you want to eat?"

"I don't care. I want to see Grandpa again. That's what I want."

This was Clarkson's first close experience with death and Kelly's too; his own mother's death had seemed less significant. Maybe when they had cut him from their lives, he'd experienced his family's emotional death, but that was not relevant right now.

David Clark had become Kelly's new father, a kind man who accepted him and watched over his heart in a way Kelly had never experienced. If he let himself, Kelly could collapse to the floor in tears, but his family needed him to support them. He prepared the shower for his boy.

"The water's hot. Wash your hair with shampoo. And be sure to use soap on your body. Don't just rinse off. You need to get the salt off your skin. Careful stepping into the tub."

He placed a folded towel on the counter, where the boy could reach it when he was finished showering and collected Clarkson's swimming suit from the floor.

When he entered their room, Curt was standing at the sliding glass door, looking at the Caribbean horizon.

"I'm going to order a burger and fries for Clarkson. Do you want anything?"

"Do you believe in premonitions, Kelly?"

He paused, still holding Clarkson's damp suit.

"I believe we can know things but not realize we know them. And it can *seem* magical when we discover them."

"I had a premonition about my dad before we left. He'd had some sickness when he was an infant. He doesn't know what it was. Didn't know. He escaped death then, but now death has finally come to collect him. Somehow, I felt this was going to happen. As long as I stayed close, he would be safe. Only when I was far away from him could death catch him. I shouldn't have left him."

This was not adult Curt talking. It was the part he kept hidden most of the time. The little boy part that wanted to be held in the strong arms of his father. He was paying a heavy toll for having held his father at a distance for so much of his life.

"Don't blame yourself, Curt."

"I *do* blame myself. I'm a doctor. I should have looked into my father's health more. I knew something was wrong and I didn't act!"

"We don't know what happened. It may have been an accident. It may have been any number of things. Don't torment yourself about what you cannot know. Clarkson is going to need support too and examples of how to deal with the death of a loved one."

The shower stopped then, and they could hear the curtain being pulled open.

"You're right. You're taking my part now, being the rational one of the family. We do need to be strong." And then, "Thanks, Kelly."

Kelly called room service and ordered Clarkson's dinner and a few extra things they could snack on as the evening progressed. He didn't think Curt was interested in a meal, and he knew he wasn't.

Clarkson came into the room wrapped in a towel. He went first to Curt to give and receive a hug and then to Kelly.

"This is a sad time, Son. But we'll get through it together."

"I know, but I wish I could go to the cabin with Grandpa one more time."

Curt sighed. "We all do. We'll just have to go there with him in our memory now." He tried to smile, and he didn't suppose he was fooling anyone. But it was easier being rational when he had to be a strong father before his son.

"I ordered you a burger," Kelly said. "Should be here soon. Maybe you could get in your PJs. Maybe rub some lotion on your body. That sea salt will dry out your skin." He rummaged in his tote and found the bottle of lotion that he handed to the boy.

"Do you want to get in the shower now, Curt? Or I could if you want to wait."

"Go ahead. I'm going to sit with Clarkson while he has his dinner and try to be a good father. I think I can pull it off."

"You are a good father. And a good husband. And a good son. And I've run out of nouns."

Curt chuckled then. A brief respite. He was surprised how good it felt to smile. His hand rose and stroked Kelly's cheek.

The food came while Kelly was in the shower, and it was demolished by the time he was out. He emerged from the bathroom with a towel around his waist. Clarkson and Curt were discussing returning to school when they got back. "But not this week," Curt told him. "It's still winter break. And it's going to be hectic for a little while."

The curative power of the mundane, Kelly thought.

"I want to watch for the green flash tonight," Clarkson said.

"Not tonight, Son. We're going to have a big day of travel tomorrow and we all need to rest."

Clarkson persisted. "But pirates believe that if you see a green flash, it means someone is returning from the dead."

Kelly had to step into the bathroom to stifle a sob. He didn't know how Curt had reacted to the boy's desperate wish, but he knew they would sit on the veranda that evening to watch the sunset.

And they did. Kelly wearing fresh clothes he would travel in the next day. Clarkson in his pajamas, sitting on Curt's lap. And Curt still in his swimsuit, Hawaiian shirt, and Cardinals cap.

They saw no green flash; no one would be returning from the dead that evening. They'd sat in the veranda chairs long after the sun had disappeared beyond the sea.

Curt carried Clarkson back to their room. He'd fallen asleep sometime during their vigil. Kelly pulled down the spread and sheet, and Curt laid their son in the middle of the bed, bent low, and kissed the boy on the forehead.

to love that well which thou must leave ere long

"Dream happy dreams about Grandpa."

Kelly sat at the desk, trying to reschedule their flight. He was pleased that Curt was holding up as well as he was. That would help Clarkson cope. It was certainly helping him.

"I'm going to jump in the shower," Curt said. "And I promise to use soap and shampoo like a grown up."

"See that you do," Kelly said, not looking up. "And lotion on your skin."

Sometime later, he heard someone crying. He looked toward Clarkson on the bed, but the boy was asleep. And then he heard a loud thump from the bathroom. He rushed in there and found Curt sitting in shower, clutching his knees and crying, the water rushing over him.

"I am a terrible person. I am a terrible son. I should be the one who died, not him! Dad, come back!"

It was the emotional outburst he knew Curt needed to have.

Kelly put a hand on Curt's shoulder, which made him cry even harder.

"Why?" Curt asked. "Why did he have to die? Why? Please come back!"

Kelly shut off the water and slipped off his shoes. He climbed into the tub behind Curt, soaking the seat of his jeans, and wrapped his arms around him. He said nothing. He'd let Curt say whatever he needed to. Scream it if he had to. Or just cry for his bitter loss until he ran out of tears.

"It's all gone . . . the chance to be a good son . . . I wasted so much, Kelly . . . I didn't love Dad enough . . . and I can't get it back . . . can't do it right."

Kelly hugged him harder.

Curt cried. And cried more. Kelly held him. He would stay there all night if he had to.

Chapter Twenty

Flint and Steel

Kelly woke to Curt moaning. He knew what was happening and what to do. He threw back the quilt and hurried around to Curt's side of the bed.

"Which leg?"

"My right one," Curt groaned through his teeth.

Kelly pulled Curt's leg from under the quilt, straightened it, and rested the heel on his hip. Then he pushed back on Curt's toes until they pointed toward his freckled nose.

Curt groaned with relief. "Just like that. Just hold it there for a minute."

Curt's middle-of-the-night leg cramps were common in their married life.

"One of the hazards of being a runner."

"Which is why you don't see *me* out there running around like a fool."

Sometimes during the daylight hours, he would see Curt throw a leg behind him and then lean forward to stretch out an incipient cramp. But when they assaulted him in his sleep — "I think they could wake the dead!" — they had to act quickly so Curt wasn't seized with such pain he'd be unable to sleep for the rest of the night. Kelly was able to do this for him, and he was grateful to have the chance to do this for him.

When the cramp eased, Curt told Kelly he could stop. He rolled his foot, testing the muscles in his calf. Still taut. He sat on the edge of the mattress, his feet flat on the floor. Outside the cabin, the night sounds had ceased. It was early morning.

"A thousand years ago, in my dark and stupid teenage life, when I was being such a wretched dick to the man who was my finest friend in the entire, ever-expanding universe —"

"A little florid but go on."

Curt smiled in the darkness. "One of the perils of being married to an English major. I pick this stuff up like socks from the floor. Anyway, when I was a less appreciative son than I ought to have been, and I'd get these cramps in the night, Dad was always instantly at my door, asking if I needed help. Like he had some secret sense to know when I was in pain. And then he'd come in and grab my leg with his strong hands. I didn't even have to tell him which one. He'd stretch it, just like you do, and make the cramp go away. Remember, I was a teenaged boy. I could have been moaning in bed for a very different reason. But Kelly, he *always* showed up when I needed him in the night."

Kelly sat in the chair beside the bed.

"We'd never speak of it in the morning. If he had ever tried to do that during the day, I would have pushed him away. But in the night, when my defenses were down, maybe he knew he could approach me. That I'd let him because I needed him. And I think now maybe I was letting myself be a good son, the one I always wanted to be, deep down, and couldn't let myself be during the day. Is that screwed up?"

"You were a child, Curt. You're older and wiser now."

"Older, anyway. It makes me sad that Dad won't ever do this for me again." He hadn't cried at his father's memorial service, but here at the cabin, knowing he would never see his father there again, he wanted to.

Kelly yearned to return to his side of the bed and the warmth under the quilt waiting for him, the softness of the pillow, the delicious dark behind his eyelids. The comforting certainty of Curt's weight on the mattress beside him. But he stayed in the chair nearby in case Curt's cramp decided to sneak back.

"It's never going to be the same, Kelly."

"What?"

"Coming to the cabin knowing Dad is gone. That he'll never be here with me again."

"We'll just have to make our own experiences then. And give them to Clarkson."

"I wonder if Dad felt this same way after his father passed on. I never asked him."

"He once told me that he felt closest to his father when he came here."

"Yes. I can see that. You can come back to bed now, Kelly."

Clarkson was sleeping in the other room. So far Curt's incident and their ensuing conversation hadn't awakened him. Now that he was in puberty, they knew the boy needed as much sleep as he could get. That second great growth spurt in a person's life takes place while the body sleeps, Curt had explained to Clarkson. "If you want to sleep in on weekends, that's okay. Your body is doing the important job it needs to do. But maybe you can start taking more showers now because you will sweat more."

Curt thought Clarkson was starting puberty a little earlier than most boys when Kelly confided to him that the sheets from his bed suggested he'd "unlocked a certain developmental skill," a euphemism Curt instantly understood. "So, his plumbing works."

"It's completely natural," Curt said trying to sound clinical and not blush. "We've both been there. Let's not embarrass him about it."

Flint and Steel 207

They knew little about their son's biological parents. Were they early bloomers too? Kelly wished their boy had had a year or two more to simply be a boy, without the thoughts and urges his hormones would now trigger.

He used to sleep between them on their overnights to the cabin. Even when he grew into two long arms and two long legs that flailed about, he showed no interest in abandoning his fathers for a bed of his own in the other room.

But no longer. The first time Clarkson announced that he wanted to sleep by himself in the second bedroom at the cabin, on a chilly visit the previous spring, Kelly could see hesitancy in his eyes. The night sounds that filled the forest had been part of his life since infancy, but he'd never had to listen to them without a reassuring father within reach before.

Kelly walked into the second bedroom to get Clarkson settled. He brushed some dead bugs off the quilt and checked to see if the sheets had been changed since their last use. They had, though Clarkson probably wouldn't have cared.

"Do you want the window open or closed?"

"Closed," Clarkson said after a moment. He placed his battery-powered lamp on the table beside the bed, set to low, and stripped to his briefs, leaving his clothes where they fell. Kelly turned away while he collected the boy's clothes and put them on the chair where he could find them in the morning. Clarkson crawled into bed and pulled the top sheet and quilt up to his chin.

"We're just a room away. Should I turn off your lamp?"

'No, leave it on."

"There's an extra blanket in the drawer if you get cold. Just pee off the side of the porch if you need to in the night. Or you can call Dad or me if you need anything. Do you want the door open or closed?"

"Closed," he said, without hesitation.

Kelly leaned in and kissed Clarkson's forehead. "I'll send Dad in to say good night. See you in the morning."

"Love you, Pop."

"I love you, too."

Before Curt went in to say good night, Kelly suggested, he should knock first. From now on, he said, if they heard any sounds from behind Clarkson's closed door in the night it might mean the boy needed privacy rather than help.

Curt nodded. His son had reached the age where his bedroom door would now be closed to his fathers. "I know it's wrong to want him to stay a boy forever, but . . ."

That change in their pattern had occurred months before. Despite a similar quiet ending to this July day in the woods, it had been a trial for Curt. He still felt off balance without his father here in this place. He had wanted to use the visit to finally teach Clarkson how to split logs with the sledge and wedge. Split logs were easier to use in the fire — they caught more quickly and burned to ash sooner than solid logs — but they also needed some pieces with specific dimensions for the woodstove in the cabin. You could never have enough stove wood on hand.

But this was July. They wouldn't need a fire in the potbelly for months, he could hear Clarkson say, so why the need to split wood? Still, it was a skill Curt wanted to share with his boy, one of the traditions of the cabin. Curt was beginning to feel the weight of his role at the cabin, his responsibility now that his father was gone, to pass on David's lessons.

Clarkson dutifully learned to spot where the logs were already beginning to crack on their own so he could place the wedge and more easily split the log. Curt showed him how to tap the wedge into

Flint and Steel

place then carefully swing the heavy sledgehammer to hit the top of the wedge and force it into the wood.

Clarkson missed his first few swings and knocked the wedge askew several times after that. He was a growing boy, but upper body strength evidently wasn't on the schedule yet.

Despite Curt's encouragement and the effusive praise he offered when Clarkson finally split the log in two, Curt could see that it was a losing game. He'd picked the shortest log on the pile to start with. The one easiest to split. But he couldn't manage the hammer properly and his sweaty hands slipped.

"Well, now that we've worked up a sweat," Curt said, surrendering the failed lesson, "how about a swim?"

Clarkson had finally, hesitantly returned to swimming in their lake. Kelly had sat him down one day and explained how important it was to his dad that the boy join them in the lake. It was a family tradition, he said. "Even Grandma has been known to do it sometimes!" That brought a look of amazement and was maybe what finally convinced him to try again.

For Curt's birthday the previous August, Clarkson announced that his present to his Dad was that he would swim in the lake with him. "If you stay close and don't splash me." He *had* joined them that day, and the fish *hadn't* eaten him as he'd feared. In fact, the fish didn't seem to take any notice of him at all. And since he'd learned to swim at the Y, his only reluctance was going in water where he couldn't see the bottom. Both fathers stayed close, and he found he could keep himself afloat in this murky water just as well as in a pool. It had been a fine birthday party at the cabin for Curt. "Best birthday ever!" he had shouted to the sky.

The swimming this July had been even better. Clarkson showed no hesitation to leap from the dock ahead of his dads, no reluctance to swim off on his own. He'd even conjured enough mischief to dive under the murky water and tug their feet from below. He'd splash to the surface laughing, whip his long blond locks out of his face, and swim out of their reach when they lurched for him.

When they finally trudged up the old sandstone steps to the cabin, Curt saw Jimmy standing by the fire ring. The three of them were stark naked.

Normally, Curt wouldn't have minded, but it did bother him a little that Jimmy had probably seen Clarkson naked. Jimmy had never expressed judgment about how his neighbors lived their lives, and he knew the lake was well suited for skinny-dipping, having run off the local kids many times. But a pubescent boy's body, Curt thought, was not something he wanted an adult man to see.

"Sorry to disturb the swim in your pond."

"Lake. Not a problem. We were finished anyway." He wrapped his towel around his waist. "What's up, Jimmy?"

Jimmy made a quick scan of the area. Kelly had directed Clarkson inside the cabin rather than cavort on the porch to air dry as they normally would.

"Heard about some timber trespass over to Roscoe. Bottom land near the Osage. Thieves got away with a couple of acres of oaks. Nothing this side of the county so far. Your forest is mostly too young. And dry ridgetop. Not likely to be visited by these folk. Wanted you to know is all. Heard you drive in earlier and wanted to stop by to let you know. Sorry I interrupted your swim."

"You didn't. And I'm grateful that you told me." There was little Curt could do to prevent such a thing from happening in their woods or even know about it until after it was done. Maybe Jimmy was getting the word out to everyone in the area so that word would reach the ears of the thieves and they'd know he was paying attention on this side of the county.

Flint and Steel

And with that, Jimmy turned and began walking up the road to the top of the ridge. It was only then that Curt realized he hadn't seen Jimmy's truck. The old man had walked to the cabin, nearly a mile into their woods and even farther from his own place, and now he was walking out.

Off and on over the years they had talked about putting up a gate at the entrance to their woods, but they all felt that the only people it would stop would be them, because they'd have to open and close it each time they went in and out. Any determined trespassers would find a way around it — their forest was porous enough for that — or simply drive through a gate, break the latch, or flatten the gate and keep going. A gate certainly wouldn't stop determined timber thieves, as they often heard at the feed store.

And Kelly thought a gate would be an affront to the spirit of their forest. It was supposed to be their place to be unguarded. Not locked in and locked out. A gate would change the tone of the place No, they'd agreed, they would live and let live.

Sure, they'd find occasional beer cans scattered around when they reached the cabin. Bits of trash. Cigarette butts. Coils of fishing line. Evidence of a fire in the ring. Even embarrassing pieces of clothing sometimes. But what could they do about any of that? Call the sheriff and report a whole lot of nothing? Get a reputation for being the hard-assed, out-of-town landowners and practically invite more malicious visits? No, it was peaceful coexistence that had to rule, and it had worked for decades. For all Curt knew, the kids who made their occasional parties out here could be the sons and daughters of the kids who had done the same in his dad's time. Even his grandfather's time.

Curt mounted the porch steps and called into the cabin. "It's okay to come out. He's gone now." But once he got inside, he saw that Clarkson was already capering in his briefs, and Kelly was pulling on his boxers. No one was going to air dry on the porch that day. So Curt unwrapped from his towel and begin drying his hair.

"What was that about?"

"Oh, Jimmy just wanted to tell me about some timber trespass on the other side of the county." Curt's voice was muffled through the towel. "He didn't think we had anything to worry about since our trees are still too young for a good harvest, but he wanted us to know." He flung his towel in the corner. "Where is my underwear?"

When he joined them outside the cabin a few minutes later, Clarkson and Kelly were standing by the fire ring as though waiting for him. Curt smiled as he walked over, not knowing what to expect.

"I told Clarkson I had a surprise for him this visit," Kelly said. "And I didn't want to reveal it without you being present."

"I guess it's a surprise for me too then."

"A good surprise." Kelly reached deep into the pocket of his sweats and brought forth two objects. One looked like a rock and the other was a curved piece of metal. He handed them to Clarkson.

"Thanks, Pop. What is it?"

"Flint and steel. A really old way of starting a fire. I thought we could try lighting our dinner fire with flint and steel. Maybe a bigger challenge than even a one-match fire."

He beamed at Curt, who knew he should smile back. But deep inside, he was not pleased, and it took him a few moments to figure out why.

One-match fires were the family tradition. The skill was handed down from father to son as a rite of passage. There was no need to improve on it. Clarkson had been a lackluster student when Curt had first shown him how to do build a fire that he could light with a single match. Perhaps Curt had been too eager, but Clarkson mastered how do it most times when he tried. Often he left the job to his Pop, who had grown good at it.

Flint and Steel 213

This flint and steel business felt like an insult somehow. Like they were trying to replace what his grandfather had taught Curt's father and what his father had taught him, in order to create a new tradition that was even more exclusive. They wouldn't be doing this if David was alive.

Who were they to establish a new tradition, to sweep aside something that had brought pride in achievement and sense of family specialness for so long? What was Kelly trying to do? Create a new tradition just between the two of them? Tear Clarkson away from him? He knew it was wrong to think this way, but he couldn't stop himself.

"I read up on this, Clarkson. Watched some videos. The trick is to have the right tinder. Crumpled paper won't really work. Stuff like really dry grass works best. But I gathered some straw from that bale I got at the feed store last time we were out. We can shred it some and see how well it works."

So that was what it had been for! Kelly claimed he got the straw bale so they could sit on it around the campfire, but obviously he'd had other intentions. How long had Kelly been planning this?

Curt thought that he should get Clarkson a magnifying glass. A big, goofy, Sherlock Holmes magnifying glass, and show him how to light a fire with *that*. It would impress the boy, the showmanship of it. *That* could be the real new tradition. He could teach that to his son.

"The trick is to strike the steel against the flint to create sparks that land in the straw and dry grass and tinder and start a small flame. Everything after that is just like with a regular fire. Just like Dad showed you and Grandpa showed me."

Their first flint and steel session was a bust. Both tried, and were each able to strike some sparks, but neither could get the sparks to land right in the tinder. Kelly was disappointed. Curt was not.

"Lucky thing you have a whole bale of straw to work with," he snickered. He knew he was being bullheaded and petty, poking pins in Kelly's balloon. Failures like this could sometimes plunge Kelly into one of his spirals. Curt didn't want that.

A breeze blew through the treetops. Somewhere inside him, he heard his father's voice. *It is important that the family continue to come here, to keep it part of your lives. To bring your own experiences and richness to it.*

Kelly wasn't stealing a family tradition, Curt conceded. Not really. Kelly was *enriching* the family tradition and building on it. It had to sting a little for Kelly to fail in front of Clarkson. His big surprise reduced to a big disappointment. Actually, Curt realized, David would probably have been fascinated by Kelly's attempt and would have wanted to try it himself. If Dad had sat me down as a boy and taught me this skill thirty years ago, he thought, it would have belonged here, so why shouldn't it now? Another dad sitting down with another son and sharing another skill — isn't that what this place is for?

More importantly, it wasn't merely any father and son moment. Kelly was attempting to bond himself with their cabin. The way he studied Joe's old nature guidebooks, and tried to identify the birds they saw at the feeder, the insects, and the spiders he would see in their webs and identify as well as the fish they pulled from the lake and the different kinds of trees and scrub — these were *his* way of finding belonging, seeking acceptance and a family that would never let him go.

Did those vile people of his original family know what a good husband and a good father and a good son-in-law and a good man Kelly had become? All the battles he had to fight? All the pills he had to swallow to drive away the monsters? Did they care?

Flint and Steel

Did Curt care what they thought? "We'll leave them behind us," he'd urged Kelly when his darkness came. "We'll stride forward, you and me into the kind of world you deserve." He would say it for the rest of his life if that was what Kelly needed. Sometimes as Kelly slept beside him, he whispered that promise.

This, he came to understand, was one of those times to stride forward together. Curt would encourage Kelly as he perfected his flint and steel technique. They would use it to build fires they could cook their meals over and keep warm around. Dad would approve.

But not today.

"Pop says he wants you to light the fire today. We're hungry. I'll get the matches."

Curt's empty hand followed the boy as he turned and ran for the cabin. And it was still outstretched when the boy returned.

Chapter Twenty-one

Invisible Wounds

Curt's instep ached so bad that he winced with each footfall. It didn't stop him from going on his regular runs, but he could feel it nagging him even when he was sitting. His right knee was getting a little wonky again, too. His running shoes were worn out. Maybe he was wearing out.

He hoped he could hide it from his mother, although for as far back as he could remember, she had been able to see through him with her empathy superpower that she reserved for the people she loved. He wished he had that talent, especially when his littlest patients couldn't tell him what was wrong. Or when he couldn't puzzle out the distance between himself and Clarkson.

She didn't need one more thing to worry about. She'd faced enough in recent years, and the whole point of coming over that afternoon, sitting at the familiar kitchen table and pawing through boxes of papers from his father's orderly collection in the basement, was to help her.

"Why do you think Dad never brought electricity to the cabin?" Curt studied the notarized deed, transferring the ownership of the Ozark property to his mother after David had died. He guessed they must have made a similar transfer when his grandfather died. Some future day the property would transfer to him, and eventually to Kelly and Clarkson, and on to a succession of people he would never know. We're all just passing through that forest. Leaving a little of ourselves behind if we're lucky.

"If he had, we could have drilled a well and put regular plumbing in the cabin. Running water. A flushing toilet in the middle of a forest. Air conditioning. Actual electric lights instead of lanterns. Classy stuff like that."

Curt had the money to do that. Even with Kelly only working part time, Curt's salary kept them comfortable with enough to spare to make improvements. But Curt could feel his father's spirit at the cabin and the hundred acres. He depended on it and was comforted by it. He was fishing for what his mother, as the new owner, thought about improvements.

"Would have made it more comfortable for you, Mom."

"Oh," Kathy said. "Well." She paused, collecting some words. She'd always been careful with words, always considered how they'd land before she spoke them, but Curt thought that she was taking more time to find the right words lately, in the months since her mother had died. "It seemed like there was always something else we needed to buy, Curt. Bills to pay. I guess your father thought improvements were an indulgence he couldn't allow himself." She turned to her son and smiled. "The taxes would go up if we did. A bunch of boys in a forest don't need flushing toilets anyway."

"Dad deserved it, Mom. It wouldn't have been an indulgence. It would have been his due."

Kathy looked across the room. "Yes, it would have." And she may have been speaking to her husband rather than to Curt. "He would have liked that. But what he'd wanted most of all was for you to keep going to the cabin with your family. To enjoy it and pass it down. If bringing in electricity ensures that will happen, I'm sure he approves."

They were still settling Kathy's mother's estate. After the unsurprising contributions she had made to her church and a few causes and paying off a handful of minor bills and the lawyer's fees, it looked as though the money left to be split between Kathy and her sister was considerable. Add to that the sale of her mother's very nice Brookside house in Kansas City and Kathy would soon find herself with more money than she could imagine ever needing.

Early in her adult life she had learned to keep her wants simple. Having grown up more than comfortable and secure with her every wish indulged, then dashing into adulthood with Davey when they were both just kids. There she quickly learned what it meant to be poor, to do without even essentials sometimes, and to live from paycheck to paycheck. She had accepted all of that because she was with Davey and soon with Curt. Riches enough. Yes, regrettable choices had been sometimes required. But they had beaten the odds, confounded the doomsayers, made it work.

Kathy's choice to marry David, whom her mother disapproved, and raise their son within that financial struggle, had raised a wall between the two women. Even in later years, when the pressure had eased and the bills were mostly paid on time, when they had pulled to themselves a modest amount of security, her mother's frowning disappointment was inescapably evident in her careless choice of words or her arched-eyebrowed silence. Occasionally she would slip hundred-dollar bills into her daughter's hand, which Kathy was not too proud to accept but hid from Davey lest he be reminded of her parents' judgment of him as unable to provide for their family. A look-how-generous-I-am gesture. Her mother's dictums for how her grandson ought to be raised resulted in Kathy's mother paying for his private high school, his college, and medical school. But her largesse came with spoken and unspoken judgments, that only ceased with her death.

It was years since Kathy had to choose between paying the electric bill or the gas bill or how many times she could patch Curt's jeans or darn Davey's socks, but she had never forgotten how that felt — the meals she skipped so Curt had a snack after school and the clothes she wore until they were threadbare so he could have new school clothes. Every penny she picked up from the ground, every time she claimed she preferred a walk in the evenings rather than going to a movie, a picnic on a blanket under the maple trees in the backyard rather than a meal out. She recalled when an amazed Curt had announced that mac and cheese was just a *side dish* for some of his friends. And Davey had done the same, never complaining when a sacrifice had to be made.

All of that was behind her now. Her checking account would soon swell with a ridiculous amount of money. Years of worries and cautions and careful considerations would wash away. And all she felt was resentment.

Their coffee had grown cold, and so Curt found himself speaking of bigger things, which had been his intention. He stood, fetched the pot, and refilled their mugs. Living alone, his mother never brewed full pots. He put the empty pot back in the machine, unsure if she would want to wash it before using it again. He didn't know her routines anymore.

"Isn't it funny how the house you grew up in always seems so much smaller when you return as an adult?" he said.

"Not my mother's," Kathy said. "That place always seemed immense to me, especially when I returned to visit."

"Yeah, Grandma's house was over the top."

"I don't think she ever fully gave up her fantasy that I was going to move back. She said as much after your father died, that I could move in with her, take back my old bedroom, and help her in her golden years. I wanted to grab her by the throat."

"Mom!"

"I'm sorry." She'd spent her life insulating Davey and Curt from the worst of her mother's passive-aggressive assaults and knew Curt had loved his grandmother. And she had loved him. Even after Curt came out — revealing his "sinful" orientation (according to her mother's perspective). Even then her love for him was bedrock. The boy felt it and needed it. And maybe it was better he didn't know his grandmother more fully. Weren't all families full of mysteries and secrets?

"I was wondering if *this* old place was too big for you, Mom. Not the house so much, but the yard. Cleaning the gutters. Shoveling the walk. Raking the leaves. All the headaches of home ownership." Headaches he avoided by choosing to live in a condominium. "You don't need it."

"The neighbor boy, Grant, comes by every week to check on me and takes care of a lot of things. And I'm certainly not moving in with you and Kelly, Curt. I'm finally at a point in my life where I find the toilet seat down all the time."

Curt laughed.

"I don't need a yard. You're right. Except sometimes I look out the window and I can see you climbing your maple tree or tossing a ball with Dad. Yes, there is a lot of maintenance I probably shouldn't have to deal with anymore. But to tell you the truth . . ." She turned her wedding ring around her finger. "Well, you don't know how important buying this house was to your father, what it meant to him to be able to give you this."

It was years before Curt had finally begun to understand why his father had been so pleased that his son had his own bedroom, something so insignificant, something all his friends had. The drafty sleeping porch Curt had slept in during their apartment years had been fine and the real bedroom he got when they moved to this house was even better. It seemed a natural progression he was entitled to. Until he realized it wasn't simply a natural progression to David, but a hard-won achievement he had finally provided for his son.

"Do you want a piece of cake, Curt? I baked it this morning. Just for you, so you have to say yes."

He was running as much as he could. There was a treadmill in his garage and a weight machine at the hospital gym, and he'd been pushing back from the table more lately because he was facing the onset of middle age, and he didn't want to get pudgy or feel winded when he climbed the stairs. Except Kelly was a good cook. "He made tortellini that was so good, Mom, I asked him to *never* make it again!"

The hidden heart disease that had taken his father too early had jolted Curt. He was trying to be rigorous about his fitness and diligent about his diet because he had experienced the sudden loss of his father and didn't want Kelly and Clarkson to go through that.

"If you made it, Mom, then I want a piece." He'd be taking the leftover cake home with him later. It was her way to press baked goodness on him and his family, to be a sweet presence in their lives. "Grandma's cake?" he could already hear Clarkson cheering when he got home that afternoon, and he'd devour the whole thing if they let him.

Kathy began setting out plates and utensils on the counter. The clinking sounds took Curt back to his childhood in that kitchen.

He reached into the box and drew out a manila envelope with the word "HOUSE" penciled on it. Inside was the deed to the house he was sitting in, one of the great achievements in his father's life. The place where they had built their lives and shared the millions of quiet moments that make up the best parts of what is called living.

Curt looked at the document, then looked again. He flipped to the back and saw his mother's signature on the original deed.

"Why isn't Dad's name listed on the deed to the house, Mom?"

Kathy dropped the knife she was holding. It clattered on the floor, but she didn't move to pick it up.

"Mom?"

"He doesn't know, Curt." She turned to him with her finger on her lips. "Don't tell him."

"Mom, are you okay?"

Kathy took a moment to collect herself. She bent and picked up the fallen knife then put it in the sink. Turning to Curt she smiled, but he could see it was a mask.

"Davey didn't know, Curt." She remained at the counter by the uncut cake. "It was a condition of my mother lending us the money. He was not to be listed as an owner of the house. I kept that a secret from him."

"Yet he paid the mortgage for the house each month!" Curt slapped his hand against the paper. "How many insults did that man have to face in his life?" Insults, Curt thought, that were heavy and unrelenting. That wore him down, that slowly killed him before his time.

He *had* paid the mortgage each month, except sometimes there wasn't enough money and Kathy had to choose between paying Joe's bills at the care home or paying her well-off mother who held their mortgage.

"A bank wouldn't let you get away with this, Kathleen," her mother had snarled at her over the phone the first time it happened. "A bank would foreclose. You've made many unfortunate choices in your life. And see how you must live!"

"Well, this is who I *am* now. And most of all, this is who I *want* to be. Don't make me choose between you and Davey, Mother, because you won't like what I decide!"

"I could foreclose on you —"

"THEN FORECLOSE, MOTHER! Evict us. Do it if that's important to you!"

Her mother withdrew then. The long-overdue force of her

Invisible Wounds

daughter's words, and the strength of the choice she had made, left her mother unable to respond. She had no words. Not so much for her daughter's insolence as for her conviction. And several months later, when it happened again, she did not confront her daughter.

Kathy had juggled the books. She'd kept it all secret from Davey and Curt. She compromised here and did without there and squirreled away what she could. Eventually she caught up. She kept them afloat a little longer until things slowly got better and she could breathe again.

Now Curt had asked the question and opened a door that she had wanted to keep closed to him.

He watched her from across the tiny kitchen. She stood unmoving, unseeing. He rose and approached her. Kathy's dropped her head on her son's shoulder, and he wrapped his arms around her. She was alone now. No husband that she'd loved so ridiculously hard. No mother who, despite her flaws, did love her daughter. Even her son was grown and gone and with a family of his own. Clarkson's grade school drawings hanging by magnets from her refrigerator were how old? How many unseen tears did she shed for her loss and loneliness? How many invisible wounds did she carry? Wounds she could see so readily in others and hide so well in herself? Why didn't he know these things?

But he understood she needed to live with her ghosts. Needed their comfort. Wasn't that what the cabin was to him? A way to abide with his own ghosts?

Chapter Twenty-two

yellow leaves, or none, or few

What she refused to believe, what she had nodded in acknowledgement of as the doctor spoke, words she had repeated to show she understood, were without substance, words she'd never accepted and never would. That his heart could fail. Davey's heart! No, the doctors were wrong.

He had been alone. Unmissed until he didn't return the next day when expected. And she had called Jimmy to please check on her husband who hadn't come back from his overnight. Thus it fell to Jimmy to make the sad discovery and to deliver the unbearable news. He found David seated against a tree he'd apparently intended to bring down, as though he'd paused for a moment to rest, his chainsaw beside him. She'd later asked Jimmy to finish the task her Davey had begun. Only then did she allow herself to be led to the place in his forest where he had died to see his last contact with ground more sacred to him than any other place on earth.

That had been in the bitter cold of the preceding winter, and life, when she allowed it, had gone on. There was a son to love, a son finding his way through the emotions of loss. And a grandson, a young teen experiencing death for the first time. And Kelly. His heart a mystery to her still. And there were decisions, adjustments, accommodations. The shifting of their lives, both subtle and profound, before the void of David's departure.

The rawness eased. The emptiness slowly, though never fully, filled. Lives resumed. Responsibilities called. Laughter crept in, tentatively, sometimes guiltily. It seemed that going on might be possible, though in a bleak way that suggested no hope.

And there was one last promise to be kept.

They had ventured to the cabin, the four of them, their new configuration of family, with no spoken agenda. A day trip, eleven months later, to assess what none of them was even clear about. To take stock. To inventory what was there and what was in themselves. To see how the remaining pieces fit together in their altered lives. They would be lighthearted about it. Make no urgent decisions except that they would *never* part with David's cabin and hundred acres of Ozark forest!

Curt, new master of the cabin, poked about, finding when they looked that his father had left things for them in order, as they expected. His tools were cleaned, sharpened, each in its place. The cold woodstove held only the scant ash of his father's final one-match fire. Curt thought of rekindling it, to warm the little cabin on their chilly November visit, but the thought troubled him. Was it too soon to erase his father's final act? Even cleaning the residual ash from the bottom seemed premature. A lunch fire in the ring outside was sufficient for now.

Kathy sat bundled on the porch, staring down at the lake in the weak sunlight, letting the men inside find their way, the door and windows of the cabin open to counter the mustiness within.

"I'm afraid to touch it," drifted Kelly's words through the window.

"Dad always said that the day to stop using a chainsaw is the day you're no longer afraid of it."

An acorn cracked against the metal roof. She heard doors open and drawers slide. "Oh, I'd forgotten about that," and "When did Dad get this?" and "So that's where it went!" Clarkson nosed around with them, as open and enigmatic as always. Currents stirred within him that would never make sense to her.

"Wow," said Kelly. "Look at these!"

"Oh, Dad's old Superman comics. They must be more than fifty years old now."

"I'll bet these are worth some serious money."

A moment of silence, and then, "We're *never* selling these!"

With her men thus occupied, Kathy felt safe to embark on her own chore for the visit. The promise to be kept.

She rose from the chair and left the porch, taking herself across the weedy gravel where Clarkson had now scattered thousands of colorful marbles to the car where her daypack waited. If any of them glanced out the window and saw her, what of it? She was going for a hike on her own. Leave her to her solitude. As simple as that. Rather than shouldering the pack, though, she held it in her arms.

Across the dam, halfway up the north-facing slope and a little to the east, just out of sight of the cabin even on this leafless November day. Her destination: a boulder — what Davey had told her was limestone, though she hadn't cared at the time — waited for her late return. Her feet found their way through the crisp fallen leaves and hidden rocks. When she arrived, she set the pack on the boulder and sat beside it. Now came the hard part.

Before her, the grass at her feet was matted, pressed down in a rough circle, and her thoughts raced to a moment, a long-ago past that she clung to, still as vivid as the experience had been then.

"What, Davey? Here? Now?"

"Yes."

"But someone will see us."

"No one will see us."

"Davey, I don't think this is a good idea." But she found that she was helping him off with his shirt just as he was doing for her.

He'd made a nest on the grass with their clothes and held her in his arms as he laid her upon it. The world had stopped for them then. They became two forest creatures, natural and innocent. Alone together. And in the cool shade of a hickory tree, they soon drifted to sleep in each other's arms, cradled by the soft, yielding grass.

When they'd returned to the cabin, she had leaves in her hair, and was certain Davey's mother, who had stayed behind with the napping Curt, knew.

Her face warmed as she smiled with the memory. She found she was holding the daypack in her arms. She wished she could undress now and lie in the grass again to live within the warm memory for a time.

The matted grass at her feet held yellow leaves fallen from the nearby hickory. Davey, as timid and uncertain as he could be about everything else in his life, became masterful in these woods. He became his true self here. She clutched the daypack closer.

He had died, alone, in this forest. And now, as was his wish, spoken casually in a time when they both could barely conceive a concept like mortality, she was returning him to the forest he loved. A part of her resisted the thought of leaving him there, alone once again.

She'd waited this long so her emotions could soften, so Curt wouldn't impulsively try to contradict his father's wishes and his mother's duty. The urn, she had told Curt, was on a shelf in her bedroom closet, and that seemed sufficient for him, though really it had been under her bed all those months, positioned, she believed, directly below her heart.

Davey had always said that fall was his favorite season, a gentle hand on the shoulder reminding him to enjoy what was before him for it would not last. Thus their return in November.

But where was he to go now that she had brought him here? Scattered in the grass? Or buried at the base of the hickory? Thrown to the breeze?

"Some deer slept there last night."

Clarkson pointed to the matted grass. He had appeared, noiselessly. Kathy was no longer surprised that this boy could pass through a leaf-littered forest without a sound. Or by his clever, correct insights that he reached by no paths visible to any of them. Clarkson was to be taken as he came. And he had come to this place, at this time. To her.

"Deer," she said. "Of course."

Forest creatures. Wild, and graceful, and exactly right, she thought. She hoped they would return many times to grace the holy spot.

He sat beside his grandmother on the boulder.

"I don't know what to do, Clarkson."

"This is the right place."

"How do you know? Did Grandpa bring you here before?"

"No. I just find things in our forest." If she had pressed him, he might have told her that Scrapefoot showed him the place, but he had learned not to talk about his friend.

"Our forest," she heard him say.

He rose from the boulder and knelt before it, brushing aside the fallen yellow hickory leaves and wresting two large rocks away from the base, revealing a cavity under the boulder. He pulled a small flashlight from the pocket of his parka and switched it on.

Kathy knelt beside him and peered in. There, at the back, she saw two urns tucked in the cavity with an arrangement of marbles pressed into the dirt in front of them.

"Your marbles, Clarkson?"

"Something I read in *Tom Sawyer*. They're my great-grandparents, aren't they?"

"Yes," Kathy said, realizing only in that moment who they were and how they had gotten there. Davey must have placed them, his parents, Joe and Peg. Clarkson had never known them just as he had never known any of his *biological* family. She wondered then if the boy felt robbed, although she knew that family was what you made as much as what made you.

Kathy lifted the daypack down from the boulder and opened it, pulling out the urn that she had kept close to her heart. Davey would not be alone in his forest after all. The pain in her heart eased with this discovery.

"Give me a hand, Clarkson."

Together they guided the urn to the back of the cavity, beside the other two. It was a reach for her, but the boy managed the last part.

And then he dug in the pocket of his red parka and brought forth a small bag of marbles and began arranging them before his grandfather's urn.

"Goodbye, Grandpa. I'll visit you a lot."

Together, they moved the rocks back in place before the opening and scattered the fallen yellow leaves upon them. Kathy did not want to leave. Not yet. She sat in the grass wishing she could bring back that moment with Davey decades ago but knowing she could not. When she was finally able to speak, she said, "Clarkson, when my time comes, I want you to do this for me."

Chapter Twenty-three

Barbarian at the Gate

Curt paused, one foot on the wooden step leading to the door of the whitewashed country church. It looked ancient, sinking into the ground, in need of fresh paint, a new roof. A barbarian at the gate indeed, about to enter a place as foreign to him as the dark side of the moon. Full of strange rituals and stranger beliefs. He wouldn't know a single person within, except the dead one. The living ones would certainly wonder who this stranger among them was, with his citified air, intruding on their solemn business. Desecrating it if they truly knew him.

A winter-bare sycamore stood before the church. In the wind that had brought the clouds, its bone-white limbs clicked like a rattling skeleton.

That he didn't belong was laughably obvious to Curt. He wondered if they would even allow him through the doors if they knew the kind of man he was. If they would permit him to hide in a pew at the back and silently, respectfully sit through their service, holding a hymn book opened to the wrong page and bowing his head when he saw everyone else do so. He would be eyed from every direction. Estimated. Judged. Who was this stranger? This interloper? Why was he here? What business did he have to intrude on their sacred rites? He barely knew himself.

Curt moved out of the way as an ancient man and woman hobbled to the stairs and then struggled up them to enter the church. They seemed not to notice him as they passed, but he was sure once inside they would ask, "Who is that man outside the door?"

He'd come too far to leave, though he'd considered doing that every mile of his drive. He owed it to Jimmy to pay his respects. He would come all this way to attend a funeral at a backroads country church where he would be shunned and evicted, he was certain, if they knew he was their most wretched sinner. He could visit the cabin instead. *That* was the sacred place he knew. But instead, he was here.

"How do I look?" he had said to Kelly early that morning, having pulled from the back of his closet the dark gray suit he rarely wore. He'd declined Kelly's offer to help him with his tie but then smiled and lifted his chin as his husband's gentle hands straightened the knot.

"I suppose saying that you'll knock 'em dead would be unsuitable for a funeral."

"Unsuitable for a doctor, too."

"Well, you look fine, Curt. Modest. Neat. Respectful. Funereal. You have all the right adjectives working for you this morning." He brushed Curt's shoulders. His own father's memorial was probably the last time Curt had worn it.

"It's weird, going to a church service. I don't think I've been inside a church since high school. And I certainly won't know anyone inside this one!"

"I hope you don't burst into flames when you cross the threshold, you heathen."

"*Gay* heathen. And an unbeliever. At a small fundamentalist church deep in rural Missouri."

"A homo among the holy. A barbarian at the gate. I suppose it would also be unsuitable at a funeral for you to disarm them with your charming smile and clever wit."

"My smile isn't charming."

"Then tell them you're a doctor. If Jimmy was as old as you

say, it's likely most of the people will have ailments and infirmities they'll want to tell you all about. Work the crowd, Curt!"

"I should probably get going. I want to get out of the city before the morning rush. What are you and Clarkson doing today?"

"He said he wanted to go to the art museum. And I could come along, so I don't want to miss that! Need anything from the gift shop?"

Curt could never summon an appreciation for the museum the way Kelly could, which Clarkson knew. He was too much a man of science, where those two leaned toward the arts. Even in his own family he sometimes felt like an outsider.

"Just think of me when you're looking at the religious paintings. Especially if someone is being persecuted."

"We'll probably never get out of the modern galleries."

"Well, give me a hug now before I go."

"I'll wrinkle your jacket."

"Do your worst!"

Kelly could hear the anxiety behind Curt's glib manner. But he would be fine. He would call up the gracious, professional part of himself and wear that mask while he was among the mourners. He'd pay proper respect to the man who had watched over their cabin for decades. Then he'd skedaddle.

At the front door Curt turned for another hug, and this time holding on longer.

"You'll be fine, Curt."

"I know. I'll see you tonight."

Kelly watched him walk to the car in the gray dawn light.

"Don't sign up for the church newsletter!"

"I won't."

"Or volunteer for the bake sale!"

No other mourners had approached the church. Curt stood

alone at the bottom of the steps leading to the door. The sky had grown overcast. Appropriate for a funeral, he supposed. He hoped it wouldn't rain and freeze on the roads. That would make the drive home more difficult. He thought again about just getting in the car and leaving to beat the rain. Make up some fiction to tell Kelly. Or tell him the truth. That he was an outsider who barely knew the deceased and didn't belong among the faithful or in a church at all. He could tell him the real truth: he was afraid.

And he'd almost convinced himself to leave when the door at the top of the stairs opened and an older man peered out.

"Please come in, friend." He held the door open.

Caught between entering and escaping, Curt mounted the stairs and stepped through the door. The man handed him a folded paper, the program for the service. Curt thanked him and took a seat in the very back pew. Two people farther along the pew looked at him and nodded before turning back to the program.

There were more mourners in the tiny church than he had expected. Not many people could have outlived Jimmy's ninety-something years, though a few looked like they had. The man had clearly attracted younger souls as well old ones.

The space was unadorned, unlike the Catholic churches his mother had sometimes dragged him to as a child. Fluorescent lights buzzed from the ceiling. The walls were white, and at the front was a large, plain cross that dominated the room.

Below the cross a brown wooden casket rested on its bier. Flowers were displayed around it. Inside, the corporeal remains of James E. Larson, the program told him. Curt realized that he'd never known the man's name beyond "Jimmy." He'd never thought of Jimmy's life beyond caretaker of his cabin in the woods. He'd never thought of Jimmy much at all. Odd that he was finally getting to know him a little better after he was gone.

The few hushed conversations stopped as the man who had welcomed Curt into the church walked to the front.

"Friends," he began. "It is a sad day and a joyous day."

The minister proceeded with the funeral service. Had it been spoken in Latin, Curt might have been able to parse some of it, but it was in an English that seemed a foreign language to him. Scripture was quoted. Hymns were sung. Prayers were intoned. Amens were chanted. Memories were shared. Throats were cleared and sobs hushed. Curt followed along in the program as best he could, sitting rigid and unmoving in the back pew. Though no heads turned his way, he felt certain he was being examined, his non-participation noted in some cosmic ledger.

Near the front he saw a man lean toward the pew before him and rest his hand on the shoulder of another man, who began visibly shaking. The minister paused until the sobbing subsided. A few faces fell into open hands. One very old man silently reached for the heavens, supported by the very old woman standing beside him.

Curt understood that ritual and belief were important, especially in times of grief and suffering. He understood in a clinical way. Many times, he had counseled parents to seek their ministers or rabbis or imams. Had directed them to the little chapel in the hospital. Had stood silently at bedsides as they prayed over their sick children. When his own father had died, he grieved and felt regret and a great loss. But his grief was restrained and controlled. Might it have been eased with some kind of faith or some kind of ritual? But those small grafts in his childhood had never taken, and by the time Curt had made his escape to college, he was certain faith and ritual were useless to him.

These people were different. He did not begrudge them their faith, so he sat quietly and remained respectful.

When he'd understood the service was over, he had risen from the bench and turned to leave, but an old woman was already blocking him, looking directly at him, her rheumy gray eyes gone liquid behind her thick glasses.

"Thank you for coming, young man," the woman said, grabbing his hand and holding it weakly. She wasn't going to let him escape, Curt realized, until she found out who he was. A group collected behind her, forming a semi-circle that hemmed Curt in with their canes and their walkers and their stooped bodies.

"How did you know Jimmy?" one of them asked.

He looked at their expectant faces and calculated what he could say. "I have a cabin not far from here, and he watched over it for me unofficially. I live in St. Louis."

"Oh, you're Mr. Clark!"

"Shepherd. Curtis Shepherd. You're thinking of David Clark, my father."

"Shepherd? Are you the adopted one?"

"No, that's my son." How did they know about his son? He considered how his next words would land and said them anyway. "I took my husband's name when we got married."

"Husband?"

"Oh, sure," said a bald man in the group, jumping into the conversation. "Jimmy told me all about your family. You're Joe Clark's grandson!"

"This is Joe Clark's grandson? Let me look at you good and proper, boy." An ancient woman pushed in and examined him up and down. "Well, he sure is! You grew up straight and tall, didn't you? I remember when your daddy would bring you into the hardware store. Red-headed dynamo. Smart little tyke, too. Always so polite. Your daddy sure raised you right. Yes, he did!" She stroked the sleeve of his jacket.

"Your daddy used to sit in the café for hours and brag about you, Son. Talked to anyone who would listen."

"And a few he wouldn't."

"He sure was proud of you, Mr. Shepherd."

"Is it true you can run faster than a jackrabbit? If I were a betting man, I'd put money on that race."

"You got lots of medals from running your dad said."

"And a scholarship to Mizzou."

"Remember that time David came into the barber shop shouting that his boy got into medical school? Remember that! Practically in tears about it he was." Several heads nodded. Several smiles formed.

"I remember that! He sure was a proud papa that day!"

"You're a doctor now, aren't you?"

"Pediatrician."

"He sure is! This is *Dr.* Shepherd." Several heads nodded.

"You adopted the child of that wayward girl. Gave that little boy a family. Gave David Clark a grandson to dote on too. That was a noble thing you did, son."

"Of course, look at the kind of father he had!"

"I remember David all puffed up, crowing that he had a grandson! That he was a grandpa!"

"Are you okay, Dr. Shepherd?"

Curt was swaying. He felt lightheaded. His vision narrowed.

"Here, sit yourself down, Dr. Shepherd." Several hands guided him back to the pew he had risen from. "Just rest here for a moment."

Curt found himself seated again. He gripped the back of the bench in front of him, trying to hold himself upright. He should have eaten breakfast. He should have gone to bed earlier the night before. Maybe his electrolytes were out of balance. Maybe he was dehydrated.

He found himself crying. His hands rose to his face and stayed there as the tears came.

"Let him grieve as he needs," someone said. "This is the place for that." He felt a hand patting him on his shoulder.

Even here, in this odd little backwater of the universe, his father had prepared a path for him. Had smoothed the way for his son's unlikely acceptance in this community that ought to mean nothing to him but seemed to mean everything to them.

Even here, his father's love for him was present. He didn't know Osceola had a café, much less that his father would hang out there and brag about his son.

He would never touch the bottom of his father's love. He suddenly understood that. It would remain mysterious, and it would support him for the rest of his life.

Chapter Twenty-four

The Woman at the Fair

The middle school art show was held in the gym over two evenings. Curt missed both. The first night he couldn't help being absent. There was a conference that had been scheduled months before that he had to attend. But the second night?

"I'll be there tonight, Clarkson," he vowed at breakfast. "I promise." Except he got swept into a difficult consultation late that afternoon and forgot about Clarkson's art show. He was sitting in a colleague's office, his feet on her desk, puzzling over the details of the case, when he finally checked his phone and saw the string of texts asking where he was.

"Oh, no! I gotta fly," he said. He tapped ON MY WAY but knew that even if he ran all the red lights, he was going to be too late. When he got to the school, the janitor was turning out the lights in the gym. On his phone he saw the message he'd missed: DON'T BOTHER!!!

The art fair had not been without its own surprises. When Clarkson pinned his work on the fabric walls of the booth allotted to him — mostly monochrome pieces with horizontal, parallel lines, along with a few abstract, three-color tempera abominations on crinkling paper that he'd reluctantly made at the last-minute insistence of his teacher — he had signed them as "Sprout."

Kelly hadn't noticed at first, not until some of Clarkson's friends breezed up and congratulated him on his artist's signature. Clarkson's grandfather had been a practical man who had loved his grandson, a boy he could see was forever at odds with his dad, a boy who could probably shower a little more often and maybe cut his hair or pull it back out of his face. David had loved Clarkson in the quiet, strong way that was his vocabulary, with an open ear and an open heart until the day he died. His love was the anchor the boy needed.

Because it was *Sprout's* exhibition at the middle school gym those two evenings, his grandfather's spirit was there. Clarkson had brought him along.

It had long been obvious to proud-poppa Kelly, and soon was acknowledged by other discerning parents whose words Kelly overheard, that Clarkson had more than a little artistic talent. He had an "eye" for lines and a sense of space and negative space. This boy's works showed control, vision, depth. Kelly loved to hear this.

"How am I to read all of these lines, young man?" This came from a commanding gentleman before him wearing a suit and still looking neat and trim at the end of the day. He was clearly a man who spent most of his life in a neat and trim office somewhere.

"However you want, I guess." Clarkson stood beside his display, his hands at his sides, not in his pockets as he had been cautioned. He wore a clean flannel shirt and an obviously unpracticed smile. His face showed pale fuzz above his lip, and he was rolling a couple of marbles in his fingers to relieve his nervousness. He'd pulled his hair back in a ponytail, but strands had come loose as the evening had progressed. Kelly thought he looked a little raffish for a middle school artist. Everyone was being graded on the evening, and Kelly gently reminded him his scores in art and English were propping up his GPA. "Let's finish eighth grade strong!"

"Is this a ladder?" the man continued. "Is it aspirational, perhaps? Are my eyes to climb the lines? Or is it a barrier? A gate between here and there? Do I live within the brown and black lines or between the lines? Or behind the lines? I see you call it your 'Foundation' series. Is this stone laid down that one can build upon perhaps?"

"Maybe it's just lines. It's what comes to me when I sit down to work. If it has more meaning than that, the meaning belongs to you. Whatever you find in it."

It doesn't have to "mean" anything, Kelly thought as he stood to the side and watched his son. It just has to "be." He'd said that once to Clarkson, and the boy had laughed, asking if his Pop had changed his meds recently.

But it clearly *did* mean something to Clarkson. Horizontal lines began running through his drawings from the time he could hold a crayon. There was something in them. Something important, visceral, foundational.

Frustrated by not being given an easy answer, the smartly dressed visitor, like several before, walked on. Clarkson didn't care. If you pressed him, he'd tell you he didn't do his lines to make sense to others. They didn't have to make sense even to him. Eventually he would know what it was all about. He would understand why the lines could wake him in his sleep and came to him when he was sad.

"Is Squirt going to be here?"

"Sprite." Clarkson corrected his Pop.

"Sprite." Clarkson never brought anyone to the cabin, though Curt had insisted he was always welcome to. When Kelly picked him up after school, he was usually hanging around with a brooding, artsy looking clique, but he never introduced them. He didn't think Clarkson was embarrassed by his family. Maybe the boy just needed time alone to decompress and be himself — like his Dad. He spent much of his time in his room, on his tablet reading or doing whatever adolescent boys do. When he wanted to make a half-hearted effort at doing his homework, he'd work in the kitchen where he could

The Woman at the Fair 241

generally find his Pop and avoid his Dad. He didn't seem to need friends.

Was Sprite a play on Sprout? Kelly wondered. Sprite and Sprout?

"He's here somewhere," Clarkson said. "Or he's here in spirit."

"I'd like to meet him."

"Yeah, you'd like him, Pop. But he's not a reader. More a philosopher."

"Does he have an exhibit?"

"He wanted to. He was going to have a table and just make paper airplanes then fly them over the other booths. The elusive ephemera of the creative spirit. It was sort of my idea. But the teacher said it would just make a bunch of trash he'd have to clean up, and Sprite said that showed how much she valued his art. And that pretty much ended his participation."

Clarkson continued to scan the crowd. From the distant end of the gym, a basketball pounded on the floor a few times. A pause. The sudden shudder of the backboard. The swish of the net. A quick adult bark. One more bounce and the ball went silent.

And it was then that Kelly noticed the woman looking at them from the nearer end of gym. She was standing by the refreshment table, alone, and she almost looked frightened. She didn't take her eyes off Clarkson. She looked at the printed program, at his booth number, at him. He remembered seeing her pass slowly before Clarkson's display, stopping to study a drawing and glancing at this artist who called himself Sprout. She hadn't lingered before any of the other students' displays; he wondered if she had a child in the school.

Suddenly Kelly understood who he was seeing. This woman who had kept her distance as promised but who apparently could no longer. A public event in a public space. She had every legal right to be there and a compelling emotional reason to as well. She wanted to see with her own eyes the child she had given birth to nearly fifteen years before.

"You okay if I walk around for a minute, Clarkson?"

"Sure, Pop. Have a blast. Don't get lost in all this middle-school genius." Clarkson smiled in what Kelly knew was only *semi* sarcasm.

Kelly took the long way around to the refreshment table. He stepped beside the woman. She was unmistakable up close: the same flaxen hair, the flair of her nostrils, her thin, pale lips, her blue eyes. But she was short and even a little stout. Clarkson clearly got his gangly build from his father.

"Pretty good crowd for a middle school art fair," he ventured.

The woman startled and spilled some of the water she had in a cup.

Kelly wondered if he was violating their agreement, if they both were. She'd given up all claim to the child, and once the adoption was finalized, she could not reverse her decision. That was long ago. By agreement, they sent her his school photo each year, and Kelly included a shot of the Clarkson standing before his spruce trees at the cabin. But meeting her, even without acknowledging that he knew who she was — could that be some kind of breach that might have legal implications?

"Yes, good crowd."

"See anything you like?" It was a terrible taunt, but he couldn't stop himself.

She didn't look at Kelly, didn't make eye contact. She stared straight ahead in the direction of Clarkson.

"Does he ever ask about me?"

What had Kelly expected? He should have left her alone. Not approached her.

"No. But he hasn't said anything negative about his birth parents either."

"Birth mother. Just say birth mother."

"He lives in a good, stable home, surrounded by a small but loving family. You can see he eats well. He does okay in school and seems to have a talent for art. He's a reader and has a good imagination. He has a small group of friends. He keeps to himself much of the time. Rarely ever talks back. Sneaks the occasional ten or twenty out of my wallet. He's a good boy."

"Clarkson."

"A family name." And then he wondered how she would take that.

"Sometimes I cry," she said, and Kelly feared she was about to then. She sniffled a few times. "I know it was the right thing to do. For him. For Clarkson. I must go now. I can't stay here any longer."

On the rainy drive home Clarkson brought it up.

"Who was that woman you were talking to?"

He may as well have asked where babies came from, though Curt had addressed that with him years before. It was an inevitable question, inescapable, and Kelly knew he'd set it in motion the moment he approached the woman. It demanded, and deserved, an honest answer.

"I think she was your birth mother, Clarkson. We never actually confirmed it."

"So that's her. I guess I look like her a little, don't I?"

"You look like yourself, Clarkson. You *are* yourself and whoever you want that person to be." It seemed to him they were having one of the most important conversations of their lives, and yet Kelly didn't know what to say.

A few moments passed, and Kelly tried to read his son's face in the sweeping lights of the oncoming cars.

"She's not supposed to try to make contact until you're eighteen, Clarkson. That's the agreement. It's all up to what *you* want in the end. You'll be in control of how that goes down."

"WHY THE FUCK CAN MY BIRTH MOTHER COME TO MY ART SHOW AND DAD CAN'T?" He pounded the dashboard with both fists, and Kelly pulled over to the curb, turned off the engine. "What the fuck, Pop? What the fuck?"

Clarkson began crying. He hunched forward, maybe to hide his tears, but his shuddering shoulders betrayed him. Kelly put a hand on his back.

"He promised he'd come," the boy sobbed into his hands. "He *promised*."

"I'm sure he has a good explanation." A stupid thing to say, especially since Kelly didn't believe it. No explanation Curt had was going to be good enough for Clarkson.

Selections of Clarkson's art from the show were to stay at the school for the next two weeks and be on display in the main hall along with the other students' works. Curt could see it there. He could take an afternoon from work and stand before it, study it, but it wouldn't be the same. The few pieces they'd brought with them, sheltered from the rain under their jackets as they ran for the car, would end up in a bottom drawer in Clarkson's desk, never to be taken out or shared with anyone. "They're only good for tinder."

The moment had passed, but Kelly doubted it would ever be *just* a moment.

Dad hadn't come. And she had. Who was his family? Who really cared? Who showed up? Clarkson didn't have the vocabulary for what he was feeling or the maturity or context to make sense of it yet. The questions shook every foundation he stood on. Grandpa, the only one who ever really loved him right, gone. Dad as good as gone. Hardly there even when he was present. Pop doing his bumbling best. Fighting his own battles. Grandma trying to touch his heart and almost, almost getting there. His own mother giving him away. Throwing him away. He was alone. Somehow, he'd known it all his life. He was alone in the world. He belonged nowhere. To no one. Not even to himself. Clarkson Shepherd, a name and a family imposed on him. But who was he really? He was no one.

Clarkson sat up. He wiped his face. "He was supposed to come, Pop!" His words sounded resigned, like Curt had just missed his last chance at something.

They got home before Curt, and Clarkson went to his room without saying anything more.

"Maybe take a shower," Kelly said. "It's been a long day. Relax a little." He'd bring up a plate of something in a while. He didn't want the boy to be around when Curt got home. He checked his phone. Curt was on his way.

When Curt came through the door, he saw something in Kelly's eyes he'd never seen before. The sound of the running shower filled the dreadful silence of the kitchen.

There was nothing to be said, no defense he could give, no apology he could offer that would make any difference. Curt knew that. The tempera abominations on the table stood out amidst the general chaos of the kitchen. Curt stepped over and picked one up.

"DON'T TOUCH THAT!"

He dropped it at Kelly's command.

"Don't touch anything of his!"

Kelly stepped between Curt and the artwork, pushing Curt back toward the door he'd just come through.

"You crossed a line tonight, Curt! You crossed a very big line!"

Curt stood mutely, knowing there was nothing he could do but take what was coming and see what pieces he could pick up when it was over.

"THIS IS NOT HOW FAMILIES ARE SUPPOSED TO WORK, CURT!"

He didn't dare respond. He had no excuse. And he knew Kelly's anger came from a dark, terrible place he'd worked hard for years to escape that now surged again, confirming all his doubts.

"Families support each other!" He growled at Curt, jabbing the air with his finger. "Families show up for each other!"

The roar of the shower halted abruptly. No more shouting. No more growling.

"She was there, Curt."

"Who?"

"Clarkson's birth mother. She came to his art show."

The alarm he saw in Curt's face stung Kelly, but he let it linger. Maybe it would find a place to fester inside him so he would have to attend to it.

"He wants to know why his birth mother, a woman he's never seen before, could show up for his art show *but his own Dad couldn't*. What kind of answer can I give him, Curt? What can I tell him?"

Curt lifted his head, but Kelly cut him off.

"Don't even try. Just don't! This is a mess, Curt. A big mess, and it's not going to be easy to fix. I'm not sure it's ever going to be right with Clarkson again."

"Maybe if I talk to him . . ."

"No. That's the last thing you're going to do. You didn't sit on the side of the road with a screaming, crying boy you could not reach who was asking questions that have no answers. Words aren't working, Curt. Maybe in a few days I'll let you try. Maybe."

Curt rubbed his hands over his face and through his red hair. His next step seemed clear to him.

"Okay, I'll pack a bag and stay with my mother for a few days."

"No. I'll pack a bag for you and bring it by later. You'll stay away for a week. And we'll see how things stand. Right now, just get out of this house before Clarkson comes down!"

"I can't talk to my son?"

"That seems to be the heart of the problem, Curt."

After Curt left, Kelly dropped into a kitchen chair, seeing his darkness approaching, hoping it didn't come closer. He felt like shattered glass, but he heard Clarkson coming down the stairs, so he pulled the broken pieces of himself together and thought about what he would say.

On the drive to his mother's house, Curt wondered what he could tell her. Where to begin.

Inexplicably, the rift that he'd known had always been there had widened after David's death. Clarkson witnessed the stoic persona Curt had called up to face his own father's death, watched it and maybe he wondered if there had ever really been any love between them. He supposed it could look that way to the boy, especially when his father had gone so quickly into his shell then to protect his heart.

Clarkson looked on him with a child's eyes, predisposed by years of clumsy, muted affection that Curt had tried to pass off as love. Was that all that fatherhood meant to him in the end, a transaction with an expiration date and debit/credit columns? And if he didn't show up for the art exhibit, well, that just went in the debit column?

Curt had cultivated emotional reserve all his life. Clarkson couldn't know that his dad automatically fell into a well of non-feeling because it was his only way to cope with the onslaught of his grief. Clarkson saw Curt shed no tears at Grandpa's funeral and not speak of him since.

Curt fumbled the key in the lock of his mother's front door sufficiently to awaken her, and when he came in, she stood before him in the front room, holding her robe together.

"Oh, Mom. I've screwed up big time."

Chapter Twenty-five

The Old Man of the Forest

The forest was too dry for a fire in the ring. There had been no rain for weeks. Over the years, Curt had grown into a habit of checking the forecast for the cabin whether he had planned to visit soon or not. He just liked knowing, as though he was there in spirit. It had become a reflex, a part of his nature.

In his rush that morning, he hadn't checked the weather, and it was only after he turned off the paved road, when he knew he would soon lose a signal, that he turned on his phone to check. There were no texts from Kelly, which pleased him in a petty way yet bothered him deeply. He called up the weather and saw that a storm was forecasted for the area — he had seen dark clouds massing on the horizon. The tiny map on his phone suggested it would pass to the north and miss the cabin.

They'd sold his father's battered old truck for what they could get, and the fresh-faced kid who'd bought it seemed delighted with his new treasure despite its infirmities. Their low-slung city car got him to the cabin well enough but looked wrong parked there. But the whole morning had been wrong, starting with the usual cluttered chaos in the kitchen while Clarkson and Kelly, sitting at the table in their underwear, slurped cereal. Curt telling Clarkson to get over to his grandmother's house to mow her grass, pointing out that the boy had neglected his chore all week. When had it become easier to hide in the role of perpetually annoyed parent?

Kelly had taken him back; they needed each other. But Clarkson seemed to want less to do with him than ever.

"And wash your hair! Your grandmother doesn't want to see you with oily hair."

"Grandma doesn't care what my hair looks like."

"Well, your father does!"

And then it happened. Clarkson looked straight at him through the oily strands hanging over his face and said matter-of-factly, "But you're not my real father, are you?" before turning back to his cereal.

His words didn't sound rehearsed, but they didn't sound spontaneous either. And whether he meant that Kelly was, or that neither of them was, Curt didn't know. All he knew in that blinding, white hot moment was that the words were true and that they had pierced him deeply.

Without a word, and with the best mask of stoic indifference he could pull together, Curt had turned and left the kitchen, left the house, left the city.

So here he was, having driven the three hours in a snit, telling himself with each mile that he should turn around, go home, and apologize to his family. He wondered if they even missed him. His disappearing act probably had seemed childish to them. Had they shrugged it off and gone to do something together without his sour self to ruin their fun?

But he hadn't driven nearly three hours fueled only by a wounded ego, or to escape a family drama he didn't have a script for. He had dropped into his car, turned the key, and pulled away automatically, relying on muscle memory, not knowing quite what he was doing or where he was going until he was well on the way.

The cabin sat quietly before him. The air was still, the birds and insects in the forest hushed by the drought. Every living thing seemed to be conserving its resources to get through the present stress.

Curt was accompanied only by his certainties and his doubts. He didn't have an agenda for his visit, but since he was at the cabin, had come all that way, there were always chores he could do. Never-ending ways to push back against the forest trying to reclaim what belonged to it. "Nature always wins. But it won't win without a fight!" Curt had roared in mock defiance one visit long ago, waving the loppers over his head. Little Clarkson had been tickled by his performance, waving a stick above *his* head imitating his dad. Back then he could still impress the boy, or please him. Or something. Something that felt both good and gone.

The dry leaves gathered against the cabin needed to be raked, especially in such a dry time. He ought to do that and sweep the porch. Maybe he'd wander up to Clarkson's little grove of spruce trees to see how they were doing. He hadn't visited there in a long time.

But he didn't feel like fighting nature that morning. He'd done enough fighting for one day. Instead, Curt tucked his jeans into his socks and took himself for a hike. He wasn't dressed for a ramble. He had on the wrong kind of shoes and his thin socks wouldn't do much to keep the chiggers off his ankles. He was halfway across the dam before he thought he should have at least grabbed a cap and maybe some gloves and the loppers, and a daypack with some water in it. But he didn't turn back.

He stumbled up the south ridge, kicking over the leaves and rocks, climbing the hillside at an angle the way his father had taught him. "Easier on the heart and lungs," David had said. "Make a path straight up a hill and it erodes eventually." From here he could head west, into a part of their hundred acres he didn't visit much anymore. When he was a boy, he and his dad would sometimes hike there, and each time David would say how spooky the area felt to him. "The hillside faces north, so it doesn't get direct sunlight in the summer. That means it stays a little wetter and different plants can grow here. Stuff we don't see around the cabin. Trees grow bigger too." It was here that they could find delicate ferns reaching out of the leaf litter on the forest floor. Their unfurling fiddleheads in the spring seemed like little green miracles to young Curt. He remembered a plant with spiky flowers that they'd come upon once in a little clearing around there, and when they got back to the cabin, they looked it up in one of his grandfather's books. It was called rattlesnake master, and the name alone had been exotic. He'd repeated the name all afternoon.

There were cat's mouths in the tree trunks here — the scars from old ground fires that were now rotted cavities. David had suggested maybe forest sprites or fairies lived there. "Look quick! Did you see one?" Curt had considered himself too big to believe that kind of thing, but he had looked anyway, just in case.

Curt wondered if he could find the same cat's mouth his father had shown him years before. Why had he never taken Clarkson on a hunt for sprites and fairies? Just because they weren't real wasn't a sufficient reason not to look for them with his son. He knew it was too late for that kind of thing now.

The canopy was thicker on the south slope. Maybe that was why his dad had considered the area spooky. The odd stillness of the air, the silence of the forest, the deeper shadows. It was a suitable place for fairies and sprites. He felt it.

Ahead of him he saw an old oak resting on the forest floor. He thought he ought to know the tree from his past ramblings, but he couldn't recall it. A big wind had toppled it, and the gap it left was flooded with sunlight. The roots, ripped from the ground, were still coated with powdery dirt and rocks because there'd been no rain. He stood in the new light. "Maybe I'll find an arrowhead, Dad." His father had always hoped to find one on his land, but it had never happened. Curt studied the roots, picked out a few likely rocks, which sent a rain of dirt to clatter on the dry leaves below, but only briefly, and he, like his father before him, didn't find any artifacts.

Curt began to understand where his feet were taking him as he kicked and crunched through the dry leaves on the hillside, to understand why he had driven three hours in the wrong car and the wrong clothes to get to this place. He was going to visit The Old Man of the Forest. A giant, storm-battered cedar more than a century old. The one cedar tree in their forest they would never liberate from its earthly toil. Instead, they had cut down the oaks and hickories around it, giving The Old Man room to grow and flourish. Curt's hands couldn't meet when he wrapped his arms around the trunk. Not then as a boy and not now as a man.

"Grandpa calls it The Old Man of the Forest," David had said sheepishly one long-ago visit, as though his son would think it was a silly name. Curt thought it was the perfect name.

The tree was old when his grandfather had first brought Curt's father to it, and it had grown half a century since then.

Over the years, it had become a kind of council tree for them, far enough from the cabin, so getting there felt like an achievement and a kind of sacred place in this forest. Curt and his father had sat there many times, resting from their rambles, and talked about important things. It was where David had taken him to calmly explain the mysteries of girls and where babies came from. "It's as close as two people can ever get, Curt," David had said with quiet conviction. "As close as two people can ever get to becoming one person. That's why it's important."

The Old Man of the Forest stood waiting for Curt. The log where they sat had long since rotted away, so he rested on the soft duff beneath the tree. An ancient lightning scar ran down the trunk that had ripped the tree open long ago. Still, it had remained standing and was growing itself back together over the half dozen marbles Clarkson had wedged in there that Curt did not know about. Before he sat, Curt ran his hand down the wispy bark of the trunk, as he had silently watched his father do many times, with many trees in their forest. Whatever wisdom, or insight, or peace it had granted the man eluded Curt this visit, but the gesture seemed important.

Curt seated himself, resting his back against the old tree, feeling its warmth through his thin shirt relax his muscles. He realized he was exhausted. He could just drift. That would be easy. But he wanted to recapture the mood of the place, what it had meant to him as a child, before he'd imprisoned himself in his aloofness.

He let the stillness of the forest enfold him. After a moment, he spoke.

"I walked out on my family today, Dad. I just turned and left. What kind of husband does that? What kind of father?"

He grabbed a twig from the ground beside him and mindlessly snapped it in two.

"I'm not sure what's worse, Dad. That I did it or that it was so easy to do."

One piece of the twig was longer than the other, so he broke off the extra length and laid the three pieces on the bed of cedar needles. Two longs and a short. Clarkson, he knew, would arrange and rearrange them. Lines had always fascinated him. It was something Curt noticed early on. The lines he drew with his crayons, on scraps of paper and the walls of their house.

"He said I wasn't his real father."

Curt rearranged the sticks.

"I knew this day was coming, Dad. I've been waiting for it. I didn't expect it to be quite like this, though. Not so . . . surgical. I'd always envisioned something more explosive and drawn out. Clarkson barking his grievances about me being an inadequate father, and me barking back, with pain. Shouting and banging furniture around until the neighbors complained and the police arrived. A lot of noise and commotion but never getting to the point."

"Except Clarkson did get to the point this morning, *straight* to the point and in the fewest possible, most unequivocal words. He lacerated my heart, and I walked out when I should have stayed and got it all into the open. Showed him I wanted to. I don't know what Kelly thought. Maybe he agreed that I'm a crap dad. I ran away too fast to learn anything."

He listened to the breeze in the treetops but didn't hear any words from his father.

"Sometimes I feel like Clarkson sees me as just the guy who pays the bills. I come home from the hospital in the evening and speak a few pleasantries over dinner. Ask a few safe questions about his day, and that's all I get. I'm a generous provider and an emotional cheapskate and I've settled for that."

Curt picked up the sticks and held them for a moment before arranging them on the ground again. One long stick apart from the other two.

"The thing is, Dad, Clarkson is right. I'm not his father. I don't love him like a father should. Not like you love me. I try. Just like you said. I try. I really do, but it just isn't there! I don't love my son."

There. He'd confessed his secret. Except it wasn't very secret. Clarkson clearly knew it and felt it. Kelly probably did too.

"I do his laundry and help him with his homework. I ask about his friends and try to be interested in what he's interested in. I make sure he brushes his teeth and eats right and takes a shower now and then. I even tell him I love him, but I have to *make* myself say it. The words aren't spontaneous. I don't *feel* them. He's like a neighbor boy to me. Some kid I see around the block who's nice enough, even fun sometimes, but not someone I want to live my life for. Not someone I would walk through fire for. It's shameful, but it's the truth."

He looked up, speaking into the trees. "You did me a great disservice, Dad, by being such a good father!"

Curt closed his eyes and rested his head against The Old Man. He wasn't used to being open about his feelings. Even with Kelly, there were some things he couldn't discuss. It was only with his father that Curt could expose his darkness.

"I'm paying the price for being such a poor son," he said from behind his closed eyes. "I see it now. All those stupid years of trying to keep myself at arm's length from your love, not betraying any emotion. It turns out I wasn't protecting myself. I was *limiting* myself, Dad. I was holding in my feelings, thinking I was strong and instead I was retarding their growth. I hid and failed to become a full person. I don't know how to fix this, Dad. I don't know what to do."

The dry forest remained quiet, not yielding any answers. His visit to their council tree had been a bust.

Yet when Curt opened his eyes, Clarkson was standing before him. Like a beautiful vision. His hands in his pockets and a gentle smile on his face, under the shaggy the nimbus of his unwashed hair. Curt blinked once, and the boy was still there.

"How . . . ?"

"Pop tracked your phone. We were about a half hour behind you the whole way."

"But *here*? At The Old Man of the Forest?"

Clarkson leaned back and looked into the branches of cedar. "Is that what you call it?" He considered this and nodded. "Good name." And then, "I followed your trail, Dad. The obvious path of destruction you left in leaves on the ground. Grandpa taught me how to do that."

So his father had led his son to him.

"I'm sorry I walked out on you this morning, Clarkson." He was surprised at how easy it was to say the words.

"I'm sorry that I made you do that."

"I'm sorry I never took you hunting for arrowheads or forest sprites."

"Storm's coming, Dad. You need to get back to the cabin." He winked. "Time to wake up, Dad."

Curt opened his eyes. Clarkson was gone. Of course, it was just a dream. A fantasy. A wish fulfillment in a forest where his problems were supposed to go away.

Clarkson had been right nonetheless; even if the boy hadn't been there, the storm soon would be. Leaves blew across the ground, tumbling over Curt's outstretched legs. The branches high in The Old Man swayed as the air hissed through them. The midday light was fading.

He pushed himself up from the ground and swiped at the seat of his slacks. A roar from the southwest, strong wind pushing its way through the canopy, growing louder as it got closer. Soon branches would fall, and he had a long race back to the cabin if he was going to beat the rain. The shortest way was across the south-facing slope, on the other side of the creek below him. He thought back to his cross-country days in high school. Could he summon that boy now?

The descent to the creek was steep near The Old Man, and he wanted to get down and across the creek before the rain came. But the storm's roar had arrived and, as the trees began to sway and complain in the wind, rain fell on him, a sudden torrent that turned the forest gray as it hissed through the trees and slapped the ground. The rocks beneath his feet were wet. The exposed dirt would soon be slick, inviting his loafers to slip, and he would tumble down the hillside.

Curt grabbed at branches as he slid his way down, and he managed to hop across the creek without getting his feet wet, but he knew that was pointless. He had too far to go back to the cabin. He'd be soaked before he got there.

He wondered what Clarkson and Kelly were doing back home as he parted the dense scrub, ducked under branches, and maneuvered across slippery rocks. Had the boy mowed his grandmother's yard after all, his hair oily or not? Or had he and Kelly just looked at each other, shrugged, and gone to a movie? Whatever they were doing, they'd be dry and warm.

Much cooler air rolled into the forest. Curt knew he was racing the cold. He had to get back to the cabin before his body began losing heat too fast. He wasn't likely to get hypothermia. He knew that. But he would get a good dose of misery.

The sky grew darker. No jags of lightning to stab his eyes, no peals of thunder. His thin shirt stuck to his skin. His slacks were getting heavy. His shoes were filling with water. He slid on wet leaves as he pushed through the undergrowth beside the creek. His foot slipped out of his shoe, and he stepped directly on a sharp rock. He cried out with pain. He still had to climb at least some of the hillside before it leveled and then trudge across irregular ground, rocks hidden in the fallen leaves, branches slapping his face, thorny vines waiting to trip him, tear his pants, cut his skin.

He remembered one summer day, not so long ago, when he and Clarkson were caught in a downpour like this, far from the cabin. They'd gotten soaked then too, but instead of going inside to dry off, they'd peeled away their clothes and jumped in the lake, laughing like maniacs. Kelly had watched them from the porch sipping his coffee and shaking his head at their antics, their silly fun. That was the memory Curt had anyway. Was it even true? He and Clarkson splashing about in the lake, marveling at the novelty of getting soaked by the rain and the solution being to get even wetter.

"Not without a fight!" he shouted to the storm as he slid across the hillside. "Not without a fight!"

But he had a long way to go.

Chapter Twenty-six

Running Naked

Curt had laced up early on Saturday morning because he had a full day planned. When he got back from his run, he wanted to price wood stain at a couple of places in St. Louis and then call the hardware store in Osceola to see what the same brand would cost there. Grandpa Joe had always said he would rather spend his money in Osceola than in the city. Another week of clear, sunny weather and the cabin would be dry enough from their pressure washing to start slopping on the stain. It was long overdue.

He had an appointment to get their older car in for a new muffler after lunch. It was becoming less of an embarrassment and more of a road hazard by the day. He had told Kelly several times that they ought to trade it in and get something decent since Clarkson would be driving in another year. Not put any more money in the cantankerous thing. "Maybe we could even join the 21st Century and get an electric!" But Kelly, who paid their bills each month, suggested they try to get another year or two out of it. An old beater was the perfect car for Clarkson to learn with.

Kelly had suggested that he take Clarkson with him when he ran the errands. Low stakes. They could be together for an hour or two in public so there wouldn't be any explosions (on Clarkson's part) or withdrawals (on Curt's part). His campaign to be better with his son, better at something he couldn't quite define, though he thought about a lot, had sputtered. He felt that he was on trial within his own family, and maybe, he thought, that's exactly how he should feel. He'd not behaved well.

Most of all this day, Curt wanted to see his mother. This March Saturday was his father's birthday, and Curt wanted to spend some of it with her. Kelly was going to bake a chocolate cake for him to bring, and he'd pick up a carton of the mint ice cream that his dad had always liked. He'd hold her hand in her quiet kitchen and sit in his father's old recliner that he could never convince her to part with. Maybe he'd even spend the night in his old bedroom so she could know there was a second heart beating in the house again.

He'd left his running watch in his dresser drawer; he hadn't worn it in a long time. Kelly had asked him many times if analyzing and dissecting and quantifying and inspecting his runs — "and a few other multisyllabic verbs I could use" — robbed them of their spontaneity. And Curt had realized he was right. He wasn't training for another marathon. One was enough for his lifetime. He wanted to try not being analytical all the time. He would just run to feel alive. Doing that meant he didn't miss his watch.

He was running his usual loop in Forest Park, sticking to the roads on the north side that were flatter and farther from the zoo and art museum traffic. He wore the bright orange tech shirt Kelly had given him so he would be visible. Curt had run here once or twice with his father long ago, but he'd never really developed into a runner. Maybe he'd come to the sport too late. Curt wondered if it was his dad's heart that had limited him. Had it begun affecting him years before anyone knew? Maybe his dad did know and tried to keep it hidden it from everyone. His father should have looked after himself better. Or at least prepared them, somehow, for the inevitable.

Maybe he didn't want to know himself. Maybe he didn't bring it up, whatever it was, at his annual checkup because it seemed minor. Some occasional twinge in his chest. Rare moments of dizziness. A little shortness of breath. Just getting old. That's all. Maybe he dismissed any symptoms because his own father had lived so long. Specific memories of moments with his father came into his head more frequently these days when he ran, and he liked to live in them for a while. He could remember his father boosting him into the branches of a tree one time. He could feel his father's strong hands under his arms, on his bottom, cupping his foot. And the tears David could barely hide as he cheered from the sidelines when Curt was running a race in high school. He'd had to train himself not to look at his father, to stay serious.

Quiet little moments. What his mother called the substance of life. These were what he remembered now.

His father was not a great man by any conventional measure. He'd never attained the trappings of success. No fame outside his little family. No wealth. He didn't lead people or run a great corporation or discover a new formula or cure a disease. But he was kind, even when Curt gave him reason not to be, and present in the quiet moments when the important bits of life happened.

It was a late lesson for Curt. It didn't help that Clarkson had long since become another version of himself. As emotionally withdrawn to him as Curt had been with his father. A few grunts of acknowledgment before he left whatever room Curt entered or turned back to his drawing. Monosyllabic answers when asked about his day. Often it was just easier to let Clarkson retreat to his room with the door closed and not pursue his unanswered questions. Settle for a dismissive gesture rather than even a half-hearted hug. What they had was an uneasy truce, one he was too willing to use as his excuse not to try harder. He thought long about that.

Curt had closed his bedroom door to his father every evening and his father had let him. He tried to have chats sometimes, knocked on his door and sought permission to come in. But Curt had turned his back when David sat on his bed, wrinkling the spread and doing his simple best to find something, anything to talk about that would engage his son.

"Why did you let me get away with that, Dad?" Curt pushed the words out of his running lungs. "Why didn't you try harder? Why did you settle for such a shitty son?"

His father should have muscled his way into Curt's life, whether he liked it or not.

Curt knew he would have resisted. But why did it have to be that way? Why did there have to be *any* barriers between them? Why had the father allowed the son to be that way? To waste so much of their lives?

Yet as his pounding feet covered the pavement his thoughts took him further. He had allowed Curt to be that way because he had a secret weapon. One so subtle Curt didn't even realize when his dad used it. It was so effective then, and so obvious now, that Curt had to stop and lean against a lamp post to gasp with his amazement.

Their humble, beautiful cabin. That had always been his dad's secret weapon in the war of their hearts. "Let's you and me go to the cabin this weekend, Curt." And he could rarely resist. Curt had felt its gentle release then and understood its mighty power now. That was how his father had kept the door open, how he had nurtured their love, kept it alive through the fallow times. Their sanctuary, where they could shed their defenses and just breathe the same air together in quiet peace. Where they could be their true selves with each other, where they could just *be*, for the time they were there. Where the simple act of clearing cedars allowed unguarded conversations about matters large and small. Where, Curt knew without knowing, that the secret pride he felt building his one-match fires for their meals was felt equally by his father looking on. Where they *really could* strip naked before each other, saunter down to the lake, swim and float and splash each other, then sit in the chairs on the porch to dry and talk about things that Curt would never allow anywhere else. Or just savor without words their unfettered togetherness for the time. He wished he could have one more swim like that with his father. One more visit. He could feel that wish pounding heart in his, swelling in his throat.

And he wished it could be that way with Clarkson. That the cabin could be their mutual ground of respite, too. Where whatever ailment was between them could go into remission and maybe their hearts could do some healing. Yet despite his cleverness, and despite his desire, it took Curt another quarter mile before he reached the obvious conclusion.

Why couldn't it be? Why couldn't he and Clarkson begin their journeys back into each other's hearts at the cabin? Not just go there. Not just do chores together. But make the effort there. Go to their woods deliberately. Why couldn't he be more like his own father? Bring out this same secret weapon? Let their defenses fall in its presence? Why not? Why not?

The journey wouldn't be easy. It would take time and effort. They'd have more failures than successes, he guessed. At least at first. But the cabin was there, was always going to be there. Their chances to try were infinite. It made sense.

"Maybe I need to strike the steel of my soul against the flint of Clarkson's resolve until I get some sparks." He realized that he had just come up with a metaphor. He'd have to tell Kelly when he got back.

When Kelly got home from dropping off some books at the library, where he couldn't stop himself from lingering and browsing and sampling in the stacks for a while, and then the grocery store, where he did much the same in the aisles, and then drove wistfully past the used bookstore and paused at the light and thought about stopping in for just a minute, he found the house empty. He'd gone to the store to get a mix and some eggs for the cake he was going to bake for Curt to take to his mother. And more milk because Clarkson drank a gallon a day now, generally straight from the jug. And a Three Musketeers bar because he wanted one. When he called out that he was home, no one responded. He guessed Clarkson had joined Curt on his chores for the morning, though it would have been nice if they'd left him a note.

Kelly had just put the cake in the oven and set the timer when Curt came sweating in the door and shucked his featherweight running shoes and thin socks.

"Where's Clarkson?" Curt gasped as leaned over the sink gulping water. He was panting.

"I thought he was with you."

"With me?"

"Didn't you two run some errands this morning?"

"The only running I've been doing has been in Forest Park. Is Clarkson in his room?"

"No."

Kelly darted to the door that led to their garage and yanked it open. "If you and Clarkson didn't go out, where's the other car?"

"What?"

Curt hurried over. Their second car, the better one, the one more suited to the gravel roads and washes at the cabin, was gone.

"It was there when I left for my run."

"It was there when I left for the store."

"Is it in the driveway?" But when they looked out the window, the car was not there either.

Curt pulled his phone from the tiny pocket of his tiny running shorts and tapped some buttons. "I don't even want to think about what I'm thinking about."

When Curt was able to track Clarkson's phone, it showed him on the highway, already several hours from home.

"He's going to the cabin, Kelly."

"What? He doesn't have a license. What makes him think he can drive a car?"

"My father letting him drive his truck all over our forest when he was a tween. That's what."

Kelly didn't add that Clarkson had once breathlessly confided that Grandpa had let him drive all the way into Osceola staying on the back roads and switching drivers when they got near town. Curt would have been livid had he known, but David would have been a good driving instructor.

"At least he had the sense to take the good car. How far is he?"

"He's nearly there, Kelly."

"So, I guess it's too late to call the Highway Patrol. But I think we can still panic. Can we panic?"

"No. No need to panic yet."

Getting the police involved would be exactly the wrong thing to do. An underaged, inexperienced driver was a hazard on the road, no matter how capable he imagined he was, but getting the boy arrested or detained would only raise another wall between them. He was nearly to the cabin anyway.

Curt considered the provocation Clarkson was presenting. And provoking him was exactly what the boy was doing. Clarkson had left his phone turned on, which, Curt realized, was the key to understanding this mess. If he'd really wanted to run away, even if for a day, he would have switched it off. He was smart enough to do that. He'd done it before. But he'd left it on. Knowing his dads would be able to track him all the way until he lost the signal a couple of miles from the cabin. He knew they would come after him.

That was surely his plan, Curt saw. Set up a fiery confrontation with the parents who would be angry by the time they reached him after driving three hours. Curt knew his son well enough to know Clarkson could match their anger in full measure in an ugly, monstrous argument where tears would flow and firewood might get thrown around. Gravel would be kicked at each other. Words would be shouted that could never be unheard. Accusations made worse by being true.

Yet Curt grew aware as he stood silently in the kitchen, staring at the blip on his phone, watching it move farther away from him every second, that it could be different. It could be accepted as a gift that was also a cry from his son. "Listen to me, Dad!"

And he could. Curt could try to be like his father and let himself do that. He could get to the cabin. He could sit before the fire ring with Clarkson and they could just talk. And maybe voices would be raised, but they could be calmed again. And maybe it would be hard to hear some things, but healing was never easy. And maybe some painful revelations would be made, but that would be because they needed to be. And certainly things would never be the same between them, but things weren't so great now anyway.

The only question left in his mind, then, was why this day? Why had Clarkson chosen this day to raise the stakes?

"Kelly, could you pack us a bag? Some sweats. Underwear. Toothbrushes."

The oven clicked as the cake baked. Kelly looked through the oven window. "It's rising nicely. Only another twenty-five minutes. Do you want to get a shower?"

"Yeah, I guess so. I'll stretch first."

"So you think it will be an overnight?"

"I hope so."

But Kelly didn't leave the kitchen. He wiped a rag across the counter, cleaning some of the mess he'd made from mixing the cake. When he spoke, his voice was casual, and he didn't look at Curt.

"You remember, way back, when my witch doctor told me I should share some of my ugly parts with you?"

"Yes, of course." He looked up from his phone. "Wise woman."

"I was terrified you would push me away, Curt. I was truly, truly terrified. But instead, you held on. You wouldn't let me go. Curt, that may have been the most important chapter of my life's story. I'm not sure why I'm saying this now. It just seems important."

Kelly rinsed the rag, took a last peek at the cake, and walked out of the room, making a list in his head of what they would need to pack.

From the kitchen, Curt heard drawers being opened and closed upstairs in their bedroom.

From the bathroom, Kelly heard the unmistakable grind of the garage door opening. He rushed into Clarkson's bedroom to look out the window and saw their old beater rumbling down the block.

Curt had tricked him. Sent him away to pack while he made his escape to the cabin wearing nothing more than his sweaty running clothes. And in a moment Kelly understood why. The coming confrontation needed to be between Curt and Clarkson, just the two of them.

They had a clever son. And their son had a dad who was beginning to see something new in the boy and in himself. Kelly thought it might be rough at first and even painful, but at the end of the day, maybe they'd have built a new foundation together that just might bond them.

"Well played, Curt. And well played, Clarkson."

When Kelly returned to the kitchen, he found a note waiting for him after all, hastily written in Curt's finest doctor scrawl.

"Be sure to get a carton of mint chip ice cream to take with you to Mom this evening. Tell her anything you want. Maybe tell her that her degenerate son has finally gone in search of his soul. Let's have Clarkson's favorite dinner tomorrow night. Save us some cake."

Chapter Twenty-seven

The Liminal Animal

Did anything ever last at the cabin?

It was a losing battle, Clarkson thought, looking through the windshield at the old place. They'd lose their low-key war with nature in the end. They'd tire of the fight and surrender bit by bit. Or nature would tire of the fight and send a ground fire to reclaim it all at once. Or it would just slowly sink into the ground after they no longer cared, yielding to rot and weather and gnawing critters, and then the scrub and banished cedars would creep back. Get large. Block the view of the lake that would choke with silt anyway. In a hundred years, probably less, you could stumble on this little clearing in the forest and maybe see some evidence that lives had once been lived here — the circle of stones in the fire ring, maybe, or a cracked slab where a little cabin might have once stood — but you'd move on to find your own special place in the forest and forget about this one.

The cabin, all their efforts around the place, stood in between what people called civilization and what people called the wild. Made of wood, like the forest, but cut and trimmed and nailed and domesticated to suit civilization's needs. It was made of forest, but if the family had to fight to keep it, did it belong in the forest?

He'd gotten himself to the cabin on his own, which left him feeling untethered. Whether *he* belonged there or not remained to be seen. Lucky the car had a half a tank of gas when he took off. He hadn't thought about that. His Dad always pointed out the cheapest gas on their drives to the cabin, filling up in the sticks to save a nickel. But Clarkson hadn't brought anything more than the handful of change he'd scooped from the old floral bowl by the door on his dash to the car. He couldn't tank up and get himself home on that. He would have to wait. There might be some food in the cabin. Or one of his great-grandfather's guidebooks could tell him what bark he could eat. He'd survive for a few days.

He'd told Sprite and Scrapefoot that they would talk about some things as soon as he got there. He would meet them at The Old Man of the Forest. But then he paused. Why had he called it that? His dads had never used that name. Nor had Grandpa that he could remember. It felt like the name had come to him in a dream. Or the forest had whispered it in his ear. Maybe that was the same thing.

Clarkson sat in one of the camp chairs and stared at the black ash in the ring. He could light a fire, even use his flint and steel. The sun was out, but the March air would cool quickly if the sky clouded up. Except he had no burgers to cook. Another oversight. He reached into his pocket and brought out the coins, poking them with his finger. There were said to be quarters under the stone steps going down to the lake; although this was another thing he wasn't sure how he knew. Grandpa had put them there with Great-Grandpa Joe. Those might be there a long time. Might be what some wanderer found in a hundred years.

One by one, Clarkson took the coins from his palm and pressed them deep into the ash inside the fire ring, as far down as his fingers could go. "First the old nails from the fence you burned, Grandpa. And now my coins." Maybe he *would* have a fire. Seal his offering properly with fresh ash so it could belong there too. He wiped his sooty fingers on his jeans.

When he turned, he saw Scrapefoot sitting in the gravel nearby. She had approached silently as she always did. Not there, and then *there*. Her fluffy tail was wrapped elegantly around her front paws. Her ears pointed primly, and her white bib glowed. Her red fur reminded him of his dad's hair. She sat beyond his reach; she would never let him pet her. Something wild in her wouldn't allow it. She, too, was between worlds. But she would sit with him. Sometimes they talked. Mostly he'd talk and she'd listen.

The scuff of a boot in the gravel told him that Sprite had arrived now too.

"I went to the other place first," he said. "But no one was there, so I came here to wait. I see I almost missed the party." He nodded to Scrapefoot who may have nodded back. Their acquaintance was new, Clarkson had only recently introduced them on one of his rambles in the forest.

"You didn't miss anything. We're just sitting here. Waiting. Somewhere between what came before and what comes next. Stuck in the now. But something's coming."

"I thought philosophizing was my job."

"You're part of me. So same thing."

"Fair enough. Mind if I sit?" Sprite dragged a chair closer to the fire ring, but opposite Clarkson. The noise and scuffle made Scrapefoot move and settle herself a little farther away.

Once they were assembled, he began.

"My grandmother told me something the other day." Clarkson poked a stick in the black ash then used it to draw lines on the blocks that made the fire ring. Dad didn't like when he did that, but usually the rain washed the marks away. Nothing lasted long. "Something I'd never known. Something I wish I had known years ago."

"Grandma Kathy?"

"Yeah, she's the only one I have. I should have four grandmothers, I guess. Lucky me! I should have four sets of grandparents spoiling me. The biologicals I'll probably never know. Pop's parents. Not likely I'll ever know them, and his mother is dead anyway. Only Dad's mother left. But she's enough."

"What did she tell you?"

"That Dad was an accident."

"We're all accidents. Happy little evolutionary accidents."

"No, more than that. She and Grandpa were just kids. She said they'd come out here one day to do what kids do."

"What you should be doing, Clarkson. You're a little behind the curve on this. No longer a boy. Almost a man."

"With the right person, I will. Say what you want about them, Sprite, but my dads have given me the best example of what a committed relationship is. How powerful it is. That's what I want when my time comes. More than just parts touching parts. More like hearts touching hearts."

"That's sweet."

Clarkson eyed him. Sprite seemed sincere, and they were there to talk, so he let it go.

"Anyway, Dad was an accident. A mistake by a couple of kids because they weren't careful. She told me because she hoped it would help me understand him better. She said Dad's spent his life trying to understand what that means to him. That he was an accident. A good one, but an accident. But she said he's still not sure who he is. And where that leaves him in relation to everyone else in the world. Especially to me, she said."

He rubbed the stick against the blocks and sliced it through the gravel. He didn't feel like he was making his point, but Sprite and Scrapefoot granted him silence so he could continue.

"Funny. Something like that *should* bring us closer. I guess that's what Grandma hoped. Him an accident. Me an accident. We should bond over this fundamental thing we share. Except we don't. I'm sure Dad wouldn't want me to know this about him. Anyway, I don't want to feel like I'm just an accident that happened in the back seat of some car. Like I'm some random kid that popped into the universe and they had to figure out what to do with me."

"But you were adopted," said Sprite. "Gathered into a family on purpose."

"Except that hasn't worked out. It's not a family to me. Pop does his best, and he's a good guy. But he has his demons. Times when he's lost. And Dad thinks there's a formula to fix every problem. Some behavior he can turn on when he needs it and then off when he's done. He's so withdrawn he won't let anyone in to see what's real inside him. I'm his obligation. His assignment until I'm eighteen. I think he adopted the wrong kid. Pop let slip once that they had tried to adopt another kid before me, but that one didn't work out. So I was their second choice. Their consolation prize. They must have looked at each other and said, 'I guess we'll have to make do with this one.'"

"Aren't you being a little ungrateful?"

"Ungrateful for what? For a roof over my head? For food and clothes? That's the basics. That's expected. Any kid at an orphanage gets that. Oliver Twist got that much."

Clarkson flung the stick over his shoulder toward the cabin. He heard it cartwheel across the gravel and hit the wall of the cabin. He turned in his chair and looked. There was a smudge of black soot on the clean siding. He studied the smudge for a moment.

"I suppose it will wash out," Sprite said.

"I hope not." Something was forming in Clarkson's mind that felt important, and he intended to stay open to it. He looked toward Scrapefoot, dependable, inscrutable Scrapefoot, but she gave him no guidance.

He grabbed another stick from the wood pile and dug it into the black ash. If he kept his hands busy, maybe he could talk better.

"I finally got that DNA report from Jordan's brother."

"I wondered if that was why we were here."

"My bio dad is listed on it. No doubt we're related."

Clarkson had spit in a vial and given the specimen to Jordan's older brother, who had sent it in as his own. Then the report came back. Clarkson's biological father was out there. He'd taken the test too. He had to know what it said, had to know he had a child, even if it was just an accident. Had he been looking for his lost child? Was that why he took the test?

What was the man going to do with the information? Was it good news that he had family waiting for him? Was he eager to be a father to a kid who needed an eager father? Would he come for Clarkson now that he knew he was out there? Would he grab him and hug him and act like he never wanted to let him go? Would he speak real love, whatever way he could? Would he take Clarkson, or whatever name he wanted to call him, out of the loneliness and take him somewhere that was certain and warm? Would he love him?

And when would he do this? It shouldn't have to take long. Jordan's brother knew what to do. He was waiting to be contacted. It would be confusing at first since Jordan's brother was too old to be the man's son, but they'd clear that up. And then Clarkson would get to meet his father. See if he was tall, gangly, clumsy, maybe with a big toothy smile. If he read books or made paintings, liked stir fry or spaghetti. Was he a runner like Dad or a chef like Pop? Maybe his dad was uncircumcised too. Did he have other kids now, brothers and sisters for Clarkson? A whole family might be waiting for him. He wanted so much to believe those things could be true. They could spend the rest of their lives getting to know each other. Stuff Dad didn't share and Pop tried to share when the darkness wasn't on him.

Clarkson had needed nearly four months to pay Jordan's brother the last of the money he'd been taking from his dads' wallets before he got the report. But his bio father had to have seen it earlier. It shouldn't have taken this long. When would he hear? He was stuck in the middle, waiting for his bio dad to approach him. His bio dad had to seek him out. Look for him. Come for him. Want him.

Clarkson jammed the stick into the black ash and stood. Something told him to turn and face the cabin that sat incongruously among the trees. This odd thing his great-grandfather had made in the forest where it belonged but didn't belong. The place that kept them warm and dry and shaded them from the sun. Where they could sleep in each other's arms.

Such a strange thing in a forest really. Not a cave to crawl into. Not a cat's mouth in a tree. But a sort of defiance. All those unnatural horizontal lines among the true verticals of the trees.

All those horizontal lines!

Clarkson stood transfixed. Those lines the siding made, horizontal lines that had haunted his art, his thoughts, his dreams. *There they were. There they were!* Right there! The cabin. Their sanctuary where all that was wrong could be made right within those horizontal lines of the siding his great-grandfather had nailed up decades ago. His name was Joe. His ashes were under a boulder across the lake right now. Joe's ancient horizontal lines had stretched far into the future and had touched the soul of a boy who desperately needed touching.

Maybe he *was* part of this family, Clarkson thought. Maybe before he'd even been born, he was supposed to be part of this family. Could this be how the universe worked?

He began to cry. Sprite remained silent. Scrapefoot did too, of course.

This was what he'd come from. *This* was the heritage that made him who he was. Not something to come. Something already here. Here all along. It was in his skin. In his genes. In all his memories, with such odd fathers who maybe really did love him in their clumsy ways. Who welcomed him and wanted him to be a part of them. Who brought him here and cried, "Be a part of this with us. Let's start from here and go as far as we can together. I'll bet we can go far!"

He needed to protect this cabin now. He knew that as deeply as he'd ever known anything. He needed to keep the cabin safe and whole. It was a part of him. He needed to protect it so he and his fathers could keep coming back. He belonged here, and he needed to make the cabin belong here, so the forest wouldn't fight them any longer.

Clarkson walked up to the cabin and felt the wood under his fingers. He looked at the smudge he'd made with the stick. The freshly cleaned siding, waiting to be sealed with stain, was now marred.

But was it marred? The cabin was supposed to be lived in and used, carried on to each generation. It was a living thing, like Dad and Pop and Grandma. And Grandpa. And Joe and Peg. Their hearts were beating in it. And now his heart could too.

And the forest needed to agree with that.

With the stick he fetched from the fire ring, Clarkson jabbed the siding again, just below the first smudge. The dry, clean siding took the soot readily. He stepped back, and then stepped back farther. A cabin in the woods. A collection of unnatural horizontal lines in a forest of vertical lines. It made sense now. He knew what he had to do.

Clarkson reached as high as he could toward the eaves and dragged the stick down the side of the cabin. It left a long black streak. He ran to the fire ring and plunged the stick into the black ash again. Then he returned to the streak and darkened the lower part.

This was it. This was how he would merge civilization and wilderness. How he would stop the war and wage the peace instead. He would make the cabin *belong* in the forest, make it fit in and look right.

He looked at his stick for a moment, looked at the siding, then dropped the stick in the gravel and marbles. He jumped onto the porch and went inside to cabin to fetch a large bucket that he took down to the lake and filled with water. Half of the water sloshed out as he dashed up the sandstone steps. He took a hand shovel from the cabin and began digging in the fire ring, into the decades of ash that he understood now had been waiting all those years for him.

He splashed great chunks into the bucket of water, then stirred his black slurry and carried it to the cabin. With one hand he scooped out a goopy mass and spread it down the siding making the beginning of a vertical line. Black trickles raced down the boards, and he felt the rough texture of the wood beneath his fingertips. "Dad probably would not approve of my technique," he shouted to Sprite and Scrapefoot. "He'd wash my hands carefully when I was done. Pick out the splinters. Apply ointment. Maybe bandages. Suggest using surgical gloves the next time. Pat me on the shoulder. Maybe even kiss me on the forehead and say something like, 'Let me know if you feel any tingling or swelling or soreness. Probably need a tetanus booster.'" He understood that this was Dad's way of showing love.

Once he'd worked out his technique, the verticals lines went fast. He'd finished the side facing the fire ring and he started on the back, though he needed a second bucket of slurry to finish that side. It was beginning to look right. Like it belonged, this odd wooden thing with its horizontal lines among its vertical trees. Not exactly like the trees, but maybe it could still belong.

Sprite and Scrapefoot watched him work. They offered no help but made no suggestion or complaint either. Not all the lines were exactly vertical, but neither were some of trees in the forest when you really looked at them. Clarkson was absorbed in his work, protecting the cabin, finding a way to make something that didn't seem to belong, *belong.*

A forest is full of sounds. Birds and insects and frogs, wind in the treetops, cattle on the ranch to the east, even a distant chainsaw. But when Clarkson paused and listened, he heard an unlikely sound.

"Time for you to go," he said to Sprite and Scrapefoot. Sprite smiled, got up, and turned to leave. Scrapefoot may have nodded. Together they walked away, disappearing into trees that marched on forever. He would never see them again. He no longer needed to.

Coda

Two-Match Fire

"I'm no good at this."

"It takes work."

"I don't want to give up."

"Then don't."

Curt was kneeling before the fire ring, his bare knees pressing into the cold gravel, striking steel against flint the way Clarkson had showed him. The boy's fingernails and cuticles were black with ash slurry. Curt was throwing sparks, but he was not getting a flame deep in the tinder.

"Don't try to hit it. More like slice past it. Maybe switch hands. You're a lefty, so you should have the steel in your left hand, Dad."

Curt had arrived and parked the beater next to their good car on the weedy parking pad. He turned off the engine and looked out the window. In that instant he understood he wasn't in control.

On the long drive he had rehearsed a half dozen scenarios for how he could approach his son, the sensible words he could say, the sensible ways he could say them. He tried to anticipate how Clarkson would reply, sensibly or not, and tried to come up with a measured, patient response for every reaction he could imagine. He wouldn't raise his voice or flash his eyes. He wouldn't clench his fists or shake his head. But he would let Clarkson do those things, not because he intended to look like a long-suffering father, but because *he had it coming.*

What he hadn't prepared for, however, were thick black stripes painted down the freshly cleaned siding of the cabin. His prepared arguments no longer seemed sufficient in the face of this.

When his father pulled up, the noise of the rotten muffler announcing him a half mile before he got there, Clarkson turned and looked at him briefly, then continued his urgent work of slopping the ash slurry onto the cabin.

Curt got out of the car. In the March air he felt the skimpiness of the running clothes he was wearing. He hoped there was something in the cabin he could pull on because he wouldn't stay warm enough in running shorts and his orange tech shirt.

Clarkson stopped his work on the cabin. He sloshed his hands in the slurry bucket before wiping them on his jeans. Curt saw smudges on his face, black streaks in his hair. War paint? He hoped not.

"You're going to freeze, Dad."

"I left in a hurry."

"So I see. We should get a fire going."

"Teach me how to light a flint and steel fire, Clarkson."

"Sure, Dad."

Clarkson walked over to the fire ring, not in a hurry but with purpose. Whatever he might say or do that afternoon, he wasn't going to let his father freeze.

They assembled the tinder and kindling quickly. Curt didn't comment on the holes dug in the ash. But the flint and steel were defeating him, and it felt important that he do this thing right.

"I can only do it about half the time," Clarkson said matter-of-factly. It sounded like he was giving his father permission to fail.

Curt continued to strike. "I need to get closer." I need to care enough to master this because this is important. This is life and death, he thought.

"I have a better idea," Clarkson said. He stood and went into the cabin. When he came back, he had two matches: one for him and one for his father.

"You light it there. I'll light it here. Our flames will meet in the middle. We'll get you warmed up, Dad."

For the first time in his life, Curt got to light a two-match fire.

"There's a smelly old flannel shirt in the cabin, Dad. It might help till the fire gets going."

"Thanks, Clarkson."

He watched his son return to the cabin. He was inside for a minute or two, and Curt looked at the stripes Clarkson had drawn on the siding. Would they come off if they pressure washed again? Or would they have to stain over them? Seal them in? Let them become a chaotic part of the lore of the family cabin? Clarkson's lore. His son had not added those lines without meaning.

Clarkson emerged with the old shirt, an orange cap, and a blanket.

"This ought to help for a while."

Curt dropped some larger sticks on the fire. He pulled the shirt on carefully, popped the cap on his head, and settled in one of the camp chairs, spreading the blanket across his lap. There were gouges in the gravel where the chair had been pulled close to the ring.

"Vertical lines."

"I finally figured it out, Dad." He heard relief in his son's voice.

"I'm glad."

Curt wasn't sure why, but he knew it was time to forget his scripts and to improvise, to be in the moment, to wing it as his father had said so many times. Nothing rehearsed. No logical arguments or sensible solutions. It had to come from deeper and be better than that.

"You came a long way dressed like that. You must have some purpose for being here besides shivering. Why did you come, Dad?"

Yes, time to wing it, though he had no idea how. Other than trying to be himself.

"I wanted to tell you about someone I know, Son. It's a long story." He looked at the unfinished work on the cabin. "Do you have the time?"

"I have the time, Dad."

"Like most good stories," he began, plucking at the blanket until his voice steadied, "it started long ago. It's about a little boy who had a lot to learn. He thought he knew everything, you see. He thought he was smarter than the people around him. And the problem was, he was just smart enough that it seemed to be true. But it was brain smarts, not emotional smarts. He believed that since he could think fast on his feet, he was a thinker. That because he could use big words, he was eloquent. That since he got straight As, he was wise. He thought if he acted bored around those he considered inferior, it meant they *were* inferior."

Clarkson eased himself into the chair opposite his father and stared into the orange flames of their fire that had begun climbing the logs. It wasn't that great a story so far, not like the stories Pop had spun for him so many bedtimes. But it seemed to be going somewhere.

"This boy had a secret. He was gay. And he feared his father, a good man that he didn't really know, might not love him because of it. Might throw him out of the family. He'd seen it happen, and everything he allowed himself to believe about his father told him it would happen to him."

His words flowed as though they had been rehearsed, and Curt realized he had needed to tell this story for a long time.

"So he hid himself from his father. He put up a wall between his hidden self and his father's open self. He crawled deep inside his cave and thought he was safe. Then he found he couldn't crawl out."

"It took him a long time to find his way, Clarkson. When he finally said the things that he needed to say, *his father still loved him*. It was one of the most important moments of this boy's life, and it happened because he had found the courage to talk about things that needed to be talked about. His words had the power he needed to free him from being locked inside himself."

Curt adjusted the blanket on his lap. The fire was beginning to warm his bare legs. There was more to say.

"Now, I know you know where babies come from, Clarkson. Well, this boy's parents were just kids, not much older than you, when they got pregnant. But here's the thing. And it's a big thing. A really big thing, Clarkson. They were told to give up their baby. To hand him over to other parents. People who, on paper, by every logical, objective, sensible measure, were much more suited to raise him. He was almost taken from his family, Clarkson. Raised by strangers." He needed to pause a moment. "And maybe it would have turned out all right. But that boy will never know because those two teenagers didn't listen to logic; they fought to keep him. They weren't going to let go of their son. They believed some things, like families, are worth fighting to keep together."

"It was a close call for that boy, Clarkson. He didn't know for a long time, but once he was told, he's thought about it every single day. Thought about how fragile and how strong family bonds can be. That boy still has trouble finding his way out of his cave sometimes and still feels alone and pulls away. I think he knows a little bit about how you feel, Son."

"I've been stealing money from you and Pop."

"I know. It's okay." He's talking. Let him talk. Follow his lead.

"I used the money to buy one of those DNA tests."

"You can do that? Even though you're underage?"

"Jordan's brother submitted for me. Don't tell anyone."

"I won't."

"I found my bio father."

"Oh." This hit hard, but Curt held on. "Have you met him?"

Clarkson paused and stared into the flames.

"No," he said flatly. But then with more animation he said, "He has to know I'm out here, Dad! I took the test. And he took the test. He has to have the results that show me."

"How long have you known?"

"Only a couple of weeks. When I had enough money to pay off Jordan's brother."

"You're not eighteen yet, Clarkson. But I won't stand in your way if you want to pursue this. I don't think Pop will either."

"Yeah, but Dad, I took that test more than four months ago. *He's* had the results for four months. Where's he been?"

"Maybe it's a pretty big shock to him."

Clarkson frowned and stared into the flames. "Great. I'm a shock."

Curt wanted to rise from the chair, carry the blanket over to his son, wrap him in it, swaddle him as he had the birdlike newborn he'd once been, kiss him on the forehead, and tell him everything would be okay, that they'd work it out. They'd do it together.

"But you know what, Dad?" He looked up and smiled. "You drove all the way out here in your underwear. *You* showed up."

And that, Curt thought, was a good place to begin.

Acknowledgments

There are always more people to thank for any achievement than you remember. Many kind people have helped me or urged me along as I wrote this novel. Foremost is my wife, Libby, who read each of the chapters and shared her thoughts. Rachel Johnson did the same for several chapters. The ever-patient Tonya Miles also listened as I discussed characters and motivations and tried to puzzle out what they meant. My stalwart friend Peter Anderson read the manuscript and gave me his thoughts, many that I needed to hear as much as I didn't want to. Also, all of the unsuspecting Highway Patrol officers I pestered at random gas stations in rural Missouri with my questions about the law and my crazy scenarios. I must thank, as well, the editors at the literary journals where three of these chapters first appeared as short stories. And I can never be grateful enough to my editors at Blue Cedar Press who took a chance on my first novel and now shaped this second into the finished work you have before you.